ALLIANCE

THE LAZARUS ALLIANCE, BOOK 7

BLAZE WARD

KNOTTED ROAD PRESS

Alliance
The Lazarus Alliance: Book Seven
Blaze Ward
Copyright © 2021 Blaze Ward
All rights reserved
Published by Knotted Road Press
www.KnottedRoadPress.com

ISBN: 978-1-64470-207-9

Cover art:
ID 25149562 © Philcold | Dreamstime.com

Cover and interior design copyright © 2021 Knotted Road Press

Reviews
It's true. Reviews help. Even a short one, such as, "Loved it!" So please consider reviewing this book (and all of the ones you've read) on your favorite retailer site.

Never miss a release!
If you'd like to be notified of new releases, sign up for my newsletter.

http://www.blazeward.com/newsletter/

Buy More!
Did you know that you can buy directly from my website?

https://www.blazeward.com/shop/

ALSO BY BLAZE WARD

The Lazarus Alliance

Escape

Return

Rebellion

Revolution

Liberation

Retribution

Alliance

The Jessica Keller Chronicles

Auberon

Queen of the Pirates

Last of the Immortals

Goddess of War

Flight of the Blackbird

The Red Admiral

St. Legier

Winterhome

Petron

CS-405

Queen Anne's Revenge

Packmule

Persephone

Additional Alexandria Station Stories

Siren

Two Bottles of Wine with a War God

The Story Road

The Science Officer Series Season One

The Science Officer

The Mind Field

The Gilded Cage

The Pleasure Dome

The Doomsday Vault

The Last Flagship

The Hammerfield Gambit

The Hammerfield Payoff

The Bryce Connection

The Science Officer Series Season Two

Alien Seas

Shadow of the Dominion

Longshot Hypothesis

Hard Bargain

Outermost

Dominion-427

Phoenix

Princess Rualoh

PART ONE
ZHOONARIM

ONE

LAZARUS

LAZARUS STUDIED the image of the squadron as he sat on one side of the bridge. They were aboard the captured Westphalian Scout Wall Phalanx *Swift*. One of three vessels that Aileen's *mob of galumphs* had taken at Zhoonarrim Station.

Addison was commanding the Archer *Intruder* nearby, likely to his eternal embarrassment, while Aileen had moved the two commanders from her escorts, Deni Wallace and Juan Aroñezz, to the Phalanxes in order to train up crews.

Lazarus was mostly just along today to provide moral support. And because both Kuei and Wybert had flatly refused any sort of promotion or transfer than might remove them from their spots on *Ajax*. At least for now. At some point, that might change, but Lazarus himself would likely have to come under proper military command again first.

Piracy really was more fun.

"Sir?" Commander Wallace speaking perked Lazarus up now, as it did the various crew members around them. About half of this crew were human, with the Pilot that Wallace was overseeing being a Kdari named Jemsik Marraw.

The two protectors' crews had been thinned down, but after the battle for Zhoonarrim, a huge pool of volunteers had stood up to be inducted into whatever various navies would take them.

Another thing that Lazarus would probably have to sort out at some point, but not today.

Lazarus turned to the Commander expectantly.

"So we're really just on a long scout here, sir," the man began, speaking on a somewhat personal level, but loud enough that everyone around them could follow along.

Lazarus nodded to prompt him.

"What happens if we do run into someone?" Wallace asked.

"That's up to the Commodore," Lazarus smiled. "But this squadron contains roughly the equivalent firepower of a Westphalian GunWall, and not just a ScoutWall, since *P-4282* and *P-4317* are along. I'd rate us down a little, only because so many of the crews are just now starting to gel into something useful, but we can do a lot. It also depends on who we find. Another ScoutWall patrol of five might be too much for the Commodore to take on. And it might not."

"And her orders to clear the entire Nebula of Westphalian vessels?" Wallace asked, again mostly for the benefit of everyone else.

"If Westphalia can't take the time to locate other corridors through there then we can defend the Phraettis Alliance with the ships we have, at least until such time as Rio sends more," Lazarus spoke louder than necessary. "And patrolling like this gets everybody better trained for what comes next."

"What comes next, sir?" Wallace asked.

"Pretty soon, I think this squadron will be worked up to the point that we can go back and get *Ajax*, Commander,"

Lazarus smiled. "Then we'll go find some friends and take the war to Westphalia for a while."

The Pilot rotated his head back to look now.

"Will the Innruld let that happen, sirs?" Marraw asked.

"All those guns and systems that the Commodore brought back from Brasilia mean that the Species Underground can start attacking Security Barcs anywhere they find them, Lieutenant," Lazarus said. "Part of all this training is to prepare you so that some teams can stay here and continue this battle, while others help in Human Space. Only together can we achieve our final victory."

"How soon?" the man asked.

"That's up to Aileen and Admiral da Silva," Lazarus nodded.

TWO
ADDISON

ADDISON WAS STILL GETTING USED to this bridge. Westphalian ships tended to be shaped strangely by the need to have that big, metal shield forward, providing shelter as well as a better parallax on sensors. At the same time, the central column was hinged in the middle, so that the ship could maneuver sideways, almost like a Churquen slithering.

The Star Lance was forward, with this small bridge tucked in behind it, and that made the whole bridge a long, narrow cylinder. Extremely cramped in here, for reasons he really didn't understand, especially since Addison had been aboard the ship while it was being repaired. They could have just as easily moved all the walls out several feet and not lost anything particularly important.

He shrugged as he looked around. At his order, the repair crews had also nearly doubled the amount of lights in here, so that it was less a dreary, quiet chamber and more like the various command spaces on *Ajax*, or his old bridge on *Shiva Zephyr Glaive*.

What did it say about Westphalian mental processes that their ships were uncomfortable and dark? Except that Lazarus had assured him that their Starcruisers were more like Rio ships.

Weird, but it did show a tendency to social stratification that Addison found distasteful. More distasteful than Westphalia itself.

"Sensors, what is your status?" he called, mostly just to pass the time.

They were surveying in the Nebula today. Akeley's Passage was getting a thorough mapping, since that was one of the things a ScoutWall did better than almost anyone.

Lt. Rister Pera. Yithadreph female. Louder than Aileen, but nowhere near as supremely confident.

Everyone was operating under something closely approximating the Rio Alliance Navy, if only because Lazarus had training materials and videos that covered a frightening level of detail for how to do things.

After all, it wasn't like the Innruld had a navy worth mentioning.

She looked up now and frowned. Uncertain, but everything was new to almost everyone. Addison only had a year's head start.

"I'm seeing indications of a ship's transit, sir," Pera said sourly. "Recent, I think. Recent enough that I have echo marks of them dropping into space nearby and then jumping again."

"Show me," he ordered her.

Westphalian equipment wasn't anywhere near as good as what Lazarus had installed on *Ajax*, but still better than what the Species Underground had had before.

Yes. That was a ship with jump drives, navigating more or less down the central lane of Akeley's Passage. It had jumped out and spent a while triangulating as well as it could against visible stars, then jumped again just a few hours ago.

"Sound the alert and roust the Commodore," he ordered.

"Transmit your findings to the rest of the squadron and tell everyone to stand by for jump."

That would be what Aileen ordered, so he felt okay anticipating. He smiled at the thought that she was in charge here, instead of him or Lazarus. Of course, Lazarus would step in if he felt the need, but this was just supposed to be a familiarization patrol.

"Signal from *Swift*, sir," Pera said. "Captain Lazarus."

"Put him through to my screen, Lieutenant."

And there he was, the man responsible for such upheavals in everyone's life.

"Coming or going?" he asked immediately.

"Yisan side, transiting towards Aceanx," Addison replied.

Aceanx was closer through trans-space, but Human ships could leap in a straight line, so they could go straight to Zhoonarrim when they got into open space.

Aileen arrived before they could say more.

"How big?" was the first thing she asked when she got into her own modified command seat.

Every single chair on this ship had been ripped out first thing, and replaced with modifiable seats the Species preferred.

"One ship, Commodore," Pera responded. "Unable to identify size at present."

Addison figured that they could actually move to a spot where they could scan the wave of arrival for details, but that would require more time than he expected Aileen to give them.

"Lazarus, are we ready to chase someone?" she asked, joining in on the open line.

"I think so, depending," he replied. "If nothing else, we need to get back to friendly space so we can bring in heavier firepower, assuming an unfriendly vessel."

He watched the woman nod. She'd been a mostly quiet,

introverted Cargomaster for him for years, but a change had come over her. Firefights on rooftops, commanding convoys and then armadas.

Now, commanding a patrol squadron.

"All vessels, come about to this vector and prepare to jump," Aileen said. "Oh, and battle stations."

THREE

AILEEN

AILEEN WATCHED as her new mob of semi-professional *galumphs* went to work. It helped that she had Addison and three trained Human captains grooming folks, as well as others working in engine rooms and gun stations.

Well-meaning amateurs described a lot of the recruits. Violent revolutionaries more or less covered the rest. Still, look what Lazarus had managed to do with the original crew of *Shiva Zephyr Glaive*.

"All ships show ready, sir," Lt. Pera said.

The woman was utterly in awe of Aileen, which made Aileen a little cranky at times, but she was getting used to it. The old days had been *us against the Innruld*. Nowadays she was suddenly *Important People*. And occasionally had to act like it.

"Make your jumps," Aileen ordered, wishing that Lazarus would step in and take over, but he steadfastly refused, just like Rod da Silva reminded everyone regularly that the Humans were here to help, not command.

Addison was just as bad, but that was him wanting to get himself and Eha back to Liberty so they could pretend to be living something of a normal life. Or Brasilia, which was much more likely.

So it was kind of up to her, at least for now. She might demand an end to the dress up so she could go back to her vests and capris, but until then she needed to make sure that Westphalia failed to take over the galaxy.

If that meant that she had to remain in charge for a while, so be it.

Blueshift.

After so many years of trans-space, it was still weird to just arrive somewhere light-years distant in between heartbeats.

"All vessels hard scan," Aileen ordered. "High profile. I want to know exactly where they are as soon as they realize we're behind them."

And to give her own folks time to run if they had to. There was a Security Pyramid ahead in *Vigilant,* plus any number of armed gunships, but if this was another Westphalian probe, she'd just transfer her flag to *Ajax* when she got there, since Rod wasn't around.

That's what you get for leaving me in charge.

She grinned.

"Contact!" Pera called. "Bearing noted. Vessel currently between jumps and close enough to engage."

Aileen waited. The most important information would take a few seconds.

"Uhm, they're flying Yisan transponder codes?" Pera continued, confused. "What's a postal carrier?"

"All ships, stand down from battle stations." Lazarus did take over now. Sharply. "Friendly vessel ahead. Let me contact them and get everything settled."

"All yours," Aileen said.

When had someone established a communications route through the Nebula?

FOUR

EDUARDO

EDUARDO HAPPENED to be on the bridge of *Postal Flyer Three* when all the alarms went insane with *Blueshift*. Captain Diana Garcia stopped talking mid-word and went straight to battle stations.

He approved. Piracy was likely to be a matter of fact in the nebula for a while. Especially after what had just happened at Yisan.

"Oh, this is interesting," she said quietly, leaning back from her screen and gesturing him closer.

Eduardo wasn't strapped down yet or anything, so he could move.

And he agreed.

"Is it real?" he asked, looking around.

"Stand by," the woman on the sensors panel spoke up. "I have comm traffic from Lazarus aboard one of the Scout Wall vessels."

"Patch it through," Diana said.

Yes. Lazarus.

"Eduardo?" the man recoiled somewhat on the screen.

"Indeed," he smiled. "Might I inquire as to the nature of things, such that three ScoutWall vessels and two Rio Protectors are pouncing on me?"

"Westphalia captured Zhoonarrim Station," the man said, relaxing. "Aileen commanded a task force to take it back, and in the process three of the full ScoutWall surrendered. This is a training patrol. What are you doing in the middle of nowhere?"

"I would feel better not discussing it on an open line," Eduardo replied. "Should I come aboard one of your vessels?"

His image froze for several seconds, so Eduardo assumed a private conference over there. A moment later his screen lit up with a conference call including Addison Wolcott and the immeasurable Aileen Enjehn, plus several humans Eduardo didn't know.

"If it is as bad as you being here suggests, I'll route you on the shortest path to Zhoonarrim from here," Lazarus said. As Eduardo watched, one of the ScoutWall mushrooms suddenly vanished. "I'm sending a messenger ahead so they're ready for you. Three jumps with these vectors."

"Got it," Diana spoke up now. "Pilot, program these and stand by."

Eduardo nodded. All the folks on this bridge were female, but he generally had his pick of competent women to fly his ships, given the way that both Westphalia and the Rio Alliance tended to be blinded by their sexism. He wouldn't tolerate any shenanigans on one of his hulls, and hired captains who agreed.

"Eduardo, just how critical is your information?" Lazarus asked.

"The fate of the galaxy might hinge on it, Lazarus," he replied.

"Yes, I was afraid you'd say that," the man nodded.
Eduardo smiled, but it was sour.
The sooner he could get help, the better.

FIVE

LAZARUS

LAZARUS LOOKED around the conference room. Unlike the rest of Zhoonarrim Station, this one had been extensively remodeled to be comfortable for Humans, with a dozen chairs of his kind handy, in addition to the usual stations that could be made to fit most of the rest of the Species.

He was at Rod da Silva's right. Aileen was across from him on Rod's left. Addison and Eha were there, as were Oluchi and Anya. Grace and several others who were more civilian had also come, as well as Antonia Veracruz, herself a little nervous that her unapproved excursions in Phraettis Alliance Space might be coming back to haunt her, from the way she held her shoulders a little more hunched than normal.

Zhoonarrim's new governor—Chrine Lexand, a Zentra male of middle-age who had been a shopkeeper until recently—probably should have been in charge, but he'd only been an active revolutionary for weeks now. The man was a darker crimson than most Zentra with less black and more white highlights. Solid, but not able to think quickly on his feet, at least as far as Lazarus had been able to tell.

Eduardo was at the far end of the table, with his Captain, a woman named Diana Garcia.

"Okay, Señor Martìnez," Rod began as everyone was settled. "We're private, and you've gathered all the major players into a single room where we can talk. What emergency compels you to Zhoonarrim?"

Lazarus expected the man to make a power play of some sort. He'd been in complete control during that first poker game, a man so wealthy that he dominated entire sectors of space centered on Yisan, outside both Rio and Westphalia, but trading with both.

Instead, he turned to Lazarus now and his face was solemn but open.

"I'll start with the high points," he explained simply. "Then we can deep dive into all the details. Put simply, eight weeks ago a Westphalian force attacked Yisan, capturing orbital space and landing troops on the surface."

He paused and Lazarus almost heard the man growl under his breath.

"I was able to activate contingency plans nearly thirty years old and smuggle myself off the surface," Eduardo continued. "Given my options, and their presence in and about Yisan, that suggested a major push through Akeley's Passage into Innruld Space. I know that Rio has moved many of their ships out of position to help, but was hoping that I might find you, Lazarus, and we could do something about it."

"We?" Lazarus asked, a bit taken back by the word.

Up until now, Eduardo Martìnez had been merely a passive observer. A politician working all sides for his own apparent profit. Something had changed.

"I have already begun negotiations with Brasilia that would see most of the Yisan worlds eventually join the Rio Alliance, Lazarus," the man continued. "No doubt, that was what made me and my world a target for Westphalia. Rio will help, and I have sent messengers that direction, but I needed the man who has already proven himself capable of upending the entire galaxy."

He paused there and Lazarus drew a breath to reply, but Eduardo scanned the rest of the room.

"And all of his friends," Eduardo continued.

That was the other shoe. The room went sideways for several seconds.

Lazarus watched Rod finally get everyone quiet by the simple expedient of slamming a palm down on the table top. It sounded like a gunshot in the closed room and most folks jumped. Not him, because he knew it was coming. Not Grace because nothing ruffled that woman.

He shared a secret smile with her.

"The room *will* come to order," Rod said quietly in the aftermath.

He scowled at everyone, but most of them were sufficiently cowed by the man.

"Moving on, I will remind everyone that my resources are somewhat finite," Rod explained. "One Light Starcruiser. Two Protectors here and the three that Lazarus brought with him, but those three are clear around the rim protecting Oton Mari right now if we need them. That's it. Ambassador Dunham, given the situation, I will turn this meeting over to you and Governor Lexand now."

Lazarus smiled as Eha looked both directions. Addison had called it the Phraettis Alliance, a name that was beginning to stick. All the more so as reports came in of revolts breaking out in other systems as the Innruld suddenly lost control of hearts and minds.

Or rather, if people have hope, it will eventually overcome fear.

"Eduardo," she nodded in that direction.

Lazarus noted that Eduardo wasn't surprised, nor even nervous. But then again, he'd made all of his resources available to rescue her from Strav Ardna, including two people at this table in Grace and Oluchi.

Eha turned this way now and studied Rod's face.

"I will presume that you would make your forces available, Admiral da Silva," she said simply.

Rod nodded, still a little wary, uncertain where she was going. But the woman had decades as a spymaster. She gave nothing away.

Her eyes landed on Aileen now.

"I think that we need to open the call again," she told Commodore Enjehn.

"We can try, but if they took Yisan, they probably had enough force there to hold it," Aileen replied.

Everyone turned to Eduardo.

"Light Starcruisers and several GunWalls," he nodded, gesturing to the woman beside him. "Diana has all the information."

Eha nodded succinctly.

"Yeah, we can't take that on," Aileen replied. "We had *Vigilant* last time, but a Light Starcruiser would chew up even a modified Pyramid."

"She's right," Oluchi suddenly spoke up. "Local ships don't stand a chance. We were only successful here because we had tactical and strategic surprise, but you've chased the survivors of that ScoutWall out of Phraettis Space, so they might have run straight to Yisan to tell everyone what happened."

Lazarus grinned at the man, remembering the pretty gigolo who had walked up to them that first day and introduced himself.

How far we've all come since then.

Oluchi grinned back, as though reading his mind.

"What are you proposing, Pryce?" Rod asked now.

"Well, I would normally borrow Eduardo's yacht for something like this," Oluchi grinned. "But since he's here, I might have to trade him for *Postal Flyer Three* so I can run for Liberty and see if Carlos has any ships he can free up to help."

"The hell you will," Antonia snapped. "Not a chance you leave me behind on this one, Pryce."

"Maybe we should ask the boss?" he grinned.

Lazarus almost laughed, watching the byplay. All the people here were arguing about the best way to immediately drop everything and help relative strangers.

That was what *Alliance* looked like.

Eduardo's smile was knowing. Like a patriarch who had caught his kids squabbling.

"Will Carlos send help?" Eduardo asked.

"He will," Lazarus interrupted. "Because we'll send representatives of the Phraettis Alliance to ask."

"Phraettis Alliance?" Eduardo finally didn't look in complete command.

"Addison's suggestion, sir," Lazarus said. "After the Innruld fall, we shouldn't keep calling it Innruld Space, so he proposed that and most people have adopted it."

"I see," Eduardo nodded to Addison, and then Eha. "The Phraettis Alliance. Well I guess I'm here asking this Alliance for help. If Westphalia can cut the Rio and Phraettis Alliances off from easy sailing, they might just win the war. I'd prefer not."

"Exactly," Rod spoke up now. "However, we now have a conundrum."

Everybody fell silent and turned to the man. He smiled.

"Normally, this would be a major fleet action, with an admiral in charge," Rod continued, gesturing to Eha as he spoke. "But I must continue working with the civilian authorities on this side of the nebula to press our war and not lose any ground while others concentrate on liberating Yisan."

Rod turned to Aileen. Lazarus watched her bristle silently.

"Additionally, I feel like this might be larger than Commodore Enjehn is ready to handle," he said diplomatically. "In fact, I am likely guilty of keeping her at a temporary rank longer than was necessary. Partly, that was for my own reasons, and partly for the benefit of the Phraettis Alliance. That will now change. Commodore Enjehn, you are relieved of duty and will henceforth revert to the rank of Commander at your station as permanent Second Officer aboard the Light Starcruiser *Ajax*."

Lazarus saw it before anybody else, but he was the only other career naval officer at the table. Then his stomach sank when he realized where Rod was going.

The man turned his way and smiled.

"As it requires an Act of Congress to make someone an admiral, such is beyond my capabilities at present," Rod grinned. "Captain Oliveira, you are hereby ordered to raise a Commodore's flag for the indeterminate future. *Ajax* will become the Task Force Flagship for the mission to raise the siege at Yisan, with all available resources being placed at your command."

Lazarus nodded grimly. At least they couldn't promote him out of his chair just yet. He'd only barely designed and proven that his baby worked. It wasn't fair for them to take it away from him.

But that day was likely coming.

"Oluchi Pryce," Rod continued like a hanging judge with an early tee time. "You will take an oath as a temporary naval officer with the rank of Commander for the purposes of conveying messages to Admiral Nguema at Liberty, or wherever he might be found. Further, you will brevet to the rank of Naval Ambassador during that time, to establish your credentials and authority. The civilian vessel *Celestial Sovereign* will come under Rio Accords for the purposes of transporting you. Do either of you have any questions?"

Oluchi had gone white, but recovered quickly. Lazarus wondered how much time he would need to spend playing poker to get his face back to an unreadable mask. Antonia was smiling. This way, she might actually get to see combat. If she stayed with Eduardo, Lazarus would order her to stay no closer than Zhoonarrim.

As would everyone else.

"No questions," Oluchi replied quietly.

Antonia just shook her head. Eduardo seemed to sigh with relief.

"Commodore Lazarus, this meeting is yours," Rod said, standing and gesturing for Lazarus to change seats with him.

Lazarus did, feeling that heavy weight settle on his shoulders.

The Phraettis Alliance was going to come to the rescue. Not just Humans, Moah, Gnashiiley, and Atomarsk, but Zentra, Churquen, Yithadreph, Tarni, and every other flavor of intelligent life in the galaxy.

Now he just had to figure out how to do it.

SIX

OLUCHI

OLUCHI AND ANYA had retired to their suite on the station, rather than accompany Antonia back to Eduardo's cabin on *Celestial Sovereign* that they had more or less taken over. The man was staying on the station for now, and would have questions. Plus, he might still ask for his ship back.

Oluchi fixed a drink for himself and then one for Anya when she walked up and took a sip of his, leaning her weight against his back.

"Why do I feel like a teenager who got caught by their parents sneaking out?" she asked.

"Possibly because that's kind of what happened," he laughed, turning and handing her a glass.

They clinked them together.

"To being out after curfew," she said.

He laughed and kissed her.

"So, I have a problem," he began, watching her eyes suddenly get shrewd in that way that they did when he was dancing on the edge of an emotional minefield.

He'd gotten pretty good at mapping the mines by now, though.

"Go on," she prodded him in a slow drawl.

"I have volunteered to race madly across the galaxy to try to bring back help," he said. "It honestly was the spur of the moment and I should have stopped and asked you."

"If it was okay?" she said without any emotion.

"If you were ready to drop everything and come with me," he corrected her. "The Species Underground can take care of themselves for a while, if you're not here to hustle them. But I took you for granted in the heat of the moment and that was a mistake. I'm sorry, and I shouldn't do that."

Now she smiled. Leaned into him with one hand around his waist, both of them careful not to spill the pseudo-rum he'd grown rather fond of.

Anya even kissed him.

"You should never take me for granted, Pryce," she purred at him, breathing on his ear.

"That, madam, is a given," he agreed. "Will you go with me on this crazy race to summon the cavalry, not knowing where we'll find them or what might happen?"

"Without a doubt, Oluchi," she said with a smile, leaning back now. "The only problem I can see is that we've been making all these deals in Eduardo's name, and he won't know who any of these people are or what we've agreed to."

Oluchi laughed and took a sip. It really wasn't bad rum.

"That, my love, is where he gets to prove to the galaxy that he's just as good as he's always claimed to be," he said.

"Oh?"

"Mind you, I can't remember how many times I've heard Eduardo refer to coming up from nothing with only a dream and a stubborn streak," Oluchi laughed. "He was born even poorer than I was. Very much from the wrong side of the tracks, mind you."

"I was not aware of that," Anya said. "Usually those sorts

of folks are all garish and loud when they make it, having a huge chip on their shoulder to prove something."

"Oh, he was probably like that at one point," Oluchi agreed. "But remember that it was likely fifty or more years ago. The man is somewhere in his mid-eighties these days, although nobody knows for certain. Working on great-grand kids now, I think."

"Going to throw him to the local sharks and see if he can swim?" Anya grinned.

"Hey, all I got from the man initially was his business card," Oluchi projected hurt innocence. "At least Fernanda seeded you for some funds to start investing and banking in Phraettis Space."

"True, but she's a prisoner on Yisan, as far as Eduardo knew, so that might all evaporate before we can call on it," Anya sobered.

"It would not be the first time I have been running a good bluff against professionals, Anya Persaud," he grinned at her. "Besides, if he's here, his money is safe enough. All the promises you and I have been making aren't entirely lies at that point."

"What if he discovers that he doesn't need you, Pryce?" she asked, voice getting saucy now.

"Well, then I'm sure Fernanda's money will spend just as well," he laughed. "Failing that, we have some bankers at Oton Mari and Zhoonarrim that we can call in favors from. If Eduardo doesn't want to employ us, maybe he can deal with *competing* with us instead."

"I like the way you think, Pryce," she laughed and kissed him. "I knew there was a reason I let you seduce me."

"You were under orders, Persaud," he said archly with a sniff and quick toss backwards of his cape for effect. "I was the innocent one led astray by all you spy folks on Brasilia."

"Indeed?"

"That is my story, and I'm sticking to it," he said, grinning now.

"In that case, I should probably seduce you again, so you remember what this is all about," Anya grinned back, finishing her drink and slamming the highball glass down with a thump.

"If you insist." Oluchi did the same.

For a man who'd been on the verge of losing his livelihood as a gigolo two years ago, it was astonishing to consider where he was now.

But the invasion and conquest of Yisan showed just how quickly everything could all fall apart again, even for someone as wealthy and powerful as Eduardo.

Oluchi owed that man even more than he did Lazarus and Eha.

He would see Eduardo put to right.

Or burn Westphalia to the ground.

SEVEN

EHA

SHE WANTED to rant and rail against the fates, but Eha only did that in the quiet privacy of her own quarters when she was alone. Right now, she and Addison were curled up around each other in their nest, thinking happy thoughts and wondering why the light was so bright in here, even on the lowest setting. And when her heartrate would get back to normal.

"You okay?" he asked quietly.

"No," she answered honestly. "I'm losing you again, and not sure when I'll get you back."

She interrupted before he could do more than draw a breath.

"And yes, I know you'll be careful and that you've got Lazarus," she continued. "But this is a war, and I don't want Adriana to end up without a father like I did."

"I would promise you anything and everything, Eha," he said. "But you're right. It might all be a mirage. At the same time, to use Lazarus's favorite phrase, *it is necessary.*"

"And the Alliance of all our peoples will eventually be enough," she agreed. "But in the short term, I'm without my other half. Adriana is without her father. And at some point I'll have to return to Brasilia to deal with the High Council."

"Should you travel with us as far as the staging for Yisan?" Addison asked now. "Then move to one of Aileen's transports for the return to Rio Space?"

"What about the Species Underground?" she asked, twisting around until their noses touched now, unsure where he was headed.

"Chera Sonels, Niela Tersand, and Chrine Lexand are all System Governors now," Addison reminded her. "That's also the beginnings of a government of the Species, especially as more stations and systems start challenging the Innruld. Do you wish to be part of that government? To lead it perhaps?"

"Oh, gods no," Eha laughed now. "All I ever wanted was to run my networks and flirt with a certain Director. Everything since we fled Zhoonarrim was me trying to not get into water too deep to slither across."

"It might be too late for that," he turned sober on her, so she kissed him to make him stop. And got a smile. "But this is the same thing, if you squint at it. I'm off on some mission for a while and then I'll return and check in, only this time with more necking and tangling. Whether it is Zhoonarrim, Oton Mari, Liberty, or Brasilia, I will return to you."

She squeezed him tight. After so many years of dancing around the edges of it, that might be as good as she'd be able to get.

Eha placed her head on his chest now, listening to his heart beat. Tomorrow, she would have to make some hard choices.

EIGHT

LAZARUS

THE KNOCK at the door wasn't particularly surprising. Lazarus rose from the couch where he had been reading and nodded to Grace as she looked up from her chair. The woman looked utterly relaxed, but he knew better. And could only guess how many weapons she might have on her person or within easy reach.

At least Eha didn't need a bodyguard tonight.

Lazarus opened the door and nodded deeply—almost a bow—to Eduardo.

"Sir," he said. "Please join us."

Eduardo entered and smiled as he saw Grace.

"I suppose technically you've quit your old job?" he asked as they all settled on couch and chairs.

"Not at all, Eduardo," she smiled. "You ordered me to make myself available for whatever Lazarus needed, and that really hasn't changed."

"Touché," he laughed. "There have been a few times that I have had to settle on lesser competitors of yours to handle various tasks, but I was successful at those and you are correct that we are all better served to have you here. I heard about the assassination attempt on Eha."

"And the man was taken alive and named names," Lazarus said. "I expect a house-cleaning is underway back home, but chose to not dangle myself of Eha as a prize in front of anyone else for a while, so we are here. How can we be of service, Eduardo?"

"You all fully intend to go back to Yisan and do something violent?" the older man asked.

"Just as Zhoonarrim is something of a gateway to the Phraettis Alliance, Yisan is a hinge upon which all that trade would like to flow," Lazarus said. "If Westphalia controls it, then it becomes extremely difficult for Rio to reach our allies on the far side. Plus, this is the chance to really forge the larger alliance we've all talked about. Rio, Yisan, Phraettis. At a minimum, that is a long axis of inhabited worlds that have the potential to overwhelm Westphalia. Maybe bring them down."

"Can you do it?" Eduardo asked. "I talked to Aileen after dinner to get her take on things and hear about the battle that cleared local space and the throat of the nebula. But that was an overwhelming surge of ships against a partial ScoutWall. This will be a warfleet."

"I'll take *Ajax* and the five escorts we have at hand if nobody else offers to help," Lazarus explained. "At Liberty, that was sufficient. Granted, we had surprise, but I cannot imagine that Yisan willingly rolled over and surrendered to Westphalian troops, so we ought to have friction we can exploit."

"Such as?" Eduardo asked.

"Maybe those newly captured ships, *Intruder*, *Swift*, and *Drifter*, all pretend to be Westphalian ships to distract while *Ajax* and the two Protectors sneak up," Lazarus offered. "Maybe we just pull another Vilga's Stand on them. I won't know until Oluchi has a chance to find help and bring it back. It would aid the cause if you had more ships like *Celestial Sovereign* that could join."

"My yacht?" Eduardo asked. "That's not a warship."

Grace laughed before Lazarus could speak.

"Eduardo, you really need to have a chat with Antonia next," she said. "Those women have already proven that they are at least as good as a Phalanx, maybe an Archer-Class as well. I know you think of them in terms of piracy, but that's all Westphalia is doing right now. Putting a fleet out there at Yisan means that they will have to run long supply lines to friendly systems, or trust the locals not to poison them. I wouldn't."

"Would such ships be useful?" he asked.

Now Lazarus laughed.

"Nothing can stand before Kirov's Lance, Eduardo," Lazarus smiled. "At least for now. At Vilga's Stand, I had three Protectors keeping GunWalls off my flanks so I could snipe at Starcruisers. At Yisan, I suspect that terminally damaging a couple of megafreighters would go a long ways to ruining their entire invasion. An army that cannot eat cannot survive."

"I see," the man said. "You've given this sort of thing more thought than I have. Plus you have more experience at it."

"This was the way that I intended to defeat the Innruld if Rio hadn't sent help, Eduardo," Lazarus replied. "Take down Security Pyramids one by one like a pirate or a highwayman. Shatter their grip on the population and then let the people rise up. Yisan won't be any different."

"Oh," Eduardo fell into silence. "In that case, you might be able to do something crazy immediately, without having to sail as far as Liberty or Brasilia."

"Oh?" Grace suddenly leaned forward.

"Several of my armed transports were in dock during the invasion," Eduardo explained. "*Celestial Sovereign* is a yacht, but the rest are cargo carriers. Westphalia might just put new commanders aboard them for the time being. Political officers, as it were, to keep them in line, while the rest of the company worked. After all, without shipping, Yisan's economy falls apart rather quickly."

Lazarus started to say something, but the look in Grace's eye stilled him.

"What about Heechua?" she asked. "Are you still hauling contract materials there from Yisan?"

"We are," Eduardo nodded. "It is about a year from turning fully profitable at this point and repaying all the investments to date. Why?"

Lazarus watched her eyes light up. And he could see her plan take shape.

"Martìnez ships coming into port, armed against pirates, Eduardo," she said. "Perhaps several of them. If we could sneak in and capture their political officers, that might be a whole wing of rugged escorts for later when Lazarus attacks Yisan."

"You'll need Oluchi," Lazarus told her. "Distraction while you work. Take *Celestial Sovereign* and we'll redo the transponders to something innocent. He can pretend to be a tycoon on a jaunt. If they try to capture you at Heechua, all the better, because I know what kind of crew Eduardo hired."

"I'll need to recruit some sailors here to help communicate with everyone," she said. "Species Underground reps, not Humans, so that the Humans at Heechua understand who came to help."

"Agreed," he said, before turning back to Eduardo. "Should you join us, or remain here?"

"I am too old to be hying off on adventures, you youngsters," he laughed. "Like Admiral da Siva, I shall remain someplace safely behind lines, either here or Oton Mari, where I can figure out all the damage Pryce has done and the promises he has made in my name."

"None of them are bad, Eduardo," Grace chuckled. "He's a hustler, same as you. Just don't alienate him, because unlike Strav or Fernanda, he's actually good enough to compete."

"We shall see, young lady," Eduardo replied archly. "We shall see. Now, Lazarus, what do you need from me to make this work?"

"We'll pull everyone together in the morning," he decided. "Something from you that will tell your captains that Oluchi is on the level without telling Westphalia what we're up to. If we can do this quickly, we might more easily dislodge Westphalia from Yisan. One of these days, they have to start feeling the pain from all the things *Ajax* and others have done to them since they started getting more aggressive."

"Are they desperate?" Eduardo asked.

"Not enough for me," Grace answered.

"Nor me," Lazarus echoed her.

Quickly, they got the older gentleman on his way, and Lazarus found himself standing at the closed door with his arms around the tall woman.

"It's not fair," he muttered.

She just laughed.

"You gave all that up to become a proper scientist and naval officer," she replied. "At least that's what you always claim. Seems to me you like being a pirate a little too much, though."

"No comment," Lazarus chuckled back. "When this is all done, I might have to resign my commission and find something else to do, because I've spent so much time not answering to orders these last few years that I'm probably feral."

"Well then, I might hire you." Grace looked him right in the eyes and smiled. "I remember what you did to Strav Ardna and his friends. And what you've done since."

"What would we do?" he asked.

"I have enough money saved up," Grace grinned. "And a few contacts. Maybe we start a security company and get paid to hunt down pirates. Law enforcement rarely travels beyond sector borders, or even system borders. I expect that there will be any number of new colonies planted over the next decade, especially if we're successful here. Maybe we get them to pay you to be a traveling lawman on a roan horse."

Lazarus started to say something about buckaroos and gauchos, but stopped himself.

"I hate it when you're right," he muttered, leaning in to kiss her. "But you're right."

"Get used to saying that," she smiled. "I'm nowhere close to done with you, *Lazarus of Bethany*."

He liked that. And he had a feeling that he'd need something to do with the second half of his life.

Maybe he'd trade the uniform for a badge.

After all, he doubted that all the specist shits in Westphalia would wake up one morning and decide to turn over a new leaf. A lot of them would turn to piracy and crime.

And everyone else would need someone to come along and crack heads together.

He could do that.

NINE

OLUCHI

"SO EXPLAIN IT TO ME AGAIN," Oluchi said, looking around the conference room. "Using small words this time, so I make sure I understand."

He didn't appreciate the smiles on the the faces around the table, but there wasn't much he could do about it.

"You'll sail into Heechua aboard *Celestial Sovereign* and pretend to be a big roller," Grace said. "While you and Anya distract them all with razzle-dazzle, I'll slip aboard one of Eduardo's ships and liberate it."

"What if they have removed the crew and replaced it with Westphalian sailors?" he asked, seeing all manner of bad outcomes that seemed to be eluding all the crazed warrior berserker ninjas around him.

But then, Grace was the one person everyone agreed was the deadliest person they'd ever met. She probably could do exactly that.

"I would find that extremely unlikely, Pryce," Eduardo replied. "Most of these ships are designed to carry heavy loads, so tend to be in excess of two hundred yards long and have crews of around forty, most of whom have served for years."

"And we'll just waltz in and take them?" Oluchi asked.

"You waltz," Grace smiled at him evilly. "I'll take them."

"Then what?"

"Then we take the next one, and the next," Grace continued. "Eventually, either we get them all, or someone gets away and warns Yisan what we're doing. I'd almost rather like that more."

"I beg your pardon?" Oluchi snapped.

"They might be dumb enough to send a ship or a patrol over to try to do something, thereby reducing the forces holding Yisan proper," Grace said. "In fact, I'd almost be willing to chase one off just for that reason."

"But I'm just a sideshow?" Oluchi asked.

Anya leaned in now and flipped his opera cape up and onto his shoulder, from how he'd put both wings back earlier.

"You're the pretty distraction," Anya said. "The flash in the pan gambler who probably won the ship in a poker game and has more money than he knows what to do with. You should start an epic poker game on the station and invite various big shots to try their luck."

"Yeah, but then I don't get to kill anybody," he said sourly. "I feel like I'm not carrying my weight in this thing."

"Pryce, I promise you that you'll get all the blame for capturing Heechua and all the ships at anchor there," Eduardo said. "In fact, if Ardna's successors-in-interest have any ships handy, feel free to commit acts of pure piracy and keep one. After all, I would like to get *Celestial Sovereign* back at some point."

Oluchi grinned as Antonia blushed. She'd been perfectly silent up until now, unwilling to draw any attention to herself as folks discussed Oluchi's role in things.

But then, they made a pretty good team, him and her.

This was just going to be an entirely different kind of con than the sort he'd run on the suckers at Bajerlie and a few other places.

And maybe, just maybe, he needed to go into the shipping business now.

He turned to Anya and leaned close enough to kiss her.

"Pick a card," he whispered. "Any card."

TEN

ANTONIA

ANTONIA DIDN'T LIKE IT, but there wasn't much she could do about the subject without quitting her current job and taking up any of the offers that would probably be banging on her hatch by the morning.

Bajerlie had been something of a lark. Proving to the Innruld that any Human ship might be able to destroy anything less than a full Pyramid. Until she'd given the order, Antonia hadn't really believed that *Celestial Sovereign* could blow up an Innruld Station.

Human manufacturing ran to more durable alloys, but mostly it was better shield generators against more deadly guns. Heechua would be a Human mining station more like Oton Mari. Big, tough, and well protected because pirates played hard core.

But then, nobody else understood how deadly her ship could be.

So she sighed heavily and looked around her bridge as the various engineering lights finally all checked green and she was no longer aboard *Celestial Sovereign*. Instead, the ship would identify itself to the galaxy as *Limited Liability*.

She supposed that it even made sense, a limited liability corporation being perhaps the greatest con game ever invented by sleazy businessmen.

Antonia turned to Pryce as the last light turned green on her board.

The man just grinned all the more. He'd had that Necherle tailor work him up a whole new outfit for this con in something that looked remarkably like silk for having come from Zhoonarrim's stores.

Black pants tucked into knee-high boots polished to an ebony shine. Bright azure stripe, about four inches wide, down both outer seams of his pants, just to draw the eye. White shirt with a button-up front and a short, standing collar. That same azure fabric as a vest, highlighted with black to frame pockets, seams, and buttons. The cape was a little longer that his other ones, black on the outside and azure underneath.

Worse, the silly swashbuckler had added a pistol holster on his right and a slender saber on his left.

Oluchi looked like a toucan bird she'd seen in a zoo once.

"Okay, pirate king, your harem awaits," she said sarcastically.

Grace was tucked into a corner, mostly out of sight but apparently stifling a bout of giggles. Pryce was the only male on the bridge, and Lucas Lam, the security marine they'd brought from *Ajax*, was the only other male aboard the ship, but he stayed in his cabin and dressed like a sailor.

Antonia had herself, Anya, Grace, Aileen, Mafê, Adamanteia, and Esperança, just here on the bridge.

Harem, indeed, even if he only ever had eyes for Anya. Antonia had checked and the man hadn't so much as made an off-color comment to any of her women, except the occasional dirty jokes over dinner.

Oluchi rose from his chair and turned once to make sure every eye was on him, most likely. He was like that.

"Contact *Ajax* and the station," he said in a voice much more sober than the appearance he gave off.

"Lines are open, Oh Dread Warlord Of Space," Mafê replied in a musical voice, setting everyone to giggling now.

It wasn't like they didn't like the boy, but you know, ya gotta keep that pomposity punctured on a regular basis to keep a guy like Oluchi Pryce merely Human.

Finally, they all settled down.

"Any last advice?" Oluchi asked as the big screen showed several key players in a control room.

"Don't get my ship blown up," Eduardo replied in a hearty growl.

But then, Eduardo had personally approved every woman Antonia wanted to hire. Not that he was any more dangerous to them than Pryce, but the man was trusting them all with his life, any time he flew, and wanted only the best.

Antonia made sure of that.

"Working on that, Eduardo," Oluchi replied. "With that, I am now the cavalry, and will try to rendezvous with everyone in three weeks. Antonia, take us out."

"Esperança, your course is plotted?" she asked.

"Affirmative," the Pilot nodded.

"Make your jump," Antonia said.

As Pryce had called it, they were going off now to get the cavalry.

Or to be it, if everything else failed.

ELEVEN

OLUCHI

OLUCHI MADE it a point to be up on the bridge as they arrived close to Heechua Station on that last jump. Anya was with him, but she was studying the station itself.

He was concentrating on the ships. Big ones, for the most part. Rugged haulers designed to move a lot of product with low margins about the galaxy, and do it as efficiently as possible.

According to the notes from Eduardo, the man owned most of the ships that traveled back and forth, with a slice of independent tramp freighters bringing in luxury goods and such for the miners.

And the oligarchs who lived here permanently. Oluchi's targets, at least later.

He moved to look over Mafé's shoulder as she worked, noting that the woman had added a hint of perfume today that she normally skipped. He doubted it was for his benefit, except that she might be sweating with what was coming and didn't want that funk noticeable.

He'd certainly added a bit more cologne this morning.

"What am I looking for?" she asked, as if anything had changed from the last time they'd had this conversation.

"Mostly blind spots close to where they dock us," Oluchi replied. "Who's in-station now? Who is next, so we're prepared. This is the touch-and-go part of the operation, since nobody could know what to expect."

"Well, these six belong to Eduardo," she replied, marking them on her screen with red. "This one is from Leena Hernández. The little ones are all owner-operator types, from the transponder codes they are giving off."

"Any of them armed worth mentioning?" he asked.

She chuckled.

"Most of them could probably get away from an Innruld Security Barc at a dead run," she replied. "But that's about it."

"Any chance we could sneak aboard one from the station?" he asked, studying the layout closer.

"Doubtful, Oluchi," Mafê noted. "They dock the cargo deck and are working it constantly, so there will be people milling about with clipboards. However, I think that most of the crew would either be down there working or up on the bridge, about the time they are moving in to dock and opening up."

"There you have it, then," he said. "I'll let Grace know, but I'm sure she's already far ahead of me on that front."

Mafê just turned and grinned at him.

But he didn't have to be the mastermind here. In fact, he was the magician's hand waving about and causing the eyes to wander while all the others went to work.

Still, he'd look good doing it.

TWELVE

ANYA

ANYA DECIDED that she preferred this level of anonymity. It took her back to her spying days in the Planning Department, when she lived a double life that paid really well. And if she'd had to give that all up to chase a life of piracy with Oluchi, things were turning out pretty well there, too.

As befit the *girlfriend* of a gambler and rake, Anya was dressed well down today as they walked the main promenade of Heechua Station. This was where the money was concentrated, unlike Yisan. But Yisan was merely a transit point, most of the time, with a combined population of under fifty million people that didn't need big stations in orbit.

Heechua was all about mining. Either the planet below, or one of the ice giants out at the edge of the cold where some truly exotic hydrocarbons were relatively easy to get to. If you were willing to take a few risks.

The money was here on the station, where the factories were. Ore was turned into stock on the surface, downwind of the farms that fed people. Asteroids and comets and gases intersected here and got turned into exotics that were going to make the early investors, like Eduardo, even more fabulously wealthy.

Anya made a note to recruit some spies to help get her in on future deals like this. Eduardo had said more than once that being in the boardroom was the key. Oluchi might be useful as a front for some corporations, but Anya had learned that the quiet players rarely made public appearances.

They just controlled things behind the scenes. Like an ex-spy might aspire to.

Even if today she was showing off more flesh than a corporate boardroom might consider appropriate.

Black, sleeveless crop top that crossed her chest and then up over her neck, showing off most of her collar bones and pressing her breasts together but not covering anything much lower. The bottom might have been something she wore on a beach, were she someplace with nudity taboos, a bikini cloth covering front and back, but connected on each side by four cords. She had a silk sash the same fabric as lined Oluchi's cape knotted around her waist. The knot rested on her left hip as it draped and dangled around her right thigh.

It had the added benefit of covering just enough of her bottom to make people stare, which helped her hide, as they usually forgot to look up and notice that she had a face.

Anonymous, even as the sash contained any number of tiny pockets inside where she had a comm, some credits, a knife, and even the smallest palm stunner that Grace had in her collection.

Jewelry consisted of platinum. A necklace with a manufactured sapphire hanging just above her breasts. One loop around each wrist. A single chain around her right ankle above the black ballet slippers she was wearing. A clamp holding her pony tail back and making her face look a bit more hawklike than normal.

On a station, you never had to worry about the temperature changing. A gambler's moll could dress down as far as she wanted, as long as she didn't risk getting arrested for upsetting local morals. If a place like Heechua had any.

Anya smiled at the men staring and the women scowling, but Oluchi drew all eyes as he walked around and glad-handed everyone who came along with a business card and an introduction.

Heechua hadn't really been conquered and occupied by Westphalia, if only because they didn't have the manpower to do the job. At the same time, Eduardo Martìnez owned something like sixty percent of the facility and seventy-five percent of the hulls carrying cargo both directions, so the entire place was something of an armed camp trying to enforce some level of neutrality.

Most of the people were just here to make money, after all.

A man approached them now, a bit surprised from the look on his face.

"Pryce?" he asked, drawing close. "Is that you?"

"Hello, Miguel," Oluchi replied smoothly. "How are things on Heechua?"

"Well, I suppose, considering," Miguel replied nervously. "Where have you been? You disappeared a while back."

They had stopped walking when the two of them turned into a trio, so Anya leaned on Oluchi some. Just another faceless, nameless bimbo with a great bod that the gambler kept along as a prize.

And if you'll buy, that I have a mining claim on Guardda VI I'll sell you cheap.

"I lucked into one of those once in a lifetime poker

games," Oluchi replied, his voice bright and maybe a shade too loud for just the three of them, but Anya could see ears perk up around as other folks slowed or sped up and turned this way. "The pot was so great that you might call it Screw-You-Money. Worse, the silly fool was so convinced that he'd won that he had to make the final call with his personal yacht. So I took him, it, and the rest, and have been cruising rather far away from the scene of the crime, as it were."

"I see," Miguel said. "So you don't play poker much anymore?"

She felt Oluchi's shrug as she rubbed herself against him, putting on a show that had Miguel breathing a little heavy and distracted.

Whoops.

"Oh, I'm always up for a good game," Oluchi was saying innocently. "Gives me something to do as I tour around and consider investing."

"You heard what happened to Yisan, right?" Miguel asked now, distracted to the point he didn't perhaps realize he'd gotten louder, too.

"That's part of what drew me here, my good man" Oluchi said brightly. "There might be some openings that I could exploit. Fire sale sorts of things where I could swoop in and end up owning whole sectors of the economy in this system."

Anya turned to Miguel and smiled as Oluchi talked. Investments on that scale required wealth in Eduardo's league. Or Fernanda's.

How could an ex-gigolo have that kind of money? But if he did…

Miguel was unconsciously licking his lips. Anya already knew what a great team she and Oluchi made when it came to cons like this. That she'd turned it on its head this time was just the frosting.

Usually, she was the quiet one diving into the accounting to do due diligence, and he was the distraction.

However, this was another way into that boardroom with people like Eduardo and Fernanda, where deals worth planetary domestic products were done.

"Own sectors?" Miguel finally gasped, physically drawing himself away from ogling her body to try to pay attention to her gambler. "Are you worth that much?"

Oluchi smiled at the man and changed the subject.

"Any good poker games on the station I might manage to score an invitation to?" he asked.

Miguel blinked and dug into a pocket to retrieve a business card that he handed to Oluchi.

"Excellent, my good man," Oluchi said, swapping him for one they had printed aboard the ship once they docked.

They parted quickly and Anya found that everyone had suddenly moved on, almost ignoring them as Oluchi led her off to one side.

"You are a menace, woman," he said, pulling her close for a quick kiss.

Anya just smiled.

"I believe that's why you hired me?" she asked innocently.

"Poor fellow is doomed," he chuckled, growing quieter as he leaned in and pressed her against his chest. "Miguel probably ended up here because he was too broke to keep playing with Eduardo's circle of people. The man thinks he is a card sharp, but I honestly could probably take his ship and his shoes if I felt really mean. However, he will introduce us to the people he feels comfortable fleecing, so we'll have the chance to focus all eyes and minds on us while Grace and Aileen get to work."

"Good," Anya replied. "I need to do some more scouting here anyway."

"What evil are you up to now, Persaud?" he asked, leaning back to study her face.

"You might have been kidding about fire sale prices, Pryce," she purred at him. "I'm not."

THIRTEEN

AILEEN

AILEEN at least had found a place where she could mostly compete with Grace in a physical arena. Probably weren't many of those. For anyone. But Yithadreph were a semi-aquatic species, and working in zero gravity was almost as good as swimming.

They'd been docked for a day now. Oluchi and Anya had been working their magic on the station like wandering oligarchs looking for their next fix. Tonight, station time, they were at a dinner party similar to the sort of thing she'd seen on Yisan when Aileen first met Eduardo Martìnez and the others.

Food and gambling, plus the sort of side deals you got when people with money got friendly with each other.

Heechua Station kept time with the main starport on the ground below. Neither might truly sleep, but Humans weren't nocturnal creatures, so most honest folks would tend to be asleep now.

That just left the dishonest folk.

Grace and Lucas were suited up for a spacewalk. Aileen

had her own suit on but held the helmet in her hands for now while she waited.

"Strike Team, this is the bridge," Antonia's voice came over the intercom. "Your target is moving in to dock now. Tugs expect to lock him in place in twenty, that is two-zero minutes. Depart when ready."

Aileen locked her helmet down and did a final inspection as Grace cycled the airlock. Stun pistols. Zip-ties. Comms. Various trinkets for breaking and entering a spaceship in flight.

Not that Addison's crew had ever actually done something like that, but they'd planned out scenarios for such things, against the day the Innruld finally figured out that *Shiva Zephyr Glaive* was running illegal narcotics.

Running like hell and stealing another ship had been an option.

At least until Lazarus came along.

Grace moved like her name as she stepped out of the open airlock. Lucas moved like a marine, and she'd spent enough time around them to appreciate that he was better than most of them. Just not in the same league as her and Grace.

Aileen slipped out and Grace cycled the lock to close, in case anyone happened to be looking this way. There weren't many viewports on the station or the sides of most ships, but it only took one person raising an alarm at the wrong moment.

They could have jumped straight across to the next ship from here, but that would have likely set off all manner of collision alarms on someone's bridge. Human ships didn't fly into a garage to dock, like on an Innruld SkyCity. Instead, the curve of the station's outer hull let you dock while stuck out like a thumb. But that meant that orbital debris was a risk.

As a result, they went forward on their own hull in complete silence, because again, even an unexpected radio signal might wake someone up from a boring bridge watch.

Can't have that.

Antonia had gotten them docked away from the other yachts, closer to the loading bays. Something about not being willing to pay the exorbitant daily rate for air and fuel for generators, so they were shuffled off to the less-impressive zones.

Right where Grace wanted them.

The woman took the lead as they got to the station hull itself, pausing to look at each of them. Aileen and Lucas both gave her a thumbs up, so she turned back and started to traverse. With any luck, they would look like a maintenance crew moving around.

Human ships were ugly. No two ways about it. Even *Celestial Sovereign* was mundane, a heart shape upside down. Unnecessarily symmetrical.

She missed *Shiva Zephyr Glaive*, and that long curve Lazarus called a treble clef. When this was all said and done, she might commission someone to remake that ship in a Rio yard used to military standards of welding. Maybe the place that had originally built *Ajax*, as long as they understood that symmetry was dumb.

She looked up now at the enormous tree trunk of a cargo hauler sticking out from the forest floor of the station. Boring. Rounded-off rectangular tube in a dull gray.

Where was the excitement of flying in space?

But she caught herself from snorting. When hauling loads this massive, you wanted efficiency. This thing could probably land four of *Shiva Zephyr Glaive* in the main cargo bay, as long as Kuei skewed the nose around as she landed.

And still have space left over.

But still…

They moved around the ship slowly and carefully, not walking on the station skin, and instead using regular grips and handholds to propel themselves at a brisk walk.

Aileen happened to be holding a gripping bar when she felt an earthquake ripple through it. Their target had docked. Right on time. The whole station flexed, but they were close enough now to see it, having passed the first ship.

Grace paused again, looking back, then proceeded, two little ducklings in her wake.

Around them, the silence of space. Aileen had a local radio on, just listening to comm chatter as folks yammered back and forth. Nobody currently reporting saboteurs on the outside of the station, which was good.

They got to the target freighter about the same time all the noises of docking settled. Big ships moved slowly when doing this, but there were three tugs out on the far end doing all the pushing and tweaking.

Again, weird. She was used to just landing on a pad and deploying the platform.

They found a quiet spot and watched. The sun was on the wrong side, so they were all in near-total darkness here, broken only occasionally by flood lights. The nearest tug was a darker gray lump on the side of the freighter, until it broke loose and moved away from the station, lights blinking to warn everyone.

Grace reached out a hand to each of them and squeezed. With any luck, everyone would be looking the wrong way right now.

That, or they were about to be arrested for piracy.

FOURTEEN
OLUCHI

IT WAS ALMOST like being home, but Oluchi would never tell these men and women that. The last game of high-stakes poker he'd sat in on had ended with Eha kidnapped, Aileen brutalized, and the flaming wreck of Strav Ardna's yacht sinking in a hurricane gale.

His new friends didn't need to know his connection to those sorts of calamities.

Since then, the stakes had kept going up. The only thing that had remained had been the occasional bluff. Brasilia. Oton Mari. Bajerlie.

Oluchi revealed friendly smiles as Miguel began collecting cards for a shuffle. Everyone chucked in a coin to watch.

The crowd was a little nervous. However it wasn't about him. The Westphalian occupation of Yisan had everyone riled up a little too much, as most of these folks were likely wondering if their own livelihoods were in danger, given various ownership stakes.

Oluchi was up about a thousand from where he'd started

an hour ago. Along the way, he'd folded early on a couple of possible hands, just to see what the others did. Five other men, two women, so almost like Eduardo's games, save that the buffet wasn't as good.

The booze was better, for what that was worth. Still, he found himself cutting an awful lot of fruit juice into not much rum. Too much time on the other side of the nebula, where most folks considered alcohol a poison.

Oluchi could have forgotten all the other names of the players and assigned them mark designations after the first hand was played, but he was too polite and too professional for something like that. Still, Miguel thought he was the king shit as a player, when Oluchi rated him just a shade above the middle. Two of the men and one of the women were pretty much just here to lose their table stake and then watch.

That left two men and the other woman good enough to call themselves poker players. Back on Yisan, they might have even gotten an invite to one of the big games, perhaps, where they would have been like him in the old days, jumped-up pretty boys brought in for entertainment value, rather than serious money players.

"So, Pryce," Ernesto said as Miguel started shuffling. "I hear that you struck it rich and have been off touring your new investments over the last year or so?"

Ernesto was one of the marks just here to be entertained while losing. Not someone Oluchi had known on Yisan, but there were nearly a hundred worlds in this end of space, mostly free colonies and mining facilities.

Oluchi smiled, wondering about the ancient game of *telephone,* where a rumor keeps getting twisted around, the more people tell it.

"Something like that," he offered blandly. "I had my suspicions that the war might intrude more and more on this end of space, so I felt it might be time to diversify."

After all, if they hadn't any of them placed him in the same conversation with new aliens like Eha and Aileen, who was he to correct them? They might accidentally wander into the truth at that point.

Can't have that.

"Any good leads?" Ernesto asked pointedly. "With Westphalia in control of Yisan, a lot of money is suddenly up in the air and not sure where it should be invested."

"Indeed," Oluchi nodded. "A wise man once said that the best time to get into the markets was when there was blood in the streets. All prices are radically depressed, if you've got the stomach for the risk."

He watched that tidbit float around the table. Most of these folks were more marked by their uncertainty that they might be next. The Heechua might wake up one morning to a Westphalian fleet. Oluchi doubted it. Too small. Too far away from anywhere interesting. Still losing too much money as a system at present, as Eduardo had said that his local economy was only now starting to come together. And that had been before.

"Heechua?" Anastasia asked.

Like Ernesto, a middle-aged investor who had inherited a share from wealthier parents and was trying to build it up into something like their youth.

"I used to play a lot of poker with folks like Eduardo Martìnez and Fernanda Flores," he reminded them. "They might be cash-poor right this moment and need to liquidate a few assets. At present, I'm not even sure which banks are still solvent enough to underwrite notes. At the same time, a place like Heechua generates a steady revenue."

Oluchi let innocence be his byword as he studied the faces around him. Miguel had actually stopped shuffling cards to listen, so Oluchi prompted him.

He'd walked in here to distract people. However, some of

the looks around him right now suggested that he might be able to work a few deals.

Wouldn't that be hilarious?

FIFTEEN
AILEEN

AILEEN DIDN'T HAVE the chops with Human electronics that Grace did. That much was embarrassingly obvious as she watched the woman hotwire the airlock controls, having already bypassed the security alerts that would have warned someone on the bridge that an airlock was about to activate.

Aileen was in the airlock itself, with Lucas close by but staying out of the way of the two women. But then, he was a better marksman than brawler. She'd sparred with him on the mat enough times to know that, even if she did have a radically unfair advantage.

Nobody on this ship was likely to know how to handle a Yithadreph in close combat besides her two friends.

Grace reached out a hand and tapped her on the shoulder now, letting Aileen know that they were ready to trigger the hatch. It might not alert the bridge, but the system would still hoot to let people know to get out of the way.

If any crew members were close, that would bring them running.

The chamber sealed and pressurized. Aileen popped her helmet off as soon as the pressure was high enough for her, even though Humans couldn't handle it. They weren't designed for pressure extremes, which was why she was closest to the inner hatch.

She keyed seals loose and was wriggling out of her space suit before the other two had their helmets off, showing off her favorite lime capris and banana vest. With a gun holster.

Stunner in hand, she watched the inner airlock move towards her. Again, her skinniness let her get around it before any Human could, and she flowed out into the hallway as fast as she could move. Damned storks might have an advantage on a straightaway, but not maneuvering tightly like this.

This part of the hall was a dead end, so she moved outward at a lope, intent on seizing the high ground, as it were.

None too soon, either, as a crew member was clomping this way at a jog from a side corridor, probably panicky that they had intruders. Pirates, even.

They got to the intersection at the same time, only because Aileen put on a burst of speed she'd pay for later.

Human. Male. Burly in the way of folks like Xiuying, but taller.

He turned the corner as she got there and Aileen jumped up with a hissing growl. Xiuying had suggested it once, playing on Human subconscious fears when they saw all the fur coming at them.

The man staggered to a stop and took a half-step backwards, hands holding a pipe wrench coming up defensively. Just as she expected.

Aileen swept the foot that was stepping backwards instead. Just a tap, but when he went to put weight on it, it wasn't there and he landed on his ass instead, dropping the wrench.

Then, and only then, did she shoot him. Stunner. Big guy. She shot him a second time, just to be sure.

Grace and Lucas were charging now, but unnecessary. Aileen peeked around the corner the way her first victim had come, while Lucas grabbed the man by the ankles and dragged him quickly out of sight.

Clear. And no alarms hooting madly to draw everyone to the arms locker.

Humans and violence.

Of course, she'd just attacked a total stranger, but she had a mission. And he hadn't been hurt beyond his pride.

"This way," Grace whispered.

Aileen fell in third. Racing through corridors was where those long legs on Grace and Lucas let them shine, but she did a credible job of keeping up. Wasn't in any shape to shoot, but she didn't have to.

Just gasp a lot and hope she didn't pull anything from running.

The ship was huge, but they weren't all that far from the bridge, coming in this way. Grace led them to a staircase and looked up as Aileen staggered in her wake.

Damned storks and their impossible stairs. She might have even muttered that out loud, from the grin Lucas gave her.

Up the two Humans went, one tired Yithadreph pirate in their wake. At some point, other crew members might figure out what was happening and come to the rescue. At that point, she would be covering the rear, maybe with Lucas as well.

Wasn't like Grace really needed the help. Aileen had seen that woman work. And the man, come to think of it.

The folks back on Gowook would never forget the pair, that much was certain.

She caught up when they were at the top of the stairs.

"Just across this hallway and through that door," Grace whispered, pointing. "Aileen, you sit here and ambush anyone coming from a side. Lucas, you cover my back and shoot anyone holding a weapon."

Aileen nodded and settled. This was a great place to stalk storks from. She'd be behind them on this level as they tried to open the door, and above anyone trying to get to this top deck.

Her only regret was that she wouldn't get to see the most dangerous Human anyone knew at work.

SIXTEEN

GRACE

GRACE LIKED to think of herself as a geisha. An entertainer of many talents and instruments. And she was.

At the same time, she'd also spent an extraordinary number of hours on dojo floors and combat ranges over the years. That sort of thing aroused men like Lazarus, which was good.

She took a moment to confirm that Lucas was ready. He was her most reliable sparring partner, willing to step onto the mat with her without bringing any frail male ego along. Even now, he just nodded.

A man of few words who let his actions be his legend.

And today would make a few of those.

She looked out into the corridor both directions. Seeing nobody, she stepped across and keyed the hatch open with her left hand. The exterior had been secured, but she'd never been on any non-military vessel that treated the average interior hatch as important. It opened under her prodding.

Grace flowed silently and swiftly into the room, taking a moment to study everything before acting.

Her first target was obvious. The man wore the uniform

of a Lieutenant in the Westphalian Navy, like this was a prize ship and he was commanding. But then, even the idiots on Earth understood that if they destroyed Yisan's economy, they would make more enemies than they ever could friends, as well as generate angry refugee trains.

Two others besides the man in slate gray. The older man was probably the captain of this ship, while the younger had the look of a simple sailor whose job it was to monitor engineering as everything got shut down.

Grace had spent enough time on ships before Lazarus to understand things, and the time since on a well-run warship to appreciate how well his crews did things, even when they answered to a Vaadwig or a Qooph.

The Captain turned towards her at the sound of the hatch opening. His mouth fell open a second later, but he made no sound except slamming it shut.

The Westphalian turned this way now. His eyes got huge. Fool went for the pistol on his belt, under a fold-over flap that was really one of the dumbest designs she could imagine.

She shot him.

The sailor flinched at the sound and turned her way like he was about to do something.

"Hold!" the Captain yelled, moving towards his man and putting an arm on his shoulder to keep the youngster seated.

Grace gestured Lucas the rest of the way into the room. His job now was to cover this hatch. There was another one on the far side for her, but she was certain that there might only be one other Westphalian aboard. Both they and Rio had largely formalized things like prize crews, so a single officer and a single enlisted went along and everything was respected.

Pirates, however…

The Captain's eyes had never left Grace.

"*I know you,*" the man whispered in a hoarse, shocked

tone. "Yisan. A holiday party the CEO gave. You played cello…"

"I still do, Captain," Grace smiled, and even relaxed some. "However, Eduardo has tasked me and several others with retaking his fleet."

"He escaped?" the man asked. For a moment, she saw hope in his eyes.

"He did," she acknowledged. "Found help. We came here because a small fleet is planning to attack the moorage at Yisan and the commodore of that task force would like to insert friendly vessels ahead of time."

"We're one ship," he countered.

"You're six, if there is a means by which I can take out all your prize crews," Grace said.

"That would piracy, ma'am," he said, licking his lips. "Kinda like sneaking aboard my ship and capturing it."

He was smiling.

Everyone had obviously behaved up until now, as Yisan had been neutral about trading with both Rio and Yisan. Her home was still something of a neutral in the wider war, in spite of Eduardo making noises about joining up with the Rio Alliance.

"It had become a revolution, Captain," she said coldly. "Eduardo has chosen sides in the greater war. As have I. With your help, we can liberate Heechua and then go back to Yisan and kick Westphalia out for good."

"For good?" the man asked. "How?"

Grace slid backwards from the man, never taking her eyes off the two men who might be prisoners now as well as the far hatch. She did glance down just enough to key the hatch open from here.

"Aileen, could you join us, please?" she called quietly across the space.

The two Humans nearly fainted when a Yithadreph

slipped in and closed the door behind her. But then, Eha and Aileen had only been on Yisan for a day before leaving, and Grace didn't think any of the Species Underground had returned since.

For all Yisan's centrality, all the action had happened instead at places like Brasilia or Liberty.

Or Zhoonarrim.

"How many more?" Aileen asked, studying the two men, but they didn't react, so Aileen raised her voice. "I asked you a question, sailor. *How many more Westphalians aboard?*"

Grace held her start at how hard—how *militant*—Aileen sounded right then. Something had indeed changed about the woman.

The younger man held up one finger, apparently unable to formulate words. The Captain might be about to faint.

"Sit," Grace ordered the Captain. "Can we get the other up here quietly?"

"He's, uh, down helping with the loading," the youngster managed. "I could page him, I guess."

"Do that," the man ordered sharply. "Get him up here without any explanation other than to come to the bridge immediately."

The man turned this way and Grace nodded. That would put them in possession of this ship.

"Now, Captain," she smiled at the man. "How do we get the rest of the ships to revolt?"

SEVENTEEN

LUCAS

LUCAS HAD the two prisoners stashed in a forward cabin for now. From the grumbles he'd overheard, the biggest issue might be to keep any of the regular crew from going after that Westphalian officer with a wrench, although the enlisted sailor had apparently earned his keep by standing watches in engineering and helping load and unload when all bodies were needed.

The ship was close to done loading, but they hadn't solved the issue of getting the other vessels to fall into any kind of trap.

Lucas found himself back up on the bridge, standing off to one side as Grace, Aileen, and the guy in charge, Captain Gonzalez was his name, discussed things. And shot ideas down as fast as anyone suggested them.

"Hey," Lucas said at one point, mostly as a lark. "Why not have Oluchi throw a party?"

He didn't appreciate the many faces suddenly turned towards him. Or the smiles. He felt like a side of meat about to go onto the grill.

"Say that again?" Aileen snapped.

Lucas took a deep breath to find the words.

"So if I understand, Oluchi is a bigshot investor here to maybe vulture onto some of Eduardo's ships, right?" Lucas replied. "What better way to do that than to invite the captains to a party where he can meet them and talk shipping stuff. Gets those men off the ship. I would be utterly surprised if the Westie officers didn't come as well, just to make sure nobody plotted a revolution at such an event. Then you call all the crews and order them to arrest whatever peon sailors the Westie officers left behind and boom, you have a fleet."

Grace smiled at him in a way that Lucas found uncomfortable to see. But he also knew exactly how dangerous that woman really was, in ways that nobody else here probably did.

Eventually she turned her attention to Captain Gonzalez. Lucas found himself breathing easier.

"Would your orders and schedule allow it?" she asked the man.

That man looked nervous. More nervous. Aileen was standing close and the guy was a little twitchy.

"Maybe," Gonzalez replied. "If your other folks were to maybe call on us from the front door and come aboard, we could turn that around and say he'd invited me and everyone else. Whether they would go for it I can't say."

"Make it an open bar," Lucas spoke up. "No sailor will pass that up, Rio or Westphalia."

Grace looked at him again and he realized that he was the only professional warsailor on the scene.

Weird. She was a killer. Aileen wore the uniform. Gonzalez was a Captain. But Lucas was the professional.

"I assume we can afford it?" Lucas asked now.

He was in the Navy. Food and drink were provided, along with uniforms and orders to follow.

"We can," Aileen said. "Eduardo gave me codes to tap his secret bank accounts here if we need them. We also have a couple of mundane accounts we could tap, but someone might leak at that point."

"Do it," Gonzalez said abruptly. "My ship also has funds available. All of them do, and this can be a down payment on our freedom from those shits."

Grace nodded and turned to the young sailor standing a watch.

"Open a channel to *Limited Liability*," she said.

EIGHTEEN

ANYA

ANYA HAD RETIRED to the hotel room she and Oluchi had taken for their stay. He would be playing poker all night as a front, but the Plus Ones had been only invited for dinner. That was fine with her, as it let her dig deeper into the corporate quarterly reports of the folks on the station, including several at that poker table.

All manner of crimes and failures could be hidden in the text part of such things, but the numbers never lied. Already, she had a pretty good idea of various places she might be able to slip in and buy up shares cheap, as everyone's values had dropped precipitously as a result of the invasion, in spite of solid fundamentals that should have held the stock price higher.

She snorted to herself, glass of wine in one hand, as she considered how appalled most people would be when she told them she considered this sort of thing to be fun.

The comm chirped and she checked the line. Antonia, calling from the yacht.

"Hello," she said brightly.

The signal would be relatively encrypted, but a stubborn person could figure it all out eventually.

"So I just got a message from the captain of the Martìnez freighter in dock right now," Antonia began without preamble. "Thanking me for the invitation to a meet and greet with an open bar and suggesting that we perhaps might extend it to the other cargo captains in system and hold it tomorrow night on the station. What the hell is he talking about?"

Anya paused and replayed the whole thing in her mind. That he had called Antonia meant that Grace and the others had probably been successful in boarding. Especially since he hadn't called for the police to come take anybody away in chains.

That news would have popped up on the station channel she had been monitoring.

Open bar parties for sailors, like bureaucrats, was a guaranteed way to make sure everyone showed up, on time, and ready to eat and drink on someone else's credstick.

And it would fit the legend that Oluchi and she had been crafting, that of the high roller who had suddenly made so much money that he needed legitimate places to invest it.

Shares of freighters might do nicely, especially if ownership might be questionable at present.

"It means good news, I think," Anya replied. "It means you and a few girls on the guest list, if you have nice clothes to wear, so that we have a few friendly guns handy, just in case. I suspect that it is a way to get all the other captains and maybe their minders together in one place so that we can take them all at once."

"Can I turn all this over to you for now?" Antonia asked.

"Consider it done," Anya answered.

The line went dead immediately, which didn't surprise

her. The only question would be if Antonia would come, or just send some of the others in her stead. Grace was a given. Aileen would remain in hiding.

Anya shut down the report she had been reading and began looking up catering companies.

NINETEEN

OLUCHI

OLUCHI LOOKED DOWN as his comm chirped with a text message from Anya.

Party arranged for the shipping captains, she wrote. *Invite some of your poker friends? Food and open bar. 7pm tomorrow.*

He managed not to snort or flinch, but Oluchi had no idea what had just happened. At the same time, he was also cursed to be surrounded on all sides by highly-competent women who were running an even bigger scam than he was, which was a pretty impressive thing to imagine. That most of them were beautiful just made it all the better.

This time however, he just went ahead and folded his cards.

"Bad news?" Ernesto asked from across the table.

That man had been on a lucky streak and might break even tonight, instead of walking away broke like normal. Miguel was likely down to his last hand at this point. Oluchi was accidentally cleaning the rest out, one good hand in four.

But he was on stage right now. Make it good.

"So I might have mentioned that I was looking for

investments," he began, watching the others all put down their cards to follow.

Like maybe this hand would end the night. Not a bad way to go out, all things considered.

"My staff have been contacting some of the freighter captains around here, and managed to arrange a reception for tomorrow night," he said. "Open bar and buffet, it seems, although I don't have all the details. But I've enjoyed myself this evening immensely and wanted to invite everyone to join me. Plus Ones, and all that."

"Open bar for sailors?" Miguel asked now, intruigued.

"I wanted to make an exceptional splash," Oluchi assured him with a knowing grin. "This evening has been good, and I have several side projects that I'll be wanting to talk to all of you about later, so this is a chance to just relax. And maybe see about opening a wedge into shipping in Heechua."

Eduardo Martìnez *owned* shipping in this system. Everyone else fought for the scraps. If that was likely to change, they would want in.

And an act of piracy in the middle of a cocktail party seemed to be just about as big a splash as he could imagine.

Hopefully, the ladies all had his back.

TWENTY

GRACE

GRACE HADN'T HAD the opportunity to dress up for a while. Lazarus had been running for his life, then running various con games of his own, then fighting everyone and everywhere to save the galaxy from being overrun by the Innruld and Westphalia. She had played a few private concerts for various folks, but those had been impromptu things. Just grab the cello or sitar or flute and play.

This was going to be a performance. Lazarus would be a bit put out that he had to miss it, but she'd make it up to the man. There wasn't anywhere he could run that she couldn't catch him eventually, after all.

The best part had been walking right out of the cargo bay on Gonzalez's ship, crossing to *Limited Liability*, and walking in. Nobody had even noticed, let alone questioned her.

Because she was bringing the sitar and a small arsenal of firepower with her tonight, she'd gone for skin-tight leggings in dark green, with a royal blue tunic over it, drawn close with a black leather belt. Her hair was always kept at a medium length unless she needed to shave it for a wig, so she had picked it out tonight into a poofy halo of darkness that followed her everywhere she went.

Not entirely inappropriate, considering her usual occupation. And her expectations of the evening.

Aileen and Lucas were guarding the freighter and the two prisoners, back on the ship. Gonzalez was intending to show up later than everyone else and shrug when asked about the Westphalian Lieutenant that should have accompanied him. If everyone was there, Grace and some of Antonia's folks would spring into action.

She checked her outfit one last time in the mirror and grinned broadly.

"What's so funny?" Adamanteia asked.

As the Fusilier on *Celestial Sovereign*, the woman normally played with the big guns, but was also certified on everything down to palm stunners, so she would be attending, along with a handful of staff and crew that Eduardo kept around as guards.

"Thinking about the event," Grace replied, turning to the woman.

Adamanteia was average height, but exceptionally lean, with a metabolism like a hummingbird. Dark blond hair and green eyes were weird in this sector of space, where everyone tended to be so much darker of skin and eyes, but like Lazarus, her family were refugees from elsewhere. Jews, in her case, fleeing one of the periodic spasms of violence that lurched across Westphalia every generation or so.

"Some of the industrialists on the invite list are likely to show up late so as to make something of an entrance," Grace said.

Adamanteia snorted.

"Exactly," Grace smiled. "They'll miss all the fun, and have nobody to blame but themselves."

"Are any of them a threat?" Adamanteia asked. "Or working for Westphalia?"

"Possibly the latter," Grace acknowledged. "But not the former. There are no threats tonight except us. You'll all have stunners on your person. Shoot first if anyone gives you any reason at all to wonder. Oluchi and Anya can sort out the bodies afterwards."

Adamanteia blanched a little, that pale skin showing all of her emotions, but Grace didn't figure the woman had ever actually killed someone with her own hands, usually relying on ship's guns in big turrets to do the job.

But nobody had to die tonight. That a few fools might *choose to* was an entirely different thing.

"Go round up your girls," Grace said, checking her chronometer. "I'm going to go now and make sure the sound system is adequate and my lines of fire are acceptable."

Adamanteia nodded and vanished. Grace lifted her sitar case with all the weapons carefully hidden in it and exited the ship.

Heechua Station was just like most mining platforms, a long, gray curve around a central hub of generators and control spaces, with all the factories on the first ring and the warehouses beyond that to make it easy to do things with the fewest number of steps. A few wolf whistles and a lot of stares accompanied her as she walked, but nobody wanted to chat her up after taking in the glower of carefully-contained rage on her face.

Yet another act. She was practically dancing with the chance to show off tonight. And if her cover might end up being a little blown, she didn't think it would matter much. At some point, Grace Savidge would formally resign her position with Eduardo's organization, once she and Lazarus worked out what they were going to do next.

Anya and Oluchi had infected both of them with that

most forbidden of wild dreams, a *happily-ever-after*. And it really didn't matter how many Westphalian bodies either of them had to pile up in a roadside ditch to accomplish it.

She reached the hall where the reception was, certain that she would have to argue with someone about being on the list, but Anya was there with a man holding a tablet computer he was checking names off against..

Grace relented and smiled when Anya suddenly got nervous. Defense mechanism in public.

Anya relaxed as well.

"She's on the list," Anya said to the man, then promptly ignored him and gave her a hug.

Anya Persaud was a tactile person. Grace had learned to accept that and smile.

"We have a low stage for you, or a corner, depending on your needs…" Anya tapered off at that point.

That woman was a spy. She had a much better understanding of assassins than most folks.

Grace smiled at her and entered the hall, wondering where to best inflict her surprise on the mob that would gather in another hour or so.

But only after entertaining them a bit first.

TWENTY-ONE
ANYA

ANYA HAD DRESSED as a personal aide tonight, forgoing one of the outfits designed to outrage people's sensibilities with lust. As if any of them might somehow compete with Oluchi. No, tonight she looked more like Collin Lau, Eduardo's right hand man who was currently on Liberty, working with the Species Underground and the colonists.

Sober, even somber. Slacks so dark as to be almost black. A short, kimono-style tunic in maroon over a black shirt. Her hair was up in braids, just because she'd felt like it and had a budget this morning for a quick spa trip.

All part of her cover. Honest.

Grace and Oluchi were deeper inside the hall, supervising their areas. Adamanteia and three other women from the ship were handy in dark colors, as though staff, but none wore aprons marking them. Still, the act of wearing matte black at an event like this meant that they would be pointedly overlooked by people with wealth and ego.

That was why you made all that money, wasn't it?

She snorted under her breath. This staff was better than competent. She'd been to enough department-catered events to appreciate that as everything had come together so smoothly. A few extra folks had managed to score invitations somewhere, without being on a freighter or at the poker table, but she wouldn't begrudge them. She would need agents and contacts on this station later when she and Oluchi invested.

It would be even better if they understood just how dangerous the pair of them might be, starting now.

She smiled at the next group entering. One of the captains, along with her first mate and then the requisite punk in Westphalian gray.

Those men were armed. Part of their uniform. There really hadn't been an easy way to enforce or even suggest otherwise without raising suspicions, but they were also going to be outnumbered tonight.

And in for a rude surprise.

Still, she greeted them, welcomed everyone, and got them checked off the list. One more set and all her victims would be in place.

Oluchi was holding court in a corner, not that far from the bar. Everyone had immediately entered, gone for booze, and then maybe remembered to sidle over and thank their host more sedately. Anya wondered what it would be like to do the same thing someplace like Zhoonarrim.

Probably need to have one alcohol bar and two different tea shops set up, just because steeping would take a while and only the Humans would drink the alcohol anyway.

She counted noses. Thirty or so guests. Fifteen more staff working the buffet and floor, plus a small team of experts in the kitchen. Grace playing from the stage. Adamanteia and the others just meandering in a way that even looked random.

And the last group arrived. With a problem.

"Captain Montague?" she asked, as the man stood at the door. "Just you?"

Anya didn't want to sound alarmed, but if they were missing one, the man could possibly commandeer the ship he was on at gunpoint and order the crew to fly him to Yisan. The surprise would only partly be ruined, because they had never expected to be able to get everyone here, but Anya had been hoping.

Surprise opened up so many more options later.

"Lieutenant Schmidt believes alcohol is a tool of the devil," Captain Montague fumed. "The man almost refused to let me come, but finally relented. Sorry I'm late."

"You are exactly on time, Captain," she said, gesturing him into the room. "Welcome and enjoy yourself."

Once the man was gone, she turned to the door keeper.

"Captain Gonzalez will arrive soon, presumably alone," she said. "Admit him immediately and then nobody not on this list. Understood?"

"Yes, ma'am," the man replied warily.

Anya nodded and turned. She walked towards Grace, catching the woman's eye and quietly holding up four fingers, when they had been expecting five.

Grace studied her for a second as she played and then nodded.

Anya found Adamanteia and stepped close.

"One remained behind," she murmured to the quiet woman. "Can we take them all without anyone giving an alarm?"

"I'll handle it," Adamanteia said.

Anya relaxed. She was not a killer, like so many of these women. She planned and researched.

Oluchi separated himself from his mob now and walked close for a hug and a quick kiss.

"Everything under control?" he whispered in her ear.

"One of our targets decided not to attend," she replied. "We need to get to him before anyone says anything here."

"There are two main exits," he said in a suddenly-hard voice. "You cover the front door, and it looks like Adamanteia is going into the kitchen to keep them from panicking. When Grace takes a break, make sure nobody leaves."

"Understood," she said, breaking the clench and circling back.

Nobody here was paying much attention to her, so it was a successful party so far.

"Is everything okay, ma'am?" the man at the door asked when she got back.

"It will be," she replied carefully.

Up on the stage, Grace finished a song and put her instrument carefully into the case.

"I'm going to take a small break and be back in a little while," the woman announced to polite applause.

Anya nodded to herself and remembered to breathe.

The crowd was circling randomly, with some folks gravitationally bound to the bar, others the buffet, and a few around Oluchi. The four men in gray were standing in a small cluster over near a corner, plates in hand and glasses resting on a nearby table.

Anya watched Grace nod to Oluchi and then to one of Adamanteia's women, Rafaela, who normally worked in the engine room.

Anya didn't stare, but watched out of the corner of her eye. Her job would be to somehow prevent anyone from fleeing this way, although that might involve tackling them at this point. She wasn't sure.

It happened so quickly that Anya almost missed it.

Grace and Rafaela met like they were having a quick chat, heads together.

Both turned inward towards the men in gray, drawing hidden pistols at the same time.

Shots rang out, but quietly because a stunner didn't make nearly as much noise as firearm. Had Grace still been playing, the amplifiers might have covered them up.

But four men collapsing suddenly, plates falling to the deck and scattering, created a clatter that caused heads to turn.

"Ladies and gentlemen, your attention please," Oluchi suddenly roared over the silence and murmuring. "My apologies for the excitement, but I must ask you to all remain present and out of contact with anyone for the next hour or so. Agents of the Rio Alliance Navy, the Phraettis Alliance, and the government of Yisan are in the process of capturing all Westphalian agents on the station and in the system, as part of a wider liberation of Yisan Space."

"Pryce," one man asked. A poker player. Ernesto, that was his name. "What's going on?"

"Eduardo Martìnez sent me to capture this system, Ernesto," Oluchi replied. "I brought friends."

"So all this was a scam?" the man screeched a little.

"All of this was a military operation, my friends," Oluchi called back in a big voice. "Rather than dropping a war fleet into orbit, we decided to do it quietly."

Anya grinned, imagining the result of the first ship that might have ignored an order by *Ajax* to heave to for boarding. The survivors would have fallen all over themselves to comply after that.

"Captain Montague, would you join us please?" Anya called now, cutting out one captain like a calf to be branded.

She met the man halfway, with Grace joining her while Oluchi drew others into his orbit for distraction. This operation belonged to her and Grace, after all. Oluchi was just the pretty face.

"Captain Gonzalez will be along shortly," Anya explained. "We captured his ship yesterday and he helped plan this. How do we get a team aboard your vessel?"

"Eduardo sent you?" he asked.

Grace stepped close and the man paled.

"You," he whispered, then his brain shifted gears. "Okay, never mind, stupid question. I've got a box shuttle on deck three. It will hold four people plus me as a pilot. Is that enough?"

Anya turned to Grace and caught her nod. Grace was probably enough, but there would be two targets to take down.

Still, they might just be able to pull this off after all.

TWENTY-TWO

GRACE

GRACE WOULD HAVE LIKED to bring Aileen and Lucas with her, but time was critical. Lucas took orders well. Aileen thought well outside of any warehouse, to say nothing of any box.

But Rafaela and Adamanteia were more than sufficient.

They had boarded the shuttle with Captain Montague and quietly departed. It helped that he didn't feel the need to contact his ship and let them know anything was wrong. Just back away from the station with permission and scoot over to his own lock-in bay.

The man still needed a little more hand-holding than most, but that was the shock of walking into a second revolution when he hadn't been expecting the first. But he flew the little ship like a pro.

"So you'll just board and take him?" Montague asked. "Then what?"

"At the very least, Eduardo gets a chunk of his transport fleet back," Grace reassured the man. "Lazarus has other missions and plans he would like to ask you about, but only after we've liberated Heechua."

"Okay, well we're about ready to dock," he said. "What do I do?"

"You can choose to stay here, or join us, Captain," Grace smiled at the man. "Your choice."

"It's my ship," he replied. "And my crew will react better if I'm with you."

"There you go," she smiled to reassure him. "You follow me and the two women will trail you. That way you'll also be safe if we run into any troubles."

"Safe?" he asked.

Grace grinned as the man suppressed his chauvinism. The three women were armed and he wasn't. And they were planning to assault his ship.

They docked quietly and Grace let the hatch open.

"Forward to the end of the hallway, then there is a stairwell up," Montague said as he powered everything down.

"Yes," she reminded him. "Just like when we captured Captain Gonzalez."

The man blushed, but shut up.

Grace boarded and moved like a ghost, with one slightly noisy male behind her and two more quiet women.

Forward and up, just like before, she found herself in that same spot across the hallway from the bridge.

"Captain, you lead now," Grace instructed him. "Whoever has the watch will be less excited and I presume your minder will be in gray?"

"Starched," Montague grumbled. "The man has taken to doing his own laundry because we're not up to his expectations."

Grace grinned. It probably didn't have anything to do with Montague being Hispanic in skin tone and the other Westphalian prisoners all being as pale as Lazarus, but she wouldn't put it past them. Westphalia had very specific ideas about caste that needed to be slapped out of their heads.

She was looking forward to that part.

Montague took a deep breath to steady himself and stepped into the hallway.

"Captain?" a female voice rang out from the left.

Grace had paused out of sight. Montague froze like a child with a hand in the cookie jar and turned to look that way.

"I thought you were at the party," the woman over there said, apparently walking this way.

"There have been some changes, Jane," Montague dissembled. "Where's Schmidt?"

"In his cabin, last I knew," Jane said. "Jokum is off duty, too, with us in line to dock and nothing else to do."

"Excellent," Montague blew out a breath. Then turned back this way. "Grace, could you join us, please?"

Grace stepped out and Jane gasped. Possibly at the pistol in her hand.

"What's going on?" Jane asked nervously.

"Eduardo's rescuing us from Westphalia," Montague explained. "He sent friends."

"Oh, shit."

"Exactly," the man said.

Grace stepped forward so Adamanteia and Rafaela could also see. Jane's eyes got huge.

"Can you take us to the man's cabin?" Grace asked.

Jane nodded mutely.

"Adamanteia, you go with Captain Montague and keep him safe on the bridge," Grace ordered. "Jane, we'll follow you to round up our two prisoners, and then we'll be out of your hair until Oluchi has a private meeting with the captains."

Everyone nodded and Grace got to work.

PART TWO
YISAN

TWENTY-THREE

LAZARUS

LAZARUS WAS on the bridge when they made that final jump to *Task Force Station*, designated for the spot that he hoped Oluchi would join them after his run to Heechua. *Ajax* and four of her escorts, more or less forming the equivalent of a Patrol, with two Phalanxes, and two Protectors.

Addison in the Archer named *Intruder* had gone ahead to scout quietly, just so they had some idea of what they were facing.

"We've arrived," Kuei announced as the blink of *Blueshift* faded. "Cormac?"

"*Scanning,*" the NavCrawler replied.

Lt. Lòpez was doing the same, head down over his screens.

"We're first," the Human announced quickly, answering the key question Lazarus would want.

Cormac would take his time and search a larger window, but that was fine.

Lazarus had intentionally jumped ahead of everyone else on this last hop.

"*Support vessels arriving,*" Cormac said now, indicating everyone but *Intruder.*

They would be along soon.

"What about the rest?" Lazarus asked, unable to help the hint of nerves in his voice.

"*Estimated first arrival in fourteen minutes, Captain,*" Cormac replied.

Lazarus nodded. That was the rest of the task force, twenty-odd ships that had decided to enlist themselves as the core of the Phraettis Alliance Navy, and in turn join the Rio Alliance Navy as *Auxiliaries.*

None of them had any business being in a major fleet action, even if many had been upgraded some with new guns, generators, and shields that Aileen had originally brought.

They were still eggshells around hammers.

But they had volunteered, even after surviving the battle at Zhoonarrim, where casualties had been heavy. Not as many deaths, because Aileen had won, but still brutal.

With any luck, it would be different at Yisan.

"All escorts take up a defensive ring and stand by for everyone else," Lazarus ordered. "We won't know anything until Addison gets back, so make sure everyone takes this chance to run last minute maintenance before they arrive, because we might be stepping straight into combat at that point. Kuei, you have the bridge."

He rose as everyone acknowledged and moved to his office.

It was suddenly lonely, without any of his closest friends around. And yet, he'd known none of them more than two years.

Still, with their help he could take on the galaxy.

TWENTY-FOUR

ADDISON

ADDISON WAS GENERALLY IMPRESSED with the Westphalian design that put the hinge in the middle of all GunWall ships, including his own *Intruder*. It gave the ship tremendous maneuverability, but it also cut space significantly and made everything strangely shaped.

He hoped that he and Lazarus could come up with a better design later, once all this stupidity was done and they could build yachts or something for tycoons like Eduardo.

For now, he was a mushroom or a nail, hiding in the darkness with those exceptional sensor arrays that were part and parcel of a ScoutWall, even if the Archer-class wasn't as good as the two Phalanxes he'd left behind. Either would have been a better scout here, but Addison understood what Lazarus was doing.

Phraettis Alliance. All of the Species together doing this thing, rather than relying on the Humans. It had been his idea to call it that, so he needed to get his keelscales involved. There would be time to retire to someplace like Liberty or Brasilia when this was all done. Build yachts or something.

Stay involved with starflight, but stop killing people on

wholesale scales. That would be nice. Even if the Innruld deserved it. And Westphalia to a lesser degree.

"Sensors, what are we seeing?" Addison asked, mostly to break up the tense silence that had descended on the bridge around him.

He had a good crew. Mixture of Human and Species, but everybody was getting along.

Spacer Second Class Aanthos Park had come over from *P-4282* as part of the thinning of crews to provide space and trainers. And done his job exceptionally well. Addison could see a promotion in his future, and possibly a commission at some point into an officer if the man wanted it.

"Sir," Park said, looking up just long enough to make eye contact. "Yisan didn't have any orbital defenses prior, correct?"

"That's right," Addison said. "A few warehouses and such, but no ship yards capable of building or repairing anything big. Most traffic passed elsewhere, while the money lived here because it was a good place where smaller ships could land and swap cargo without worrying about who was in the next bay. At least until recently. What do you have?"

"They're building an armed platform, Captain," Park replied. "Or dragged one here from somewhere else, like a monitor. Hard to tell from this range."

"Show me," Addison commanded, slithering over to look at the man's screen.

It wasn't a design he was familiar with, so he had Park dial up some comparisons. In space, you could build any shape you wanted, as long as you didn't expect it to land on the ground at some future point.

This was a flattened sphere. Not as big as some of the smaller orbital stations he'd known, and not even as big as the couple of warehousing platforms in orbit already. But it looked like a ship.

He turned his attention to the catalog file of a thing called a monitor. Small engines that moved it hardly any faster than a tug might. A great many Star Lance turrets evident from the various targeting sensors the vessel itself was generating, watching nearby space.

Out here they were more than a light-hour away and running quiet, having emerged in the shadow of one of the outer planets, where hopefully nobody had thought to look. Or didn't have a good enough parallax to view.

They were still poised to run at the first hint of trouble, and damn the consequences.

"How tough is a monitor, Park?" Addison finally asked. "I am unfamiliar with it as an entity."

"Built rugged, sir," the man answered. "The core is all generators for shields and weapons, with engines being an afterthought. Heavier than any Starcruiser. Almost immobile once you set them in place."

"Defensive firepower?" Addison asked.

"Crap ton of Star Spears and Powerbolts covering all approaches, Captain," the man nodded. "They expect to be on their own, so they dig in like a tick and fight you to dislodge them."

"Understood," Addison said. "Everything else?"

"Some Light Starcruisers, but they look like they are on patrol deeper into the unknown, sir," Park said. "It's like…"

He paused.

"Go ahead," Addison prodded.

Kuei or Wybert would have just spoken, but the Rio Navy was more strict about enlisted crew members having opinions, which was stupid. Since he was only planning to do this as a temporary gig, it wasn't worth the effort to change those people.

"So they know we kicked them out of Zhoonarrim, sir," Park said. "Maybe not Rio directly, since it was just the two

Protectors and a bunch of native ships, including a Pyramid. However, the ones that escaped most likely came here. I'd want to have some bigger ships out looking around, in case someone was coming along to sneak attack them. Like we are."

"Are there any of the survivors of that battle here?" Addison asked.

"Negative, Captain," Park replied. "Either they came and got sent back out, or more likely they have been sent home. We did a pretty good number on them at Zhoonarrim."

Addison had to agree with that assessment. Aileen's herd of *galumphs,* as she still called them, had unleashed surprise on the Humans and savaged them badly enough that three ships had surrendered, including this one.

He still wondered if any had been destroyed in the process of trying to get home. Or lost somewhere. The Nebula was a complicated place to navigate, especially when you had to move in straight lines that would still get deflected by gravity.

"Do we have enough information for Lazarus?" Addison asked.

"I think so, sir," Park nodded. "The only changes at this point would be ships coming and going, but that's always the risk when scouting like this."

"Very good, then," Addison nodded, turning to his Yithadreph Pilot now. "Pera, take us out."

The time was nearly upon them.

TWENTY-FIVE

OLUCHI

OLUCHI FELT like something of a conquering general, looking around at the small squadron that had accompanied him from Heechua. Invoking Eduardo had gotten all six captains to practically fall all over themselves to join up, so *Celestial Sovereign* was sailing along like a chihuahua escorting a herd of buffalo.

Antonia was even acting like he was in charge or something, which was new from her. Or maybe she was treating Anya as the boss and he was just the Plus One here?

Maybe.

He leaned over and kissed his new boss on the cheek, just in case.

"Mafê, how are we doing?" Antonia asked the room.

"Everyone accounted for and ready for our last jump," Mafê replied.

"Oluchi, what are we expecting?" Antonia asked.

"*Ajax* and Lazarus," he replied. "Five escorts. A herd of country craft. These six aren't warships, but they are built to absorb damage and all are armed enough to harass any small time pirate that wants to bother them. What Lazarus does with them, I'm not entirely sure."

"Good enough," Antonia nodded. "Esperança, take us into jump."

Blueshift.

Oluchi was off to one side in his usual station, seated next to Anya and watching as Mafé's sensors started tracking everything around them.

"We're being hailed by *Ajax*," the woman said quickly.

"Main screen," Antonia ordered.

Oluchi looked up and saw Lazarus visibly relaxing by the moment. But he supposed that having Grace and Aileen gone would wear on the man.

"We are successful," Oluchi announced, just to take that last edge off and give the man a reason to smile. After all, Lazarus was the reason Oluchi Pryce was here today. Without Lazarus, Oluchi would have been just another local on the ground, slinking around someplace like Tershuvi Port, in the middle of a military occupation. "Six ships rescued and accompanying us here, Commodore."

And Lazarus did smile now.

"Six?" he asked. "You got them all?"

"Grace got them all, Lazarus," he corrected the man. "I was just along to distract everyone. But we're ready for whatever you have planned."

"Excellent," Lazarus replied. "We'll have all the captains gather on *Ajax* as soon as possible, and then I have a few ideas."

There was a twinkle in his eyes as he spoke. Oluchi wasn't sure he liked it.

TWENTY-SIX

LAZARUS

"AND THAT ABOUT COVERS WHAT everyone has been up to so far," Lazarus said, coming to rest from this part of the briefing.

He looked around the room at all the new captains seated in front of him. It was crowded, but that was fine. He'd gotten one long hug and kiss with Grace when she came aboard, like a life preserver on rough seas, and that had grounded him so hard he felt like he'd just awakened from a long nap. Aileen was seated on his right, taking the spot that Addison had vacated when he took command of *Intruder*. All the other captains and directors were here as well, for a working dinner and to hear the insane plans Lazarus was about to unfold.

The wardroom had outdone themselves, and he'd make sure to thank Khyaa'sha personally and to let everyone else know.

Losing her as a chef would probably be the thing that made him retire entirely from service.

He rapped his knuckles on the tabletop to get everyone's attention, but they were down to pretty much licking dessert plates for the last crumbs anyway, so all eyes remained focused this way. Humans and eleven other species, just with the officers looking back at him.

The Phraettis Alliance.

He drew a deep breath and gave thanks to his Creator for threading that needle such that he had fit a camel through to make it there safely.

Lazarus of Bethany.

"We're not sure how they are handling cargo over Yisan right now, having not tried to sail up and ask," Lazarus said, focusing on Gonzalez and Montague and the others. "Since all of you have volunteered to serve, my plan is to sequence you in slowly over the course of a single day, as if some of you sailed here faster than others from wherever. Without orders or bills of lading, they will probably orbit you off to one side, close in to the warehouse but not that close to the battlestation they are using for defense."

He waited for all of them to nod before turning to Oluchi, Anya, and Antonia.

"You three are going to be the pea in the shell game," he smiled.

Anya smiled back. Oluchi shrugged. Antonia grimaced. Exactly as he had expected.

"Sail in as *Limited Liability* again and pretend to be a wanna-be tycoon with money and a willingness to let Westphalia bend all the rules to get what they want, so I get what I want?" Oluchi asked.

"Whatever cover story you need to give them to focus eyes and minds your direction," Lazarus said. "You won't have to actually do anything, as we'll be dropping in less than two hours behind you and launching our attack. You and the freighters should have time to take up innocent-looking positions on the flanks, because they won't want you anywhere near militarily-sensitive ships. That's fine.

You'll all wait until the battle is running hard and heavy and then fire into any ships that drift wrong. Ignore civilians, as they'll just be trying to get out of the fray, but any wounded or distracted GunWall ship will hopefully be surprised."

"What are we facing?" Oluchi asked, sounding like a young commander just handed an important flank assignment in a major fleet action, and nothing like the man who'd walked up and sat down in that bar to chat about the future of inter-species trade.

"A monitor, which is a class of slow warship just too big for anyone to handle, including *Ajax*," Lazarus replied. "But I don't plan to get close to him. Two full GunWalls have been noted, but they are generally split into eight, separate Patrols. For the most part they seem to be running customs enforcement and possibly search and rescue, though I doubt they would put much effort into it. Addison's team did track three different Light Starcruisers, but only one is currently in system, so that's why I propose to move now. All three might cause me to hold off, and I'd rather strike them while we're ready."

"What about us, sir?" an Aknaan captain called from the back.

Like the others, she had an armed freighter rather than a warship. Squishy, even by Innruld standards, but one of the vessels that had been upgraded.

"Captain Inian Carte?" he confirmed. "*Ziame Traveler?*"

She nodded, maybe a little surprised that he knew her on sight, but all of these director/captains would be the commanders of a future Phraettis Navy, one of these days, so he'd taken extra time.

"Aileen will be in charge of your tactics and operations," Lazarus replied. "I'll let her explain."

He looked to his new First Officer and watched her turn

off the introversion and turn on the charm before she focused her attention at that end of the table.

"Just like Zhoonarrim," she announced. "Slowest ships will launch first, because they will take the longest to get there. We'll sequence them down on runtime, but there will be a big difference this time."

"What's that?" Carte asked.

"Instead of an out-gunned Security Pyramid on the verge of being overwhelmed, *Ajax* and the five escorts will go in as a single unit at the beginning and draw all attention to them. That means GunWalls pointed the wrong direction for the vectors you'll arrive on."

"Why do they use that design, if it is so inflexible?" the Captain asked.

Lazarus laughed and all eyes turned towards him.

"Because in the old days, all of two years ago," he said with a smile. "Two fleets would sail up to each other and open fire. GunWalls have an advantage there, because they get better parallax firing forward, and the shield itself protects sensitive command and power systems farther back. Then a Churquen director taught me a new way to fight."

Lazarus appreciated the way Addison's scales around his face all flared out in embarrassment and the man sputtered.

"Since then, we fly backwards, sideways, and *Ajax* can even do something just about nobody else can, last I looked, which is short-hop within an orbital region. Not very useful in most situations, but a great tactical surprise if we have to use it. Here, we're going at them like normal. Sail right up like we're going to throw punches at each other."

The Humans nodded. The Species captains all shuddered. Even the most aggressive of them wasn't as violent as the average Human, and his naval officers had been selected for a willingness to use violence as a tool, rather than a last resort.

"However, once we have their undivided attention, we'll

stop dead and begin a retrograde action, seeing if we can entice them away from that monitor where we'll have a much greater advantage when all you folks show up a few minutes later. Then we'll hopefully have them between a rock and a hard place."

"They'll flee?" Carte asked.

"They may have no choice but to surrender," Aileen spoke up now. "Depending on the map when we arrive, I'll be assigning target values to any Westphalian freighters that might be hauling cargo and food for the fleet. Without those, the rest probably cannot make it back to safety easily. These are not ScoutWall ships like ours, designed to sail extreme distances without support. They are intended to operate out of a base, with food on a regular basis. It is a great many light-years home for them. And just like at Zhoonarrim, you should expect the order to harry them when they do break. They'll have more options than they did in the nebula, but that just means that they might disintegrate entirely as a unit, with every ship for itself across all that distance."

Lazarus nodded and smiled reassuringly at everyone. Aileen had pushed them out of Zhoonarrim and Aceanx. He would push them out of Yisan space, and back across their own borders.

And maybe, with a little luck, Carlos Nguema and Admiral Santos would let him go on the offensive against Earth itself, one of these days.

TWENTY-SEVEN
ADDISON

ADDISON STUDIED the plot that they had scanned just before leaving yesterday. *Intruder* had watched long enough to have a solid estimate as to where everyone was likely to be. As with the Innruld, many of these ships were just there to intimidate the civilians into behaving, rather than being a serious threat to anyone in orbital space.

They were there to control Yisan, and presumably prevent the merchants from throwing the weight of their wealth and influence behind the Rio Alliance. With so many Rio squadrons shifted towards Westphalia, there might not be forces that could suddenly shift this direction to dislodge them.

"Sir, what happens after all this?" Pilot Pera asked now, her whiskers and ears pushed forward in concern. Just like Aileen.

He turned to the woman and smiled.

"I was just thinking that same thought, Lieutenant," he replied. "Did Westphalia do this because they were desperate? I think that is the case, feeling the need to seize this system and bully these worlds into surrendering to them."

"What do they gain?" she pressed.

"It keeps Yisan at least neutral, and cuts off the Nebula from helping," Addison said. "Lazarus has knocked the Innruld back onto their coils, and given how fragile their hold is, they might not recover for a generation. And that presumes we let them. I have no intention, since even this ship we are flying in right now is the better of any Security Barc in existence."

"So we'll push the other Humans out of Yisan and then go home?" she asked.

"No," Addison replied. "If it was that easy, I'd be there for my daughter growing up on Liberty."

"Then what happens?"

"Then we might need to go to Earth, the homeworld of the Humans, just like Innruld spawned that species," Addison said. "Take a fleet and break them entirely first, so that we can send ships to do the same at Innruld."

"Can we?" Pera asked.

"We're going to try," Addison assured her.

Intruder wasn't as tough as any of the GunWall ships they would be facing. Nor as well armed. They were probably as sturdy, but unable to fight it out with anybody. The Alliance ships that had come were eggs, easily cracked at the slightest mistake.

But *Intruder* would be leading the way. *Ajax* was the tool that would protect everyone else, hopefully, so that they could actually win.

"Can *Ajax* beat a monitor?" Park asked now, monitoring his sensors and all the communications channels between the many ships.

"It doesn't have to, according to Lazarus," Addison turned to the young Human now. "The Kirov Lance can strike from exceptional distances, but he needs to not be fighting all those GunWall ships at the same time he is trying to defeat that beast. That's our job."

Park nodded, eyes suddenly not focused as he listened to something in one ear.

"Countdown update from *Ajax*, Captain," Park said.

Addison had the old counter on his screen, but they still had a few minutes.

"*Ajax* informs everyone to be ready to jump in twenty seconds, sir," Park repeated.

"Engineering, we're moving now," Addison said to the folks on the other side of the hinge. "Stand by for combat."

His boards went green, which was a silly color, but how the Humans did things. Addison kept expecting blue dots everywhere and never saw them.

"Pilot, jump on the new mark," Addison ordered. "All defensive gun teams prepare to open fire. Star Lance stand by for a target from myself and the Pilot."

More green. More silliness.

Addison drew a deep breath and gripped his coil tight around the chair.

Blueshift.

They'd come out right on the plane of the system's ecliptic, just like all navigation manuals said was the correct and proper way to do it. A little farther out than normal, but that let the five escorts around their Light Starcruiser shift into position. The two Protectors were forward, with both Phalanxes on their outer flank and *Intruder* forming the point of a pentagram at the rear. *Ajax* was in the center, but up about two vertical layers.

Nobody was higher in orbital space at this point, so they should be safe, and they'd come out nearly a quarter of an orbit away from the monitor that had generally remained on station above Tershuvi Port.

"Orders from *Ajax*," Park called. "Moving down and left towards the group marked One on targeting plots."

"Pilot, conform to *Ajax* and see if you can find me anybody to shoot at as we move," Addison called.

The battle for Yisan had begun.

TWENTY-EIGHT

OLUCHI

OLUCHI DIDN'T ALWAYS like sitting up on the bridge of *Celestial Sovereign* or *Limited Liability*. The only times Antonia needed him forward involved blowing things up or running colossal bluffs on people.

Both of those were likely to happen today.

He was dressed in that same black and royal blue outfit that Thadrakho had worked up for him. It just seemed to settle him into the mindset he needed, in order to pull off something this big. *Limited Liability* could handle any single GunWall ship by itself, but the whole point of the GunWall was to gang up on you in sets of five, pounding away at anything and everything until it broke or fled.

Oluchi turned to Antonia, noted that the woman was already looking his way. All of the women were, including Anya. Not even remotely fair, because with Lucas back on *Ajax*, he was the only male aboard.

Couldn't be helped.

"So I won the ship in a poker game," Oluchi began without preamble, drawling his voice out sideways as he spoke.

Antonia just nodded, but they'd gotten into a lot of trouble together before this, and she seemed to understand how his mind worked. Maybe even better than he did some days.

"I hired the crew because I like surrounding myself with beautiful women," he continued. "But I'm a bit of a lucky fool, rather than a calculating mastermind like Eduardo, so I didn't hire anyone nearly as competent as he did. You all following me so far?"

Nods, but they were the pea in the shell game.

"We've gotten orders to take up position close to the main dock, but not that close because everyone wanting to come aboard the station or land on the planet right now has to be boarded and inspected," Oluchi reminded them. "The place is full and running with the speed of bureaucracy."

Nods. Reminders. War would be breaking out soon.

"I don't remember any guns on the platform, because any pirate coming here would normally be swarmed by private escorts owned by the tycoons, and then hunted down and executed by people like Grace," Oluchi kept going, mostly just to work them along the path he was seeking. Anya squeezed his hand. "So let's drift some as we come in to orbit."

"Drift?" Antonia asked.

"Yeah," Oluchi smiled brightly at her. "Whatever the technical term is for hiring a second rate crew and not watching them like hawks. Those two ships over there look a lot like the military cargo freighters that Aileen brought to Liberty and Oton Mari. And they're alone. How about we find a spot just inside the edge of Star Lance range and park for now. When all hell breaks loose, you spin in place and start taking potshots while they try to figure out where they're supposed to go. Montague and the others are below and farther out, but they move like moons, so maybe we drive these two like a sheep dog into the guns on those big ships before they realize they are surrounded."

"We can't board them in something like what's coming," Antonia pointed out.

"Lady, I want them hurt so bad that they surrender anyway," Oluchi turned cold. "I don't figure you can destroy them, but how about you blow up their engines entirely and maybe they don't have the power to run?"

"What about us?" Anya asked now.

"We're all set to run," Antonia explained. "Esperança has a course plotted that gets us to safety as soon as any serious warship decides to bother us."

"Good," Oluchi said. "Since we're as dangerous as an Archer, we should put that to use."

He noted the grimness on the women and understood it.

This time, they were fighting foes who could hurt them.

TWENTY-NINE

EHA

EHA WANTED TO BE ELSEWHERE, but it was a futile complaint on her part. Neither Lazarus nor Addison would allow her to be aboard *Intruder* for this battle. *Ajax* was the second safest space she could be, after all. The only place better would be to have not come at all, but that would never do.

She needed to get back to Liberty to see Adriana and Alla. And then get to Brasilia and finish everything she had started a year ago. So much had happened.

She and Grace were in the front room of the Ambassadorial Suite, with tea and music as they waited for the battle to begin. The next battle. Not the last one. Just the next one in an apparently-unending stream.

Grace put down her sitar now and just studied her.

"Sorry," Eha waved a hand.

"I understand," Grace nodded. "There is so much to do, and we're both impatient to get to it."

"Are we winning the war?" Eha asked. "The revolution had always been such a theoretical thing, moving in scales measured in decades and generations. Since Lazarus arrived, we've gotten a decent start, but I don't really understand war like you do."

"The Innruld, according to everything everyone has told me, are static," Grace replied, waiting for Eha to nod before continuing. "That means that they cannot recover quickly from what Lazarus and the others have done. The news of revolution is still rippling across their old empire, where it might take another several years for everyone to even understand that a threat has emerged. With so many Pyramids captured or destroyed, their hold is weakened, and they must work to shore it up."

"Such was the original plan," Eha said. "But we have accelerated things precipitously."

"Humans are excellent at doing that sort of thing," Grace smiled now, which Eha found comforting. "So they captured Oton Mari and liberated Bajerlie. Zhoonarrim is now a major base of revolutionary operations, guarded by a growing fleet of ships as the Species learn Human technology to fight. Yisan is next on a chain."

"Does the chain ever end?" Eha asked, giving voice to the one fear she could not conquer.

That this war might never end. Westphalia and the Rio Alliance had been fighting for centuries.

"I believe so," Grace intoned simply. "Westphalia capturing Yisan will anger a great many people. Not just Eduardo but all of those other tycoons. They own a lot of ships, including armed ones. When we liberate it, and we will, I expect to see them all turn against Westphalia. That means that Rio gains a third ally, in addition to Phraettis. That will be enough to push Westphalia back. If they chose to fight to the bitter end, then it might take a generation to complete, but I also expect that factions within Westphalia will tire of the war and sue for peace."

"Will the High Council allow it?" Eha asked.

Politics was ground where her keels were much better gripping.

"They will encourage it," Grace said. "War is an expensive waste of resources. The only thing worse than fighting a war, however, is losing one. If they can get Westphalia to crack, they will demand political changes and then sit back and hope it will be sufficient."

"Will it?" Eha asked the key question that still kept her awake at night. "Can that culture change enough to matter? From how everyone on your side talks, they are just another Innruld."

"For the longest time, all Humanity was unified in exploration," Grace reminded her. "Then an Atomarsk miner came along and suddenly the galaxy was filled with intelligent aliens. Westphalia came about when the Humans who wanted to work with these strangers were pushed out, to become the Rio Alliance. The old salts were convinced, like Innruld, that they should rule and never share power with non-Humans. But the two sides were largely balanced before now."

"Balanced?" Eha pressed. "I though Westphalia was winning."

"Slowly," Grace nodded. "But only slowly, and *Ajax* would have disrupted things, but for the spies that Lazarus was right about. Then he found more aliens. And convinced the neutral planets centered on Yisan that there was more money to be made from Rio than neutrality."

"Because neutrality will no longer be allowed," Eha nodded back.

"Westphalia invaded Yisan itself," Grace smiled, picking up her sitar again.

"And convinced Eduardo to take sides?" Eha asked.

"Pissed Eduardo and the others off," Grace corrected her. "There is nothing worse than an angry Human."

Eha shuddered, but also understood.

Those angry Humans had helped liberate Zhoonarrim. Now, they were going after Yisan.

And maybe Earth would be next.

THIRTY

LAZARUS

LAZARUS WATCHED THE SCREENS. Everything was in readiness.

"Captain, the last trans-space ship has departed," Lòpez called from his station, after a quick glance at Cormac to see who would speak.

It was good that the man was treating his counterpart as another crew member, even if Cormac was a silicon-based life form. The NavCrawler was also the second oldest crew member, after Ereshkiki Nisab.

Lazarus checked his boards. Seven minutes to jump, letting everyone else stack up to come out after them.

He didn't believe in the bogeyman, nor angry ghosts.

Spies like he had once been had to be tough. Self sufficient. Trusting their instincts, because they had nobody to talk to.

And he was unsettled.

"Contact the squadron and jump in sixty seconds from now, instead of waiting," he decided. "Prepare to come out firing and expect that we have that much longer to deal with the enemy fleet defending Yisan."

He was tired of waiting. All those years spent designing and building a ship to carry the Kirov Lance. Then having to run for his life from a GunWall on the day he was ready to start showing that it worked.

At least Addison had proved everything. Since then, he'd struck a few blows, but all of them had been defensive in nature. Liberating Vilga's Stand. And Oton Mari. That one strike at Esmer had mostly been a counterpunch to pay them back for attacking Vilga twice.

This felt like the beginning of his war. The time he got to stick it to Westphalia in the most painful manner possible.

"Wybert, I have a change of firing preferences for you," he said, waiting for that head to spin around so all five eyes could focus on him.

"Sir?" he asked in that high, bird-pitch voice that didn't sound like the deadly killer he was.

"Addison identified several Westphalian cargo transports among the various vessels at moorage here," Lazarus said. "Six or eight, depending on their load cycle."

"That is correct, Captain," Wybert acknowledged formally.

"I want you to kill them with the Lance as soon as we land and clear for battle," Lazarus said. "Kuei, keep our current jump programmed, but I want us to go after their larder first. We're technically still pirates, so I want us to act like it."

"And by damaging those vessels?" Kuei asked, mostly academically, because he'd just made her flying more complicated, and there was nothing this woman loved more than that.

"They run out of food and fuel," Lazarus said. "They are a long ways from home. They get the choice to try to make it on reduced rations, or surrender somewhere along the way. We've beaten Westphalia before, but that's been a military thing, with *Gotland* and *Warsaw*. Or even *Mannheim*. It's not enough."

"Sir?" Kuei asked.

"I want to hurt them now," Lazarus said. "Badly. Make your jump."

THIRTY-ONE

LAZARUS

LAZARUS WATCHED THE *BLUESHIFT* FADE.

"I have identified the group of vessels Addison considered cargo freighters," Cormac announced as they began to move. *"Target One on your screens."*

"Thank you, Cormac," Lazarus replied. "Kuei and Wybert, turn and engage."

From the uptight and literal person Lazarus had first met, way back on the bridge of *Shiva Zephyr Glaive*, the NavCrawler had turned into another highly-competent crew member these days. Just another person. In this case, one able to take those earlier directions from before the jump and turn them into a sequence of events and orders.

"Lieutenant Lòpez, I want you keeping everyone focused as we start maneuvering," Lazarus said. "Let Cormac handle enemy vectors. You make sure we've got our escorts in place and listen in case any of our freighters or Oluchi Pryce call for help. Bring that immediately to my attention."

"Yes, sir," the man replied, not even looking up.

They were starting to gel. This was the dream he'd had after that first conversation with Juan-Sanchez Kirov, way back at the beginning. A way to break the old stalemate with Westphalia and maybe, just maybe, win the war.

"First target acquired," Wybert called over the low, background rumble of conversations. "Firing."

Lazarus smiled as a column of blue-white light connected the two ships. The distance was extreme, but the cargo ships down there would not be expecting to be the center of attention of an invading fleet.

Sure enough, the blow staggered the vessel, like a cow being hit in the chute by the man with the bigger hammer.

"First vessel may be immobilized," Cormac called. *"Scanning for damage now."*

Lazarus watched as Wybert and Kuei muttered back and forth to each other, three pairs of hands dancing across the various controls as *Ajax's* bow drifted around a shade to bring death to a second vessel.

On his own screen, he could see the results of that first shot. A second might break even a ship that size into pieces, but that was unnecessary, even for Westphalia. He just wanted them broken emotionally.

For now.

"Stand by for second shot," Wybert called. "Engineering, prepare to route excess energy to the forward shielding array and transition to trickle charging the Kirov."

From the goofball that had nearly killed him accidentally that first day, Lazarus never would have imagined that Wybert of Capantzina would turn into the Rio Alliance Navy officer that he was today. Kuei he had no doubts about, because that woman was born to fly, but Wybert had transcended everything.

"Lòpez, prepare everyone for moving on to Target Group Three," Lazarus called, watching for Kuei's inner ear to flick in his direction as she heard and acknowledged.

Humans couldn't move their ears like that, so they'd have

to actually speak. He could watch her ears and tail and have a full conversation with the woman.

Lazarus leaned back now as the various enemy ships woke up to the terror that had descended on them. It had been several weeks, so he was certain that the crews had relaxed and started to cut corners on things. With no threats, how hard did you need to be watching your scanners, anyway?

Hard enough to react when Death came calling.

The second cargo ship was no more prepared than the first. Possibly less so, or maybe Wybert had rushed his first shot, because the other ship erupted now in a cloud of plasma and shattered metal, blown outwards by a series of secondary and perhaps tertiary explosions.

"Cormac, what happened to that one?" Wybert called, even as he turned his attention to the first Patrol of Gun Wall ships that had drawn the short straw to be where *Ajax* arrived.

"*Target vessel has suffered catastrophic internal damage,*" the NavCrawler replied with very little emotion in his voice. "*Engines and generators are shutting down.*"

"Send them a note to strike their flag or be destroyed," Wybert, of all people, called over the noise. "We're bluffing right now, but won't be in another twenty minutes."

Lazarus smiled, even as he caught the semaphore of Kuei's ears and tail as she rolled her eyes at her partner in crime.

Because if everything went well, they might not be bluffing.

THIRTY-TWO

OLUCHI

OLUCHI HAD ASKED Antonia to turn the bridge lights down a little while they sat here, mostly to help him stay in character as a thief in the night. It wasn't that he didn't have experience sneaking in someone's window quietly, but more frequently he'd been going out, sometimes with a bundle of clothes in one hand.

Today, he felt like an assassin sneaking in, which was just *weird*.

"Mafê," he said quietly. "What's everybody else doing?"

He understood electronics, but she had a three dimensional representation of orbital space showing on a flat screen, with everything coded by colors and symbols. Oluchi was completely lost at what she was seeing, but both her and Antonia had fallen into one of those long stretches of quiet and Oluchi wanted a little noise to distract himself and everyone else.

"The *rufiões* are acting just like the Innruld did when we were over there," the woman replied with a hard fierceness he hadn't heard in her voice before.

But this was her home. All of their homes. Oluchi

suspected a couple of extra layers of angry rage was going to play out today.

"The Light Starcruiser across the way was facing the wrong way and made the mistake of accelerating immediately, so they have moved even farther out of position to engage Lazarus," Mafê continued. "Or maybe he was running away from that big stick and now has to make it look like he's not a coward. Most of the Patrols were off duty and at least one has a couple of ships showing almost no power curve right now, so they had taken generators off line for maintenance."

"What about the freighters Lazarus and Aileen were talking about?" Oluchi pressed, still trying to make sense of the display.

"Wybert killed one and crippled the other," Mafê said, turning to smile at him.

It was the sort of smile he occasionally used to get from Leena Hernández, when she'd convinced Oluchi to overcome his usual reticence on the subject and give her the kind of rough sex that she seemed to thrive on much more than he did.

Predatory orgasms had looked like that, but Leena had been an otherwise acceptable partner, most of the times he'd been there. Not that he was interested in pursuing any of these women.

He turned to Antonia now, mostly as a way to deflect some of that angry energy Mafê was broadcasting.

"So what do we do instead?" he asked.

She was the captain here. Oluchi was just along to hornswoggle the locals enough to let *Limited Liability* get into a position to threaten ships that suddenly didn't need threatening.

"I suppose we could just sit here and watch," Antonia said with a laconic drawl that nearly got a rise out of him, until he saw her grin. "Or we could stay locked softly on those two CommandWall ships over there, docked to the station. They'll have to sail out at some point if they want to form a GunWall and deal with *Ajax.*"

"And?" he asked, again a little lost in the complicated geometry of orbital combat.

"And one or both ought to sail fairly close to us in the process, given where *Ajax* is right now and where I expect him to go to stay away from that monitor," Antonia said.

"Are we far enough away?" Oluchi asked, finally identifying that thing that made him nervous.

The monitor could kill *Limited Liability* with as many Star Lance turrets as could be brought to bear on any facing. Lazarus had explained that part to him.

"No," Antonia said simply. "But my hope is that they get to concentrating on those warships, and all the raiders that will be coming out of jump over the next fifteen minutes, and maybe we can get off a shot or two that they won't be able to back track."

On the screen, the red orb that was the monitor was much smaller than the nearby station, but so much deadlier. Then he saw the way the cards had been dealt.

"You're going to hide behind the station itself," he said, light bulb suddenly coming on.

"See, I told you he was smarter than he looked," Anya laughed.

Antonia smiled at the two of them.

Oluchi turned a tart look at his partner in crime and watched her dissolve into giggles that seemed to infect all the women around him.

But it made sense now. If the monitor waddled out after *Ajax*, they might not be able to even shoot at *Limited Liability* without risking the station that was between them, especially when Esperança started maneuvering to make them miss.

"Okay, so maybe I am just another pretty face," he announced, just about the time they had stopped laughing, which just caused them to erupt again. "But you people better take care of me."

"Oh, trust me," Anya leaned close to kiss him. "I intend to."

He could work with that. Now they just had to rescue Yisan and save the galaxy.

THIRTY-THREE
ADDISON

ADDISON WATCHED as all hell broke loose around them. He had commanded *Ajax* against a small pirate ship, ages ago when they had first entered Rio Space. He had been on the flag bridge at such places as Vilga's Stand and Esmer.

This made them all pale by comparison. Two GunWalls, but nobody had been expecting trouble, so the ships were in eight different locations, some at rest and some idly patrolling. It was even worse than when he had been watching a few days ago, because apparently they had been treating today like a holiday or something.

There was a term he had first learned from his studies, applying it at Vilga's Stand for an event so catastrophic that the mind simply could not process it. When gods or demons ripped open the surface of a planet and emerged to lay waste by destroying everything. And everyone.

Hell on Earth.

Two cargo freighters would be well advised to surrender now, but he also knew that Humans were impossibly stubborn creatures, so he expected them to try to escape Lazarus's terrible wrath. If such a thing was possible.

Right now, *Ajax* had already murdered them and was moving on to the next closest Patrol.

"Park, where are the CommandWalls?" Addison called over the chatter as Park and Pera conversed with others.

This bridge didn't have many crew members, and that was fine with him.

"Docked, Captain," Park replied quickly. "Both are currently attached to the orbital platform and I have not seen any *Blueshift* from them yet."

"Keep a scanner locked on them and the monitor," Addison ordered.

"That one is moving," Park replied. "Slowly rotating on axis to come this direction. That Light Starcruiser is out of position and moving away at present."

"He'll be back, as soon as he figures out which way the battle is flowing," Addison reminded them. "Without their CommandWalls present, they are at a disadvantage. Park, I want you to highlight every Archer in orbital space and begin continuously transmitting that information on one of our standard channels for the *galumphs*, with coordinates and vectors drawn from a line connecting Tershuvi on the surface with the orbital platform."

"Aye, sir," the man said, putting his head back down.

"Pera, your job is to keep us on the course *Ajax* will lay out, but then to slew the bow around as the Fusilier needs so we can hit other Archers with the Star Lance. Let our escorts all deal with the Phalanxes for now, because shortly the enemy will have their own problems."

"Sir?" Pera asked.

"All of Aileen's *galumphs* are about nine minutes out right now, Pilot," Addison reminded her.

Pera nodded and brightened, having apparently forgotten that this was a complicated battle, unfolding like an onion.

The woman wasn't as good as Kuei, but Addison hadn't

ever met that many who were even close to Kuei Akeley. Those piloting skills, anybody could learn them, but Kuei had an instinct for maneuvering, both herself and everyone else in sight, that had let her do all sorts of crazy things with *Shiva Zephyr Glaive* over the years where any lesser pilot would have run into something. And with *Ajax*.

"I have us on line," Pera said now.

"Main Gun, fire at will," Addison called. "Continue firing as you need, coordinating with the Pilot."

That was another silly design mistake, as far as he was concerned. Because of the gunshield layout, the Fusilier was all the way forward from the bridge, where he could see out a reinforced blastshield just above the Star Lance itself to direct all the various guns. A ScoutWall Archer only had the main weapon and two Powerbolts, located on the horizontal edges of the shield, instead of the four Powerbolts a regular Archer had.

But his Fusilier was seated in another room, instead of sitting next to Rister Pera like Wybert would be with Kuei on *Ajax*. As a result, Addison really didn't have the sort of relationship with his Human Fusilier, Martev Hayesell, that he had with the folks close around him all the time.

Bad engineering, which said something, when Addison Wolcott had opinions about how to make your warship a more effective, more deadly tool.

But he could also see himself taking *Intruder* back to his home space one of these days and using it as a sledgehammer to finish off Innruld control. Even a Pyramid wouldn't be all that dangerous, now that he had learned the limits of those ships and might be able to bring his own ScoutWall or maybe even a full GunWall with him.

The Star Lance fired. It was a long shot from here, but the target was only now starting that flex which would bring the bow and the gunshield around, so the Fusilier had fired first. They couldn't stand against another Archer keel to keel, exchanging punches, but he didn't have to.

Shortly, the order would come down from *Ajax* to begin backing away.

Enticing the enemy to give chase like a pack of blood-maddened *sturees*, when they were about to discover a horde of *galumphs* riding over the hill.

THIRTY-FOUR

AILEEN

AILEEN WAS FORWARD from where she felt she was supposed to be. Born to be, back counting and rearranging cargo boxes. But she had to sit on the Flag Bridge today and supervise all these folks, as well as be ready to handle communications with the Phraettis ships coming shortly to the rescue.

Wybert finished tin-canning the second freighter and Aileen suppressed her cringe. Those folks, evil Westphalian slime turds that they were, were Cargo Command, like her.

Sort of like her. Lazarus and Admiral Santos would probably force her to make a decision soon. Stay aboard *Ajax* with all her friends, or answer that wicked, clarion call to stack bigger piles of boxes and even entire Shippers.

Did she want to?

If they were successful, the stupid war might be over soon enough that she could go back to capris and vests. Maybe borrow sufficient cash to buy her own used Shipper out of service and get back to the cargo hauling business. Addison would never escape being important people, but that was his own damned fault for falling madly in love with Eha in the first place.

"Sir?" someone asked.

"Sorry," Aileen replied. "Laughing at my own jokes."

"Were they funny?" the man asked now.

"You had to be there," Aileen noted.

Funny wasn't the word she would have used. Terrifying at the time. Stupid in retrospect.

She checked her countdown clock. Four minutes to emergence of the first reinforcements.

"Order just came down to come to rest relative to the monitor," her comm guy called.

Aileen knew they all had names, and she even knew most of them as more than shapes with stork legs, but she'd only taken this job because of this battle, and would be back to her life shortly.

Right?

"What's the monitor doing?" she asked, turning now to make eye contact with Lieutenant Guyann. Human. Male. Young. Hungry. Aggressive. Working his inexperienced ass off to impress her and Lazarus, so he could stay aboard permanently.

Humans were weird, but she knew that. Wanted to make war for a living.

"The vessel has completed a turn and is lined up now to begin accelerating this direction," Guyann replied. "That was why Cormac ordered us to halt."

Cormac had? Even weirder, but she supposed that made sense. Lòpez would be watching GunWall ships and Patrols. Cormac could track everyone and everything in orbit and alert folks.

She remembered the first time Lazarus had come to understand that Crawlers were fully sentient beings. Hadn't taken it well. Something in Human history had turned them off, while the Innruld always treated them as just another species to oppress.

"How fast are they, Guyann?" she asked now.

"Slow, sir," he said, not looking up from his own screens. "Not much faster than tugboats in harbor. Even through jump. They can only go about half as far as everyone else at once."

"Really?" she blinked in shock. "How the hell did they get one all the way over there, if they had to waddle like that?"

Not that she was unfamiliar with the concept. Damned storks that could walk so fast everywhere, and outrun a lot of predators she knew of.

"They never move alone, sir," Guyann said. "Part of a squadron with a lot of support ships around. Ours don't even fly with a full crew. Instead, they have a skeleton crew aboard to fly it, and then a troop transport to carry everyone else."

Aileen leaned back now and considered what the man had just said.

If you were looking at Brasilia on a map from Yisan, Rio Space tended to be mostly on your right. Westphalia Space was more to the left, but farther away, with a lot of empty space and uncolonized stars down the left-hand corridor.

That was why Lazarus had come here from Zhoonarrim. It had been civilized enough for him to find out what he needed. And find friends. And on the way to Brasilia, more or less.

"Where's the troop transport?" she asked.

"Sir?"

"You said troop transport, Guyann," Aileen replied. "There are a lot of GunWall ships around us, one Light Starcruiser, a couple of cargo carriers. Where is that troop transport?"

"Why?" he asked, turning to look at her.

The scowl she gave the youngster caused him to snap right back to his screens.

"Stand by, sir," he said instead, suddenly remembering that she was a Commander and he was a Lieutenant, fur and stork legs respectively irrelevant.

She had herself an idea.

THIRTY-FIVE
LAZARUS

LAZARUS WATCHED the battle unfold slowly. About what he had plotted out with Addison's notes, having caught them on the equivalent of a holiday or a non-working Sunday maybe. Something that had them half-asleep when *Ajax* appeared.

"Kuei, where are we?" he asked now.

"Dead stop and H'Brige and Ereshkiki Nisab have the engines reversing now," she replied, typing furiously across her board. "The monitor is headed this way."

"He can't hurt us as long as we stay away from him," Lazarus reminded her. "Lots of Star Lances in turrets are trouble, but we can stay way back and use the Kirov on him."

"Would that actually work?" Wybert asked. "Or does that assume everyone else leaves the two of us alone?"

"Correct, Fusilier," Lazarus replied. "They're safe as long as the GunWalls can protect him. But I want to entice him this way, because we can keep blowing things up as we leave, and if we get everyone facing this way, the second wave will have several minutes of chaos where they can inflict a lot of damage on flanks, even with Star Spears and Powerbolts."

A beep caused him to look down. Aileen, wanting his attention.

"What's up?" he asked.

She looked agitated, but in a good way. The up-to-no-good way that she did occasionally.

"So, I'm not one of you people," she began, including him with the entirety of the Rio Alliance Navy. Not the first time she'd done that, so he followed with a nod. "But Lieutenant Guyann points out that a Rio monitor doesn't cross deep space by itself, like a Starcruiser can."

Lazarus nodded again, mostly to keep her talking. They had started accelerating away, and Wybert was lining up his next shot. The monitor couldn't catch them, but it didn't have to, as it could hold orbital space just fine if all *Ajax* could do was keep running away.

"And then I watched you go blow up those two cargo transports that would be hauling food for the invaders," Aileen continued. "There should be a troop transport around here somewhere where all the crews of the monitor rode coming out."

"Probably," Lazarus replied, unsure of the point she was making now.

"They might or might not be able to stop anywhere for food on the way, if we force them out of Yisan," Aileen ground out the words. "But I'm looking at the Rio design for a monitor and those things have hardly any space for cargo. Everything is generators and guns, for the most part. If they don't have a troop transport to carry most of their people, they'll be eating the insulation in about three days."

Lazarus felt like she'd just gut-punched him. Or maybe a little lower. Aileen never fought fair.

He'd been following the lessons of Wellington and Zhukov, defeating an enemy on their logistics train. But he'd forgotten that monitors were packed too tightly.

Starcruisers had a lot of space, because they were intended to fly long distances without constant resupply, but monitors were as compact as you could get them. And that included reducing the onboard supplies as much as possible, when every cubic foot wasted made your shields that much weaker in battle.

"Ah, good, you see it," Aileen said.

Then she cut the line on him. He didn't begrudge her that. She'd seen the problem and brought it to his attention, like she should. Lazarus needed to be the one to kill a lot of people, in order to implement the solution. Something Aileen wasn't really interested in.

"Cormac, locate me a troop transport or cruise ship," Lazarus called over the noise of Kuei and Wybert doing their thing.

"*Located, Captain,*" the NavCrawler replied. "*On your screen.*"

Lazarus studied the layout of ships. It was close to the place where the monitor had been resting, maybe halfway between there and the main orbital station. Ships were frantically flying every which way, trying to escape the maelstrom that was just going to get worse shortly, but maybe he could make use of that chaos himself.

"Cormac, can you lock a communications laser on *Limited Liability* and hold it long enough to transmit them a message?" Lazarus asked. "I don't want anyone having a chance to overheard and maybe decrypt it fast enough to act."

"*Analyzing,*" Cormac replied. "*Affirmative, Captain.*"

"Good," Lazarus said. "Stand by."

He started typing furiously, not even bothering to correct a couple of typos because time was short. Lazarus saved the text file and sent it to Cormac.

"Send them this," he ordered.

If it worked, Aileen might have just won the battle for him.

If not, he still had everything else he'd spent a lifetime preparing.

THIRTY-SIX

ANTONIA

ANTONIA LOOKED up as Mafê's head snapped back and turned this direction.

"Orders from *Ajax*, ma'am," she said in an incredulous voice.

Orders? That man didn't give her orders. He made suggestions and she decided if she would listen to them. Civilian gunship, thank you very much, even if she was currently engaged in lawful piracy as an armed auxiliary.

Always know the legalisms involved.

She opened the file. Read the contents. Started laughing.

"Pryce, you'll like this part," she said, routing it over to where the lovebirds had been quietly discussing banking, or some other erotica that got them all hot and bothered.

They read it and their heads did the same thing that Mafê's had. Choreographed, almost.

"Will it work?" he asked.

Antonia shrugged.

"We'll have absolute chaos on our side shortly," she replied. "That will go a long ways towards helping, but we'll have an emergency jump plotted, I promise you."

She sent it to her whole crew now, just so everyone would be able to prepare in their own way.

Limited Liability, under the cover of running for safety from a Rio Navy attack, will assault the Westphalian transport at the following coordinates and force it to surrender or flee from battle.

At no point did she read the word *Please* in there, but it also made a sort of sense. *Ajax* had identified something about that particular ship, well off from the others that they'd already bashed, that Lazarus felt was important. And she was the only person close enough to act on it, with Eduardo's six freighters over on the wrong side, but all set to start taking pot shots at the two Patrols forming up to protect them from bad people like her.

"Adamanteia, unlock the main gun but keep the turrets retracted for now," Antonia ordered. "We'll pop them out when we start maneuvering, but I don't want anyone looking our way until then. Esperança, plot us an intercept course designed to drive him ahead of us, rather than overflying if he's paying attention. Lazarus wants them running for home, so that's our job."

"Boss, that ship scans like a cruise liner," Mafê said now. "Not even a cargo carrier. Damned thing might not even be navy-built. Just not that tough. I did a hard scan of it when we landed, like everyone does, but our sensors are better than most."

"Cruise liner?" Antonia asked. "Why is something like that important?"

She turned to Oluchi and caught his shrug, but the man was a card sharp still and a successful ex-gigolo. And Lazarus hadn't seen fit to explain *why* he wanted them bashed, just that it was important enough to issue *orders*.

Anya perked up, but she'd always been a spy.

"That one was away from the others, right?" she asked. "The cargo ships."

"Separate orbit, yes," Mafê replied.

"Cruise liner?" Anya pursued.

"Affirmative," Mafê nodded.

"Troop transport for the monitor?" Anya asked.

"Why would you…?"Antonia started to say, then saw where Lazarus was going.

"They fly slow, and need a lot of cargo nearby, because they can't haul much of their own internally," she said. "Driving off or capturing the cargo ships hurts them. Taking out a place where their crew could escape maybe means that they have to surrender the ship or starve in deep space."

Anya shrugged. Oluchi shrugged. Everyone shrugged.

She was the captain.

"Lay in the course but stand by," Antonia said. "We'll start up as soon as Aileen's *galumphs* arrive."

THIRTY-SEVEN

AILEEN

AILEEN HAD her screen echoing the feed from Cormac, rather than Ulisses Lòpez. The Human was busy coordinating the five escorts as the GunWall Patrols began to coalesce, but Cormac was tracking everything bigger than a scooter in nearby space right now. She didn't need the names. Just the vectors and the colors.

Blue were civilian ships currently identified as trying to run. Humans went up when trapped, which was silly, but she wouldn't argue with it. She had, however, taken that into account when plotting courses for her raiders to arrive.

They were all coming in low, just like she'd done at Zhoonarrim.

Everyone was fixated on the plane of the system right now. *Ajax* and friends had come in that way. They were backing out the same direction.

The GunWall Patrols had been kind of all over the place, but generally centered on the station and the monitor in a big, lumpy ring.

But everyone was on plane.

How did Humans get so dangerous when they tended to be so linear and two dimensional?

Of course, she had to think in three dimensions at all times, multiplied by the need to get at boxes in a certain pattern that required the least number of movements to achieve.

Cargo Command. With *Galumphs*.

Even Lazarus's revolution had just been a bigger fist to punch people with, rather than a different way of moving around. Churquen slithered. Yithadreph swam or waddled. Qooph rolled. Kr'mari glided. Etc.

Only those silly bipeds walked in two dimensions.

"Is *Intruder* still broadcasting their vector map?" Aileen asked Guyann now.

"Affirmative, sir," he replied. "Updates arrive every three seconds like clockwork."

She let that one go. Probably was clockwork. Someone had programmed a loop to push out those signals and left it in place. None of the escorts needed it, as they had competent sensors to identify things. Plus, they were engaging with approaching ships along an entirely different axis of planning.

Addison wanted everyone arriving blind out of trans-space to know who the most dangerous ships were facing them. Not that she blamed him. Had she thought of it, she'd have done the same thing.

"Countdown is terminal," Guyann called. "One minute to estimated arrival of friendly forces."

"Remind Wybert and Kuei," she said automatically.

It was doubtful that they would have forgotten, but Wybert had started taking shots at the monitor now, firing at such an extreme distance that it wasn't clear he could hurt them.

But way farther than they could answer. At this range a

Star Lance hit had an impact somewhere between a flashlight and a sunburn.

"Contact," Guyann called. "First friendly *galumph* coming out of jump."

She didn't correct him. Technically, you were supposed to call them something like *Auxiliaries*, but these folks had picked up her term and referred to them as a *mob of galumphs* when they got excited.

Like now.

The screen started to flash purple with wormholes opening, all below them.

Humans jumped when surprised. Lazarus had told them that back on *Shiva Zephyr Glaive* at some point. Diving was an unconscious face-plant into the dirt, so they didn't go that way normally. They always went up.

Ajax had come into orbit high, but on the plane of the system. Then stopped and backed away. Her *galumphs* were arriving via the south polar region of the star. Completely alien to Human sensibilities.

By design.

"*Ajax* and escorts have transitioned to rapid fire," Guyann called now.

Right on time. They'd been sandbagging earlier, firing at a normal clip designed to not wear out power systems and coolant lines. Now Wybert and friends were unleashing everything they had, just to draw all attention up to them as long as they could.

At some point, sensors would panic and scream for help, and the GunWalls would have to figure out what was happening.

But she'd also ordered her sailors to hit hard and then be prepared to run like hell as soon as she gave the order. None of them could take on a Phalanx, one on one. Ten of them were outclassed against a Patrol. But all of them knew to sail together and everybody shoot at the same target.

In this case, the nearest Archer that Addison had helpfully marked for them.

"Give me an updated vector plot on Group Two, Guyann," Aileen ordered.

Time to go to work.

THIRTY-EIGHT

OLUCHI

OLUCHI STUDIED the tenseness of the crew around them.

"Would it help later if I was giving some sort of orders here, so you could blame me?" he asked the room in a quiet enough voice that Antonia could ignore him if she chose.

"Eduardo doesn't get to fire me for rescuing our home, Pryce," she turned and smiled at him. "Even if we damage his yacht in the process. But you could make yourself useful and bluff those punks like you did at Bajerlie."

"We weren't bluffing then," he reminded her.

"And I'm not bluffing now," Antonia countered. "That might be a warship, but if it is then they seem to be pretty damned weak. I'm not picking up any guns, and their shields aren't even as good as ours."

"Are they running yet?" he asked.

"Mafê?" she called.

Oluchi decided that he needed to be running this scam standing, so he unbuckled and rose, stretching legs that had been seated too long.

"Negative on movement," Mafê replied. "Maneuvering

on thrusters and gyros at the moment, but I'm not picking up anything else. And here comes the cavalry."

Oluchi moved to look over her shoulder, amazed as always at how much information she could pull out of what looked like random fireflies on a screen to him.

But she was a professional and Eduardo had exceptional standards among his people, one ex-gigolo notwithstanding. And there were a lot of fireflies on that screen suddenly, with more appearing every second.

"Esperança, start your chase," Antonia ordered. "Adamanteia, establish a targeting lock on them as we close. Let's give the fool an extra reason to panic right now."

"Where's the monitor?" Oluchi asked.

He'd caught the discussion among the women earlier, and seemed to remember that it had taken a safe path that didn't come anywhere near them.

"Up and across," Mafê glanced up at him. "We're also diving down and away from them to loop up from below, like all of the new attackers are doing."

"They know who we are, right?" he asked the room.

"Yes, mother," Antonia chucked at him. "And they are well away from us anyway, if they came in where they were supposed to."

Oluchi nodded. This was not a poker game, where he could see the other players. Know them after a few hands. Understand them after a few weeks, better than they themselves did.

This was a stranger across a battlefield, being evil merely by existing, much like the Innruld.

Oluchi and his friends were here to do something about it.

"Engines engaged," Esperança called to the room. "Mafê, let me know as soon as they decide to react, as we're coming at them from five o'clock low and they can still run for cover

over by the monitor if they move right now. I'm going to herd them and cut them out."

"Roger that," Adamanteia replied. "Would it help if we took a softer shot from longer range first?"

"It would," the Pilot grunted. "Anything to catch them sidelong."

Oluchi remained silent and watched them work. He'd been around Wybert and Kuei enough to see the same sort of thing happen.

Instead, he moved to where Antonia had the main screen displaying a view forward, as though they were standing on some bow sailing on a sea of stars. One ship was visible in the distance, a long, skinny bar in a bright gray, pointed up and to the right as *Limited Liability*, once known as *Celestial Sovereign,* raced after them.

He supposed that he'd have to give Eduardo his yacht back after this, but it had been one hell of a fun ride over the last year or so.

Similarly, he was going to have to sit down with Eduardo and have a long chat about everything he'd done, negotiated, promised, and delivered, over in Phraettis Alliance Space.

And maybe borrow a few million from the man, to go with the seed money Fernanda had given him and Anya.

What the hell was he going to do with his future after this?

But first, a battle had to be fought.

"Engaging now," Adamanteia growled, stabbing one hand down on a big button.

Oluchi had been on *Ajax* to see the Kirov fire, so this Star Lance wasn't nearly as impressive. At the same time, it had done a serious number on that station at Bajerlie when he needed it.

Here, it hammered into the transport's flank with an enormous splash of reflected energy.

"They saw us coming and reinforced their shields," Mafê said now.

Oluchi shrugged. It was out of his hands, but he couldn't think of a better team to handle it.

"Esperança, slow down just a little on your approach," Antonia said, overriding everyone. "If they did that, they're already nervous. Give them an extra reason now."

"Deploying turrets," Esperança nodded. "Stand by for rapid fire."

Oluchi understood that this ship was tough enough, mean enough, to stand over with all the escorts around *Ajax*, had that been a better plan; so they were protected as long as that monitor didn't notice what they were up to and take exception.

But every second he was getting farther away, and if he slowed down to engage them, Esperança would just run and let *Ajax* start pounding on the GunWalls.

That part of the battle was a complete mess. And it was good.

He moved back to look over Mafê's shoulder, watching bolts race over and slam into shields.

"Can we open a channel to them on the same sort of tight laser that Cormac did before?" he asked the room.

"Do it," Antonia said, not bothering to look.

Oluchi took a deep breath and made sure that his opera cape was just perfect.

"Give me a camera to stare at when I talk," he said.

"Use the main," Mafê said. "More impressive that way."

He supposed so. Westphalia was even more sexist than Rio, so a complete bridge crew of females probably rated right up there with angry unicorns for them.

"Attention Westphalian vessel," Oluchi intoned, going for the sort of angry toughness that came automatic to Lazarus when he was pissed off. "This is the Phraettis

Alliance Navy. You will surrender to my authority or I will destroy you. Reply on this channel."

They didn't even bother with video. The profanity that came back was perhaps a bit uncalled for, but he put that down to bad manners on their part. They were from Earth, after all.

"Adamanteia, next shot please?" he said, aware that the line was still open and transmitting.

But he also understood that Chinese water torture was most effective when it was slow and obvious. Let them see it coming, when there was precious little that they could do to stop him.

Oluchi glanced over and caught her grin as she fired the next shot. He wondered if she would hold off on the big cannon until he said something to her, torturing those foul-mouthed sailors.

Just because, he turned to Antonia and winked. She rolled her eyes at him so hard that he thought she might pull something.

"Nearest shield is down," Mafê announced in a great, big voice that they probably heard over on their bridge, over the sounds of their own engineers screaming in frustration.

"Maintain secondary fire," Oluchi ordered now.

He had no idea what the phrase meant, but he'd heard it on a vid show once and it sounded like the sort of thing to say here.

Oluchi ignored the snickering around him as these women obviously had no taste in movies.

And since he had nobody to talk to on the vid line, Mafê had zoomed the main screen in some so they could see the impact of beams hammering into the flank of the enemy transport. Not as impressive as *Ajax* blowing Heavy Starcruisers up, but still pretty nifty, until you stopped and realized that those chunks coming off were pieces of hull larger than human size and people were likely dying over there as various cabins got opened to space.

He swallowed a quick prayer, understanding better why Lazarus was occasionally so devout that he drew his own name from the ancient religions of Earth itself.

"Hit them again, Adamanteia," he ordered.

They would surrender. Or they could flee. Or they could die.

Simple as that.

THIRTY-NINE

ADDISON

ADDISON WAS TRACKING things in his head as well as on the screens in front of him.

Three ships had come out something like five seconds early, but he supposed that the sorts of captains who would volunteer for something like this were naturally aggressive anyway. And it wasn't like the Species Underground didn't have a lot of folks with generations of pent up anger.

Eight Patrols had finally roused themselves. Six were moving in pursuit of *Ajax* and this squadron as everybody moved in reverse. The other two seemed to be having mechanical difficulties that prevented at least one ship in each squadron from moving.

Addison wondered how long it would take for the admiral in charge over there to order the rest of the Patrol to ignore them and move in pursuit. Given the damage that *Ajax* was inflicting as they moved, probably soon.

"Park, track Patrols Three and Six and let me know when they start moving," he ordered.

"Six already is, Captain," Park replied. "Slowly, but they have started accelerating this direction. Three seems frozen."

Frozen? Huh. Maybe the Archer had been offline when all this happened and they were going to cluster up to protect it?

"Park, remove Patrol Three from the target list for friendlies," Addison said. "Assume some sort of trap and route them to *Ajax*."

"On it."

Addison nodded. From *Intruder*'s position, low and aft, all he could really do was fire at anyone close enough to make a Star Lance shot worth it. Mostly, he was in place to keep anyone else from flanking the four escorts in front of him, two of them having gunshields like his and weak tails.

"*Galumphs* arriving in force," Park called now.

Addison wondered if these captains had heard about Zhoonarrim. Well, of course they had. Had they taken those lessons to heart?

"Orders from *Ajax* to decelerate and engage," Park called now.

"Pera," Addison said, but she was already nodding and typing.

Lazarus must have seen something. Or he wanted to entice them in closer. Some facet of three dimensional combat maneuvering that had eluded Addison. Probably Kuei having a stroke of brilliance.

Hopefully, it didn't involve *Ajax* jumping sideways across the battle like they had, and leaving the escorts in the open. Nobody else could do something like that.

Well, that wasn't true. A trans-space drive was just fine for that, if you programmed it to fly a hard hook for no longer than the blink of an eye, which was probably where Kuei got the idea in the first place. Addison could see that woman pulling a stunt like that one of these days.

Anything to top yesterday's crazy.

"Pera, Patrol One seems to be wanting to close," Addison

noted now. "Bring the bow around and let Hayesell know that he'll have a new target shortly."

With six such groupings, they were closing in like *Ajax* was at the bottom of a bowl and they flew on the rim, slowly sliding down the sides to catch up. Fortunately, they weren't organized enough that everyone would arrive at the same time. Instead, they were all flying at the same speed, however far out of alignment they had been when the battle started.

"Park, let *P-4317* and *Swift* know that Patrol One is trying to flank us as well," Addison said.

Cormac was probably tracking everything, but Lazarus had almost a hundred signals in front of him, with civilian ships either pretending to be asteroids or trying to fly to safety in the middle of a battle.

Speaking of…

"Park, how soon until the monitor is within range if we've slowed down?" he asked.

"Technically in range now, sir," Park replied. "Optimum for firing in three and a half minutes."

Addison confirmed that he had a line open to his Fusilier.

"Hayesell, after you fire a few shots at Patrol One, I'm going to bring the bow around so you can take some shots at the monitor," he said, waiting for an acknowledgment before he went back to tracking everything.

Ajax and the monitor were going to be the clash of titans today, but the monitor hadn't been able to return fire on them yet. Not effectively, anyway. The Kirov had been spalling off shielding on this facing and even scoring some hits against metal, but a monitor was designed to have many narrow shield facings and the ship could wobble as it approached, like they had been doing.

Slowed the thing down, so maybe Lazarus had decided to pick this as his death ground, having maneuvered effectively.

Intruder couldn't do much against ships like these, but an extra Star Lance would be annoying, and might manage to sneak in through a hole that the monitor wasn't expecting.

They weren't here to defeat the thing in combat, after all. Just annoy the shit out it while damaging everyone else around it. Eventually, it would force them to flee.

Assuming they survived.

FORTY

LAZARUS

LAZARUS HAD EARNED his command partly by being able to track an impossible number of moving targets in his head and react to all of them in the blink of an eye.

"Kuei, let them get a little closer and then accelerate again, matching their speed," Lazarus said.

There was only one *them* involved here. The monitor lumbering over to bring all those damned Star Lances to bear. *Ajax* could not survive a duel with something like that if they got close enough to fire that many beams at once. Not many ships could, which was why monitors were so effective.

You needed fleets to dislodge them.

Or trickery.

Kuei's ear flickered in his direction and he took a breath. Wybert was shooting the monitor. The three gun teams on the pylons were engaging with Patrols as they got close, as were all the smaller turrets. It was a mess, and *Ajax* would have gotten overwhelmed in the next ten minutes.

Until help arrived.

"Sir," Lòpez called now. "Should we form up the auxiliaries?"

"Negative, Lieutenant," Lazarus replied. "Stick with the plan. Cormac, just order them to make a high-speed pass, firing on targets Aileen and Addison designate."

"*Affirmative,*" Cormac replied. "*I studied the effects on human psychology from Aileen's arrival at Zhoonarrim. We are attempting to replicate it here.*"

Lazarus turned to the NavCrawler and remembered to shut his mouth before any flies entered.

He'd known that Kuei could remain in tan if she wanted, but he doubted she would. Wybert would love to, but he was a pack creature, and would rather stay with his friends, long term.

At no point had Lazarus considered a NavCrawler as a Commanding Officer on a Rio Alliance warship, which just went to show how small he had been thinking. Plugged in to the sensor data, and with the experiences in warfare that he had from these many battles, Cormac might be frighteningly good.

He smiled at the sentient—the man—and nodded. Admiral Santos would resist, but that would be a mistake. A bad one. Not that Lazarus wanted to lose his friend, but that was the nature of military service.

"Wybert, how are you doing?" Lazarus said after he tore his attention away from Cormac.

"Those are stubborn ships, Lazarus," the Fusilier growled in his bird-pitch voice. "Given time, I think I could kill it, but that's longer than we have today."

Oh? Really?

Lazarus was impressed. Monitors were functionally impossible to kill in most circumstances. That Wybert thought he might was yet another avenue to investigate, but only after this battle was done. How much Lazarus had learned from his non-Human friends and how much more he had yet to learn.

Maybe Rio, Yisan, and Phraettis needed to just form up into one massive alliance, one of these days, like the ancient empires on Earth that had assimilated so many cultures and then kept them all intact.

What could the future be, given enough time and freedom?

"Monitor has begun accelerating," Lòpez called now. "Six percent above previous approach speed."

"Bums rush," Wybert called happily. "Show me an open shield now, sucker!"

Lazarus winced at the joy in that boy's voice, but he was glad he had a killer manning the cannon right now.

Kuei had already been reacting. Now, her hands flew across the keyboard like a concert pianist committing a masterpiece.

He had trained them, taught them, and brought them to this point that they could attempt something this insane as a team.

Lazarus watched with a smile and kept his mouth shut as everybody handled their jobs like professionals.

It was all coming down to the next three minutes.

FORTY-ONE
OLUCHI

OLUCHI WATCHED their target begin accelerating away from them, but the troop ship didn't have the engine power or weight ratios to succeed. Antonia and Esperança had explained that to him before all this started.

They did turn away enough that Adamanteia was pounding on a new shield from the one she'd shattered earlier. That also made their cross-section smaller, so shooting was harder.

Or would be, for someone else. Adamanteia seemed to be listening in on the commands that the Captain over there gave, to be able to know what they were doing just as fast as they did it.

Mafê had cut the line until those gentlemen wanted to talk. The endless string of profanities they'd spewed before didn't count at present.

Oluchi looked at Mafê's screen, but still couldn't see anything useful.

"Where is the big ship and what are they doing?" Oluchi asked her.

"Going the wrong way to bother us, and he just

accelerated to chase *Ajax*, but Kuei seems to be waving a red flag under their nose," Mafê replied.

Oluchi understood that ancient reference. Get in an arena with a bull and dance with it. Macho, until you realized that the bull had frequently been drugged, blinded, or otherwise hobbled to make it all a grand show with almost no risk to the idiot with the cape. But they might still do things like that on Earth, barbarians that they were.

"Is our target running for cover by the monitor?" he pressed.

"Not on this vector," Mafê laughed. "Nothing in front of them now but deep space."

Oluchi turned to Antonia.

"Zhoonarrim," he said.

Nothing more, but she understood.

"Esperança, track him for a jump and calculate where he thinks he's going," she ordered swiftly.

Oluchi nodded. At Zhoonarrim, Aileen had managed to locally overwhelm the ScoutWall that had been holding things, so they had jumped to safety. Standard procedure, apparently.

Except that she had immediately chased them through jump, landing her Protectors right in the middle of where the ScoutWall ships had started organizing, possibly to return the favor of a surprise attack. They had been overwhelmed a second time, and fled in disarray, to the point that three of those ships had surrendered and were across the battlefield today, escorting *Ajax*.

Could they capture this troop transport? Oluchi wanted to try.

"Target has jumped," Esperança called calmly now, as the screen in front of them was suddenly void of anything but cold space and distant stars.

"Track and pursue," Antonia replied.

Oluchi decided he had done his duty and more or less staggered back to where Anya watched him with a proud smile. Let the professionals handle it now. He'd have to dig deep to find inspiring quotes from movies at this point, and didn't think he had it in him.

He collapsed into the chair and strapped himself in.

"You're stinky," Anya murmured in his ear as she leaned over and kissed him.

Oluchi sniffed.

Yes, that much adrenaline coursing through his system would do that. Not like a poker table, where everything was an enforced casual.

"You might need to scrub my back later," he murmured back and got a kiss for his trouble.

"We could probably arrange something," she chuckled. "After all, you're a conquering hero and all that."

"Not yet," he said, leaning his weight on her and letting her hold him up.

It was nice having an unindicted co-conspirator to handle things like that. Might have to marry her at some point, though, so nobody could be compelled later to testify in a court of law.

"You've done the hard part," Anya reminded him. "They fled from Yisan and Antonia will hound them. That puts Lazarus in a good spot to force the rest of the battle."

"How are they doing over there?" he asked her. "I've been so focused that I didn't even track it."

"The *galumphs* broadsided the Gun Walls and it was like a tide suddenly coming in, to watch them swarm and overwhelm Patrols," Anya said. "Not sure how much damage they did physically, but they messed up Westphalian planning something fierce."

He nodded and just let her smell engulf his.

It was out of his hands now.

FORTY-TWO

ANTONIA

ANTONIA WATCHED the lovebirds and smiled to herself. Pryce, bless his heart, understood when to stand aside and shut up. Not many men did, which was why she worked for Eduardo and why Oluchi Pryce was the only male aboard her ship.

Everyone always thought that Eduardo Martìnez had a flying harem for a yacht when they saw all the females. They forgot how many of these women had been born on Westphalian or Rio Alliance worlds, and headed to Yisan to make a living in a less sexist place.

Antonia Veracruz had hired this crew. Eduardo was allowed to suggest folks, but only suggest. She had the final word.

Like now.

Pryce had Persaud, and Anya kept him on the straight and narrow, not hitting up any of the crew for sexual favors that might have gotten his silly ass tossed out the airlock. He had done his part to bully the troop transport. She would finish them now.

"Esperança?" she asked.

"Jump calculated *now*," Esperança said, slamming a hand down on her console. "We've jumped."

"Adamanteia, locate them and keep up the pressure," Antonia called.

"Mafê?" Adamanteia asked.

"Scanning, stand by," Mafê replied.

Professionals, at the peak of their game. Still, chasing someone like this was always something of a crap shoot. At any significant distance, even the slightest error might leave you light-seconds or even minutes away at the best of times.

It helped, though, when also fighting professionals. They tended to have places already programmed. Tendencies that they would lean on.

Westphalian auxiliaries wouldn't want to go far. Especially not when they were attached to the monitor and supposed to be supporting them in the field. Friends. Comrades.

Fools.

"Got him," Mafê called now. "We overshot just a little and he's almost exactly dead astern now."

"See him," Esperança replied. "Everyone stand by for turnover."

The ship's artificial gravity would make it as though nothing happened aboard, except maybe a little swirl, but if you were watching a screen, the induced motion was occasionally enough to make someone hurl.

Someone less committed.

Antonia watched the stars reverse around them and smiled as a big, gray whale appeared on the main screen.

"Pound him with everything," she reminded Adamanteia as they came around. "Esperança, be prepared to chase him through another jump. The next one might be more random."

"Assumed that," the Pilot laughed as she typed.

"Mafê, is there anybody else anywhere nearby?" Oluchi asked now, interrupting the flow of feminine voices with his own high baritone.

But that was a good question. They'd all been locked on the troop transport, but *Ajax* had opened the game today by blasting a pair of cargo ships. What had happened to them?

Antonia didn't remember. Bad. She needed to pay more attention and spend less time teasing Pryce about things.

"Hey, you're right," Mafê replied with a touch of wonder in her voice. "There's another ship nearby. Westphalian transponder."

"Rotate the nearest turret," Antonia said. "Adamanteia, I'll take over that one. You stay with the transport."

Her Gunner nodded and the starboard twin Star Spear turret came live on Antonia's board.

She rotated it up and out and found one of *Ajax*'s targets lurking nearby, like he was trying to hide from them. Long range for Star Spears, but that was a civilian ship that had already taken a beating today. Antonia let the weapon go to rapid fire.

If they were successful here, she could pull into her own garage and have mechanics she'd hired repair everything that burned out. Not many people could say that.

"Pryce, do your thing on the comm while we're concentrating on the battle," Antonia called to the man.

He might as well be useful. Otherwise, he and Persaud might just start necking or something.

Damned teenagers.

"Mafê, put me on a wide broadcast, please?" Pryce said.

"Go ahead."

"Attention Westphalian vessels," Oluchi began, somehow driving his voice down a good third until he almost sounded like Lazarus. Probably not an accident, as that man had *Command Voice* down to a science. "You will surrender or I will destroy you. I will not ask again. If you run right now, I will hunt you down all the way to Earth in order to make sure you do not escape my wrath. We will raise the red flag and take no prisoners as this will have devolved into pure piracy and murder. All I'll want at that point will be your empty hulls to display in orbit above my homeworld as trophies. ***Do you understand me?***"

Even Antonia shivered a little at that tone.

She remembered the pretty boy who had occasionally cruised with Eduardo, years ago, to play poker, entertain, or warm the bed of one of the rich ladies in Eduardo's circle. The man had been a gigolo. Nothing more. A good time rent boy, but none of the women ever had anything bad to say about him, which was pretty impressive.

Antonia had never bothered finding out for herself, so she couldn't say, but Anya was pretty smitten, and Fernanda Flores had apparently loaned them money to get started in Phraettis Space.

However, any comparison to the man she'd known five years ago was entirely physical and accidental at this point. Oluchi Pryce had turned into something frightening.

"Adamanteia, your target is striking their colors," Mafê yelled. "Stand down on guns. And-…wait. Antonia, your target is also surrendering. Both ships have struck their colors."

Antonia could hear the mixture of awe and fear in Mafê's voice, there at the end, but she agreed.

Oluchi Pryce no longer even sounded human.

But then the man staggered over to Mafê's station and whispered something in her ear. Mafê cut the open line and nodded to him, so he stood back up and drew a heavy, tired breath.

"Okay, that's done," he said, sounding more like a poker player and less like a god of destruction. "I don't even know what orders to give at this point. Antonia, I suppose we want them to kind of cluster up like ducks or something, under our big gun, while we wait for the battle to resolve down there? How far out are we?"

"About a light-hour," Esperança replied. "They jumped mostly clear of orbital traffic, both of them, to what they thought would be safe. From anyone else."

"So in about an hour, we'll know what happened behind us?" he asked, a little lost and weak, like maybe he'd used up all his spoons bluffing those two ships.

Except that she doubted he was bluffing this time, either.

"Unless other ships panic and run, and end up on our laps," Antonia replied.

"So what do we do now?" the man asked, thereby earning a spot on her crew as an honorary woman.

A man would frequently just issue stupid orders now and expect them to be followed. Or bluster when she overrode him.

"We wait," Antonia said. "If more come, they might surrender under our guns as well. If not, we can run just as easily."

"Anything you need me for, either way?" he asked.

"Nope."

"Good," Pryce said, reaching for Anya's hand and drawing her up. "I need a shower."

Antonia watched the two lovebirds go, listening to the chuckles and snorts from her own women. She didn't figure it would be a cold shower, and Eduardo's cabin was sound insulated to the point that nobody would hear them doing whatever they were up to, but that was fine.

With his help, she might have just turned the tide of the whole war.

FORTY-THREE

LAZARUS

LAZARUS KEPT MOST of his attention on the swarm of trouble on his left. Those Patrols hadn't been nearly as harassed as the ships on his right, but that had been the luck of arrangement when Aileen plotted those arrivals. A mob of ships, coming out of trans-space and firing as soon as they could lock onto an enemy Archer, or failing that, the nearest Phalanx, and firing everything they had without bothering to slow down.

Casualties had been lighter than Lazarus expected, but only because the surprise had kept the monitor from adjusting his fire into the tin cans that he could have crushed, had he reacted more aggressively.

Ajax was getting thumped, but the bow was designed for it. Extra heavy shield generators as good as Heavy Starcruisers had, backed by a lot of excess power to reinforce them. Unused chambers for the entire first frame, so damage didn't cripple anything or hurt anyone.

Around him, the battle had turned. That much was clear.

"Aileen?" he prodded her.

Her image on his side screen showed deep concentration,

as her team was busy routing all those fragile vessels around. Mostly up and away, having strafed the living shit out of his left wing attackers and letting *Ajax's* various gunners either crush damaged ships or engage on the right instead, as they needed.

She perked up and turned to look at his image, locking eyes with him.

"We ready?" she asked.

"Affirmative," Lazarus said. "Give the order, Commodore."

"Hey now, you're in charge here," she smiled. "But yeah, time to run."

She muted the line on him, but he was listening on the other line.

"Auxiliaries, this is Aileen," she called now. "Good job and excellent shooting. Time for you to get gone. We'll meet up at Forward Position Six. All ships program and jump immediately."

On another screen, Lazarus watched those lights blink out. Nobody had been surprised by the order, or the timing. Jump in, fire at anything that moved, then jump away. They'd given better than they got, and broken a couple of Westphalian Patrols in the meantime.

"Lieutenant Lòpez, prepare the escort squadron to jump out on my order," Lazarus called.

"Already set, Captain," the man replied immediately. "Say the word."

"Everyone gets clear first," Lazarus said.

"*Captain, two auxiliary vessels appear to be too damaged to withdraw,*" Cormac spoke up now.

"Order them to make best speed away," Lazarus replied. "They can also surrender on the usual terms as needed, but I will not trust Westphalian prize crews to behave themselves, so we might need to rescue them at some point.

Remind me to bring Grace and Lucas in with Aileen at that point."

"*Acknowledged.*"

"Captain, other auxiliaries are clear," Lòpez called. "Repeat, they are clear."

"Order the escorts to withdraw, Lòpez," Lazarus said. "Position Six as Aileen picked for her people. Let me know when we're alone."

"*One damaged vessel remains, Captain.*"

"Understood, Cormac," Lazarus said. "I'm not done just yet."

And if they only had to worry about one crew, that would be good. Lazarus wouldn't win this battle. The monitor was simply too much.

However, he didn't have to win here. Just not lose.

And he had not lost.

"Captain, we are alone," Lòpez called now.

Lazarus took a deep breath and smiled.

"Kuei, Wybert, it's on you now," he said.

Wybert cheered. Kuei's ears both went straight up, then rolled forward like the horns on a bull, which told him just how much she had been looking forward to this part of the battle.

"Wybert?" she asked now.

"Ready," he said.

"Gun teams, stand by to reacquire your locks," Kuei said on the intercom.

Lazarus leaned back and hoped it would work. They were out at the edge of Star Lance range from the monitor, but the GunWalls had been pounding away. Both sides were hurt.

Blueshift.

He closed his eyes for a long second to let the scanners catch up and adjust.

There. Shit, that woman was insane. And that good.

Ajax was below the main orbital platform, behind the two CommandWalls that had been slow to undock and engage. The vessels had remained defensive, staying well behind as it had been to their advantage. This way they could give orders without rushing right into the middle of a battle with someone aiming Kirov's Lance at them.

But Kuei wasn't after them directly. Those were targets for the upper two pylon Star Lances, plus all the Star Spears.

"Ventral Gun Team, your target is our original cargo carrier victim of the Lance," Wybert ordered. "Finish him off. Dexter and Sinister, engage your CommandWalls as they lay. All other teams engage only nearby Westphalian targets. The monitor is mine."

Kuei had lined the bow of *Ajax* up with the ass of the monitor. It wasn't any weaker than the front, save that the engines limited the number of big guns that could point this direction. And the shields were the same strength, plus not having been hammered for the last forty-five minutes.

But nobody had had any reason to reinforce them until right this moment. And now it was too late.

Juan-Sanchez Kirov's original dream was to kill Westphalian ships from a long ways away. Right now, they were a lot closer to the monitor than they had been a few moments ago, but that distance was growing as *Ajax* was still in retrograde.

A lightning bolt of destruction connected two points. Neither ship had relative motion to each other, other than on that single line, so Wybert had been able to aim at the starboard engine housing.

Kirov's Lance punched through the rear shields and liberated an apocalypse on the monitor's rear hull.

"Engineering, trickle charge the jump engines and give me full power on the Kirov for one more shot," Wybert called now.

"Coming up," H'Brige replied instantly, so she had understood the implications and tactics today.

Lazarus turned his attention to the cargo ship that Wybert had hammered so mercilessly before. The other one had disappeared, which was fine. Lazarus wanted panic. The one that had remained behind was being blasted by every ventral gun turret that could reach it, everyone striving to actually kill an enemy ship.

Warships were almost impossible to kill with beam weapons. They were built too sturdy. You killed generators and engines and command spaces and made them surrender.

Cargo ships weren't nearly as tough. And *Ajax* was coming after them like a shark.

Something broke. Some fuel line or coolant failure rupture. Plasma suddenly erupted out of the side of the ship as he watched.

A moment later, the explosion engulfed the ship in a fog of white hot, expanding gas that thinned as it raced away, leaving a hull like a bent nail twisting slowly in orbit.

"Good job, Ventral teams," Wybert said on the intercom. "Everyone stand by for one last shot."

Kirov spoke again, this time cutting sideways like a samurai committing sepukku across the belly, rupturing the other engine from the looks of the damage.

It was a thing of beauty.

"Kuei, now," Lazarus called as they started taking fire from the rear-facing turrets that had been asleep until now, with nobody to engage.

Blueshift.

FORTY-FOUR

AILEEN

AILEEN GRUMBLED, but the man would not budge. Didn't help that he was forward on the bridge and she was still aft with her people. Her Human people.

Her people were out there in tin cans trying to be heroes.

"They are my people," she insisted. "I should sneak back in there with Grace and Lucas like we did at Heechua and rescue them."

"No," Lazarus repeated simply, looking around the screens showing all the captains that were still with them.

One dark screen ate a hole in her soul, but there was nothing she could do about it.

"Then what?" she demanded.

"They needed time to adjust," Lazarus said to her. "Then we'll go down and do something about…"

"*Captain, you are needed,*" Cormac suddenly interrupted. "*Screen three.*"

"Alert and charge all weapons," he ordered, but Aileen knew that was automatic.

They'd only been gone for about thirty minutes at this

point. Just enough time for everyone on trans-space drives to get here and settle.

She looked at the new arrivals that had just appeared on a screen and swore.

Two of them had gotten mugged in a dark alley they should have known to avoid.

Then the mugger arrived.

Limited Liability. Or *Celestial Sovereign*, depending on who you asked.

"Good job, Antonia," Lazarus was saying. "Tell your crew they may have just won the war for me and I owe them one."

"They know, Commodore," came the response. "But Pryce did most of it himself."

Pryce? *OLUCHI?*

What the hell had that boy done now? And why hadn't Anya or one of the others stopped him?

Except that he'd apparently captured one of the two cargo carriers and the troop transport that had been central to Lazarus's mission in the process of whatever he'd done. Must have been good.

The Yisan invasion fleet might be hobbled. Hell, they might be utterly penectomized at this point.

"What is your status, Antonia?" Lazarus was asking as everyone calmed down again, the newcomers having maybe panicked a little more than the old salts.

"Operational, *Ajax*," came the reply. "Two ships taken prisoner under standard surrender terms."

"Excellent," Lazarus purred, sounding like he'd just gotten dessert first. "I think you folks can take charge here while *Ajax* drops back down into Yisan proper and has a conversation with our friends. We'll be back in twenty minutes."

Aileen watched him cut the main line, leaving just her and him on the channel.

"Now, we're going to go see about your people, Aileen," he said.

She nodded, feeling a little better. Those poor heroes had volunteered to leave home, cross the nebula, and sign up for a war clear over in Human Space.

She needed to make sure they got home.

FORTY-FIVE

LAZARUS

LAZARUS DREW a breath and studied the two killers seated in front of him.

"Assuming the speed of the monitor when we left, calculate a deceleration curve that gets them back to the station in a reasonable time," he said to Kuei. "Then bring me out someplace safe enough to send them signals with a reasonable lag such that nobody is tempted to shoot at us, or jump into melee combat."

She nodded, her ears laid back now in a way that didn't fool him one bit. Wybert was as calm as a glacier, cool and deadly.

"All set," he chirped happily.

As if there was any doubt with Wybert, when it came to fighting.

"Same here," Kuei echoed a moment later.

"Make your jump," Lazarus ordered.

Blueshift.

They came out high. Polar orbit of Yisan, and well out. Away from all orbital traffic and any of the defenders.

Lazarus watched lights appear on his screen, down close

to the twin stars of station and monitor. Both GunWalls pulled into a tight defensive laager, just like the books said to do in a situation as untenable as this.

"Cormac, scan them hard," Lazarus said offhand. "I want full details, in case we end up hunting them all the way back to Westphalian Space."

"*Understood.*"

"Lòpez, open a general channel and broadcast a signal to the entire system," Lazarus continued.

The man nodded quickly.

"Attention, invading fleet currently occupying Yisan space," Lazarus began, letting his voice get deep and angry now.

That thing coming out of the night for your soul. Not that he'd ever done that when he was a kid.

"This is the Combined Operations Fleet," he continued. "Your troop transport and cargo carrier did not escape, but have been captured. My entire task force is sitting out at the edge of the system, ready to come down on you again like wolves and harry you to death. If you do not surrender, you will face a guerrilla uprising, with ambushes every step of the way home. And I'll be there, earnestly crippling your ships. Maybe I'll just leave them out there, slowly starving to death with their engines destroyed in the dark spaces between stars. All your firepower will not help you if you cannot eat. And the people of Yisan know that help has arrived from all directions now. You can surrender your ships and be repatriated to Earth, or you can die in an unmarked grave in deep space. I will give you five minutes to surrender or make your peace with God. Reply on this channel."

He went ahead and cut the line himself with a sharp nod.

Kuei and Wybert had both turned inward to stare at him in utter horror. But they were Species Underground. The Phraettis Alliance.

If he was lucky, they would never have to know what war on a galactic scale was really like.

"Pilot, take us to Position Three," he said calmly, staring at her until she unfroze and started typing again.

He didn't expect a response from either of them, so he wasn't offended when they turned back forward and probably pretended that he wasn't there.

Blueshift.

"Will we really do that?"

He'd forgotten Aileen was sitting metaphorically at his left elbow, watching and listening.

"We will," Lazarus replied quietly. "Yisan is still technically neutral, and I'd be willing to bet good money that either Westphalia never formally declared war on them, or the declaration was delivered by warships in orbit, which does not count in my book. Sure, Yisan was leaning our way, but if you expect civilized behavior later, you better act that way now. They are pirates, as far as I'm concerned, and you know what happens to pirates who get caught."

She gulped. Fell silent.

Best Quartermaster he'd ever know. Exceptional Commodore as a result, since it was just moving boxes around to hear her explain it. But still quite innocent in the ways of *HUMAN* warfare.

The Innruld were and remained just bullies. Punks.

Fools, if you asked him, but they'd built a structure that let them enjoy all the perks of modern civilization without having to do any work other than oppressing everyone else while having tea.

Westphalia had overreached, for which he was a little thankful, as it had galvanized the Phraettis Alliance to come to Yisan's aid.

Grand Alliance.

Lazarus liked to think of it as the forces of freedom, riding to the rescue.

"Plus, I don't think they're that stupid, Aileen," he said, speaking louder now so that Cormac, Wybert, and Kuei could hear him as well.

Most of his closest friends in the galaxy.

"No?"

"No," Lazarus assured her. "They'll take a look around. Then ask their Quartermaster, who won't be as good as you but also won't be entirely incompetent. A few might argue for running for home, but they are a couple of weeks away unless they get exceptionally lucky, and not everyone will have filled up the larder in the last twelve hours to even try. If they split, I'll even let the *galumphs* run while taking charge of the smart ones. Phraettis needs modern warships, and I can't think of a better place to put that monitor than right at the mouth of the nebula, coming out of that last hard turn before you emerge into open space and can get to Dormell, Aceanx, or Zhoonarrim."

"Right," she breathed. "Good spot for a trading post, if you ask me."

"And trading posts need defenses," he nodded to her. "Hopefully, it will all work out and I won't have to become a mass murderer."

Not that it would stop him, but he'd burn that bridge when he got there.

"Message coming in, Captain," Lòpez called suddenly.

He turned his attention to the man.

"And I quote: We surrender on standard terms. Unquote," Lòpez said.

Lazarus nodded.

Zhoonarrim. Yisan.

Next stop Esmer?

Or Earth?

PART THREE
LIBERTY

FORTY-SIX

EHA

EHA PAUSED AT THE DOOR, not opening it yet as she needed a moment to center herself. Zhoonarrim and Yisan had been liberated. Protected now, even. Lazarus was all set to take his war to Westphalia directly, and needed her.

Needed the Species Underground that had turned into the Phraettis Alliance.

The Galactic Alliance, perhaps.

Needed *her*.

So she paused to draw strength before this confrontation.

Grace stood nearby. Quiet and unobtrusive as always when she wanted to be. The fleet was one long jump out from Liberty and home. Adriana. Alla. All her other friends.

And Lazarus was going to ask her to help him unleash a war of a scale so monstrous as to frighten even someone who had spent nearly thirty years as a runner, a spy, and a spymaster.

She nodded to Grace and keyed the hatch open, slithering in as everyone rose from their chairs, military or civilian.

Lazarus sat at one corner of the table, across from

Oluchi. Aileen was next to Lazarus. Eduardo next to Oluchi. Addison. Kuei. Fernanda. Leena. Human captains representing the escorts. Species captains representing the Alliance.

All here to hear her words.

Eha came to rest behind the cone chair and studied the faces. For one moment, she understood how badly the entire galaxy might have turned out, but for an Innruld raid on a tea shop aboard Zhoonarrim station. One that had turned her into a refugee and outlaw.

And a revolutionary.

She coiled herself around the seat and gestured to everyone around the room.

"Please," she said loud enough to be heard. "Sit."

Everyone came to rest again and she considered her next words. Lazarus held out a hand and she rested hers atop it on the table, feeling his warmth.

She would ask how it had come to this, but she already knew that answer.

An unwillingness to accept the Innruld or Westphalia.

The one was sorely wounded now. Captured GunWalls and a monitor would end Innruld as a threat, although she would argue long and hard against ending them as a species, regardless of fire-breathers like Addison on a bad day.

Dead-enders she would gladly see off, but the species had not earned her ultimate sanction, just as Lazarus wanted to merely break Westphalia, rather than obliterate them.

It would be a fine ledge to slither along without falling off.

"Tomorrow," she began, pausing to swallow past a dry mouth and put some power in her tones. "Tomorrow we will arrive at Liberty. A system known as Vilga's Stand for several important battles that have been fought there between Westphalia and the Rio Alliance. It is a colony of the Species, well removed from Phraettis Space, close enough to the Rio capital at Brasilia."

She paused and let that seep into everyone's scales.

"That makes it a Rio world, regardless of where the inhabitants were born," she continued. "My daughter happened to be the first colonist born there, but there will be many others now. Some of those folks might eventually choose to return to Gowook or other places, but I will not. Creator willing, I will be buried there in a century or more, because that will be my home."

Again the pause, but nobody spoke, hanging on scales, fingertips, and everything else for her words.

For her pronouncement of doom.

"I am not insisting that any of you join us," Eha continued now, turning her attention to the non-Humans in the room. "That is a private decision, but I want you to all understand that I have chosen the Rio Alliance, and will not ever return to Phraettis as anything but a tourist and visitor."

There. An unconscious sound normally silent, but voiced by so many throats that it was a quiet groan across the back of the room. Not the front, as they represented the one already deeply committed to Lazarus's war.

"Those colonists fled Gowook when given the chance to live free, before it was a given that Rio or Yisan would commit to helping us," Eha said, nodding to both Lazarus and Eduardo now. "Before it was known that they could prevent Westphalia from taking us in turn and using our knowledge to reach the Innruld for whatever evil plans they had. The war continues, and I ask all of you to remain with us and see it to conclusion. Questions?"

There were none at present, but she wasn't surprised. These men and women were the warriors, not the diplomats. A few of the latter had joined as ambassadors, but everyone understood that she was the Phraettis Alliance Ambassador to the Rio Alliance.

Eha Dunham would negotiate the deals that would see the Innruld thrown down and isolated back onto their own world until they learned to behave. She would deal with the oligarchs of Yisan and the traders of Brasilia.

For now. Only for now. Perhaps the High Council would expand to include more members. Perhaps she would join them.

And maybe not. She had given her life to the cause. Others could carry the load for a while.

Addison caught her eye and smiled. He understood that Adriana should have siblings.

"Lazarus?" She turned to the man and nodded.

"Thank you, Ambassador," he replied, also pausing to look around the room as he lifted the weight of expectations off her shoulders and put them on his much broader frame.

Not stronger, but more willing to bear that burden.

"As at Zhoonarrim and Yisan, we will approach in a staggered pattern," he told everyone. "We've sent messages ahead, but this task force is bringing with it five captured GunWall ships, in addition to the three we already had, so we want to make sure that the locals stop and ask before opening fire. Same with unknown vessels coming suddenly out of trans-space on them."

Nods. These were the warriors. The military thinkers, already plotting attacks against Westphalia, using the exotic ability to cross jump slowly, rather than instantly. No *Blueshift* announcing their arrival, so they could sneak in if they were careful.

"With Admiral da Silva choosing to remain at Zhoonarrim and work on expanding the Phraettis Navy, I am in charge until we arrive, but then there will be another admiral there and we don't know what they will say. Most of you are auxiliaries, and thus not beholden, but I will ask your patience as we sort out Human issues. Like you, I want to attack Westphalia, but that might require negotiation, as they might not let us just turn full pirate on the enemy. Not yet, anyway."

This time, the sound was a chuckle like a pack of wild predators watching a *galumph* trip and fall. Eha shivered in spite of being prepared for it, but that was the sound of Humans in their deadliest state, even when it included Churquen, Yithadreph, Kreeghal, Aknaan, and Dreeni among others.

Killers.

"I won't ask if there are questions, but route them to me later," Lazarus said. "From here, we will adjourn for a reception and dinner prepared by my favorite Tarni chef, Khyaa'sha Ramarkhay. In eighteen hours, we will begin to cycle in to Liberty. And thank you."

They all applauded, Humans included. It was a rousing speech, both of them even, carefully underlining everything that had come to this point and setting the stage for what came next.

Hopefully, an end to war before it engulfed everyone and everywhere.

FORTY-SEVEN
LAZARUS

LAZARUS LOCKED the hatch and leaned his forehead against it for a long second, letting the cool metal soothe him. Grace stepped close and wrapped her arms around him from behind, leaning her weight just enough to let him know she was there. Was holding him.

Was supporting him.

He couldn't ask for much more in this life. Or any other.

Lazarus turned inside her arms and held her.

"For most of my life, I wanted to be a sailor," he said quietly, reveling in her strength and warmth.

"And now?" she asked, staring at him from close enough to touch noses.

"I can see a time beyond that," he offered, realizing that it was fast approaching. "When I don't have to be in the Navy. When I can do things for myself."

"And what things would you do?" Grace asked now.

"Well, I've dragged you around the galaxy for nearly two years now," he smiled. "Maybe we could actually have a vacation that didn't end up saving the galaxy or killing people."

"That would be nice," she smiled and leaned into him. "I have people to introduce you to. They'll even like you."

He chuckled, guessing what kind of folks they might be.

"What do we do after the war?" he asked.

"You will need to learn to relax," Grace chuckled. "To sleep without waking."

"Is it that bad?" he asked.

"Some nights," she nodded. "Not as many now as before. I like to think that I calm you."

"You do." He squeezed her tighter against himself, grateful for this thing he could have never imagined. "And you will hopefully continue to, because we're not done yet."

"We're not," she agreed. "But you are for tonight."

Turning, she dragged him by the hand in the direction of their sleeping chamber. He let her.

It was nice to be able to relax, even for a little while.

Tomorrow would hopefully begin the last phase in his grand war.

FORTY-EIGHT
CARLOS

CARLOS SMILED at the folks on his ship's crowded main bridge. He had given Marie a week leave on the planet below, and didn't feel rude enough to pull her back up for this. She had her own issues to deal with, and his private number if she needed to chat with him.

Paulo Quispe had everything in hand. Carlos wasn't sure if they would make an admiral of the man one of these days, as commanding a Heavy Starcruiser like *Recife* seemed to be his greatest joy in life.

Carlos only occasionally missed *Dutra*, but having steaming hot showers on demand had a lot to say for itself.

"Contact," a man's voice called out over the background rumble. "*Blueshift* detected."

Carlos waited.

"Confirmed," the man continued. "Starcruiser *Ajax* arriving in-system and announcing a battle squadron following."

Carlos chuckled. That was something of an understatement.

"More contacts detected, including Scout Wall, Gun Wall,

and non-Human vessels in close proximity and a tight formation."

That would likely be Aileen Enjehn's doing, if everyone was organized. That woman had a gift.

"Open a line," he said. "What's the lag?"

"Two light-seconds and decreasing," came the reply. "They are closing at a good clip, but not running from anyone. Your line is open."

"*Ajax*, this is Admiral Nguema, aboard *Recife*," he said grandly. "When I authorized a patrol, Lazarus, this isn't exactly what I had in mind…"

He left it at that. Around him, the bridge crew got a good laugh, but they had been briefed about what was arriving today. And how insane it would look to an outsider.

"Yeah, sorry about that, Admiral," Lazarus came back now. "Circumstances intruded."

Okay, an even greater understatement. Zhoonarrim captured and then liberated. Same at Yisan, this time forcing a monitor to surrender. But those fools should have known better than to try to stretch a supply and logistics chain that far on hulls alone. You needed stations for that. A lot of them.

Carlos hoped that it was desperation on their part that had made Westphalia gamble like that.

And lose…

"Helm, transmit moorage coordinates for everyone and make sure the eight mushrooms are tucked in close and tight against the station so nobody gets nervous," Carlos called, letting everyone on the other end of the line hear.

He had *Recife* and *Curitiba* defending Liberty right now, plus *Fortaleza* and her trio of Light Starcruisers that had originally been cycled in here so that the Admiralty could figure out how to go liberate Yisan.

And then Lazarus had gone ahead and done it for him.

But that just meant that Liberty had almost as much firepower defending it today as Brasilia did.

What could a silly admiral like him do with that many warships…?

"*Ajax*, since we didn't know exactly when you would arrive, we have a reception scheduled in twenty-nine hours aboard *Recife*," Carlos continued. "Please bring all your captains and everyone else that should be on such an invite list."

Like the oligarchs from Yisan who had seen their world invaded by Westphalia, liberated by the Species Underground, and were now forward to Liberty for…*consultations*.

Whatever the hell that meant.

"Understood, Admiral," Lazarus said. "See you then."

Carlos had the line cut and turned to the Lieutenant who was handling communications today with Marie down on the surface.

"Let Governor Dunham know," he said. "Same rules. Everyone she thinks that should come. All I need is a headcount for the caterers."

"Got it, sir."

Carlos leaned back and counted noses around him. Three Heavy Starcruisers. Six Light Starcruisers. A crap-ton of escorts. Then you added *Ajax* and his escorts, plus the forty-odd Species armed transports that had accompanied him, and things were likely to get hinky soon.

FORTY-NINE

MARIE

MARIE DIDN'T WANT to put her uniform back on, but it was dawn outside and *Lieutenant Marie Oslor* would be expected to get up, shower, dress well, and ride the shuttle up to orbit with the Governor and her entire party.

But right now, she was warm. And Collin was wrapped around her back, letting his hands wander over her front and flanks delicately enough that she was having second thoughts about the shower.

One hand cupped a breast and he kissed her ear, so she just enjoyed it for a moment before opening her eyes and reading the clock. She had time.

Marie rolled over and let him stay wrapped around her.

"My bladder is making demands," she informed him.

"Mine, too, but I'm going to steal every moment of this that I can," Collin smiled at her.

She remembered the first time she'd met the man. Yisan, after Captain Nguema had sent her with the captured ScoutWall as a prize. Where she'd been swept up by Eduardo Martìnez in all his wealth and power, and drawn into the very center of the web of international relations.

And met Collin Lau. Eduardo's Assistant Business Manager, a rather charming nerd who snored quietly in his sleep and put his right sock and shoe on before going to his left.

"It's Thursday," she reminded him as one of his hands gripped her bottom like a bread dough and squeezed it ever so slightly.

He leaned up to look past her.

"We've got thirty more minutes before your alarm goes off," he replied. "Got any good ideas?"

They were in a hotel. Collin had a permanent flat in one of the first buildings erected, but she had gotten her own room here, across the square from the government compound, rather than stay with him.

So he'd spent all six nights here with her now.

"We need to have that talk," she said now, feeling for him to flinch, but he didn't.

"Before or after potty breaks?" he asked instead.

"After," Marie decided. She needed a moment to compose herself.

She untangled herself and emerged into the cold air.

Looking in the mirror, she had no makeup on, her hair was a mess, and her eyes a little bloodshot from staying up too late last night, also fooling around.

But this was as good as it was going to get.

She came back and crawled into the warm spot he'd left. She waited, wondering what it was she did want.

Collin slipped back under the covers before she came to a conclusion. His hands were warm, wrapping around her.

"That conversation?" he prompted after a few moments.

"I have to go back on duty in a few hours," Marie reminded him. "Hair up. Uniform pressed. Military everything."

"Yes," he kissed her on the tip of the nose. "I knew I only got to steal you away from Carlos for a few days."

"What's next?" she asked, staring at him.

"I have a message from Eduardo that he's part of that mob, so like you I will be on one of the transports to orbit today," Collin said. "Like you, my goofing off subsides for a bit."

"You have been working fourteen to sixteen hours a day from the moment you got here," Marie reminded him. "Stopping only to chat with me on the comm in the evening."

He nodded.

"There is a lot to do, if we're going to make this colony successful and then get that big of a head start on everyone else in trading into Innruld Space," he said. "I understand that your war takes precedence on that, at least for thirty-one months, assuming you don't re-up for another four or six years between now and then."

"And you think I shouldn't do that?" Marie asked.

Even before she'd met Collin, she had always been on the fence about making a career out of this job.

"I want you to be happy, Marie," he replied. "If that's in tan, fine. If not, then hopefully I'll get a shot to convince you that there are fun things to do in Yisan and such places."

"Give up Rio?" she asked.

Patriotism was ground into her bones, several generations of sailors, even before Rio split from Westphalia.

"Yisan might be joining the Rio Alliance," he reminded her. "In that case, you don't have to give up anything."

"You'd want me to move to Yisan," she probed.

"Only because that's where my job ultimately lies," he nodded. "Eduardo lives there, as do most of his kids. I'm not entirely sure what his Last Will and Testament contains, but he's made it clear to me that I won't go hungry. More likely that I'll have to spend a generation reining in Oluchi Pryce and Anya Persaud after he's gone."

"What do you want, Collin Lau?" Marie asked him, point blank.

"You," he replied without hesitation. "For you to find a way to include me in your life, so I can include you in mine. If that means you take regular vacations from Brasilia, or save up all your leave and I meet you somewhere, that's just part of the adjustment Eduardo will have to make. He sent me to Liberty to help set up industry here, and to give me a chance to woo you. At least as much as I could, with you on *Recife* and me on the ground. The war is going to be over one of these days, but trade with Zhoonarrim and Oton Mari hopefully won't. What do you want?"

There. That moment of hesitation, like a missing tooth she kept probing at.

Marie realized that she didn't know. That in itself was a revelation, because Collin had been tenacious since he'd met her, as had Carlos in wanting to keep her on his staff and set her up for her own command one of these days.

She'd joined the Navy because that was what you did in her family. Serve.

But she could suddenly see a future that didn't involve tan uniforms every day.

"I want you," Collin whispered quietly, when it was clear she wasn't going to answer.

"You just lust after my mind," she retorted

"Well, duh," Collin laughed. "Boobs and butts are nice, but they're a dime a dozen. Not many women can break down a complex quarterly report and distill out the essence."

"So business, huh?" she teased now, pressing herself a little closer against the man.

"Not just," he said with a quick kiss. "All work and no play makes Collin a dull boy. But I hope you'll consider me."

Consider him.

She was a blue collar kid from the wrong side of the station. He was among the top five most powerful people on Yisan, given that the only person he answered to was Eduardo, who trusted Collin to run vast swaths of his empire.

Money.

Marie finally understood.

Collin was made of money, and she'd never had any. The man could literally swim in a pool of gold coins if the mood struck him, while she'd been hard scrabble growing up.

He could do anything he wanted, because he had that much money, either himself or on call.

She finally understood what had driven Oluchi and Anya to make some of the choices, some of the gambles they'd done, like stowing away on *Recife* that first time, coming out of Brasilia to Liberty, so he was in a position to influence things, and then go on to Innruld Space.

"I don't know how to be rich," Marie finally admitted.

Collin laughed.

"What?" she demanded.

"Very few people do," he finally subsided. "But I know someone you can talk to about that."

"Who?"

"Fernanda Flores," Collin sobered. "She was born rich, but never let it go to her head. Always striving for something new. Some new adventure. She took up windsailing on a surfboard when she turned fifty, just to stay in shape with women half her age and have fun. That's why Oluchi likes her so much."

Marie thought about it for a long moment. Flores was here as well, according to the briefing packet Carlos had sent down for her, even though it was her week off. But he could have also ordered her back on station had he wanted, so she'd gotten this with Collin.

Maybe she'd need to take Madame Flores aside and ask her some questions.

FIFTY

LAZARUS

LAZARUS WAS DOING PAPERWORK. It never ended. Even with Aileen handling much of it, and much more of it than most First Officers he'd known, there was always another report to read and approve.

"Captain, I believe you should join me on the bridge," Cormac's voice intruded.

They were parked close to the station, with all the captured Westphalian ships hiding behind them, thinly manned up until now. Lazarus was still hoping he could borrow a few hundred sailors from the various ships in orbit to bring a combat Patrol GunWall up to full strength for what he had in mind next. Given how many times he had already done something similar, he knew that it would be a touchy subject.

He'd managed it three times so far. Of course, he kept stealing more ships and needing crews for them, so it had all worked out.

He rose and made his way out of his office. Cormac had the watch alone right now, but that was fine. He could sit more watches than any two other officers, freeing up Wybert,

Kuei, and the others for training and relaxation. Still, Lazarus wanted everyone rotating through regularly anyway.

"What have we got, Cormac?" he asked.

Cormac adjusted the main screen and Lazarus felt his breath catch.

"Holy cow," he whispered.

"Beautiful, isn't it?" Eduardo said from where he'd been sitting off to one side, not hidden but not immediately in sight.

Lazarus spun around in shock. That man wasn't supposed to be on the bridge, but that was a formality more than anything.

"I asked Cormac to let me know when they arrived," Eduardo smiled and gestured to the image displayed.

Six Rio Alliance Navy Heavy Starcruisers flying in two lines astern, led by Fleet Flagship *Guarulhos* itself and *Campinas*.

"You knew they were coming?" he asked, still catching up with the wavefront of information.

Eduardo nodded with a knowing grin.

"I might have sent a fast boat to Brasilia as quickly as I could talk to everyone on the ground at Tershuvi," the oligarch replied. "It wasn't quite a demand that they meet me here with a fleet, but it wasn't that much short of it, either."

"You issued demands to the Admiralty?" Lazarus gasped.

"To the High Council itself, Lazarus," Eduardo corrected him soberly. "If they wanted that grand alliance that you and Addison always talk about, they needed to put their money on the table right now, or shut up forever. I'm pleased that they listened."

"But that fleet…"

"Yisan will soon become a member of the Rio Alliance, Lazarus of Bethany," Eduardo turned serious now. Patriarchal in the old sense. "We will bring with us fifty or maybe one hundred lesser colonies and inhabited worlds. We will cease most of our piratical ways, and focus on trade with both Rio and Phraettis. That was the deal I offered. Fernanda actually has the draft of a new treaty to hand to Roald Cavalcanti when that man arrives."

"*Most* of your piratical ways?" Lazarus keyed in on that phrase.

"Westphalia has earned my eternal wrath, Captain," Eduardo replied with a hard, deadly gleam in his eyes. "I might be an old man and not long for this galaxy, but I can promise you that much younger folks are even angrier than I am. Yisan was always a neutral nation, welcoming all ships as long as captains and crews behaved. Westphalia broke faith with me. I will not abide it."

Lazarus saw the man now as he must have been fifty years ago, when he was Lazarus's age. Saw that fire that had taken a poor, teenage kid and made him one of the wealthiest and most powerful players in space.

And now turned him into an avenging god of interstellar destruction.

Lazarus gestured to the screen.

"And that?" he asked

"Westphalia must be broken," Eduardo pronounced. "Simple as that. I told them in no uncertain terms that I was committed to the task, and that they needed to be, as well."

He paused and smiled.

"Blackmail is such an ugly term, Lazarus," he continued. "But *necessary* here."

"We could overwhelm any planet in Westphalian Space with that force, Eduardo," Lazarus replied. "Including Earth."

"Yes," the man agreed. "And I have sent out the call to my captains, as have Fernanda, Leena, and others. If the Phraettis Alliance could add ships to your task force that had no business being in the middle of a major fleet battle, then I could do no less. I expect them to start arriving in the next three days. It was going to be a surprise, but Rio showing up a few days earlier than I anticipated meant that I needed to tell you and Eha. Cormac already knew. I would appreciate if nobody else was in on it, though."

"Permission to warn Carlos Nguema?" Lazarus asked.

Eduardo got a twinkle in his eyes.

"Yes, I think he would appreciate it, but again let's keep it compact."

"Understood, sir," Lazarus replied.

"Now, with that, I will be on my way, so you young people can get on with things without us old duffers interfering."

He rose as a man much younger for all that he was tall and portly. The man smiled like Santa Claus with a full bag of toys and nodded, first to him, and then Cormac.

"Thank you, Cormac," he said.

"*It was my pleasure, Eduardo,*" the NavCrawler replied brightly.

Lazarus supposed that it was.

Quickly, they were alone, the two of them.

"Cormac, since you have the bridge, you go ahead and make sure everyone in our squadron is aware and prepared," he said, turning to head aft.

"*What about you, Captain?*"

"You're in charge, sailor," he laughed. "I'm going to go take a shower and put on my good uniform for what's coming."

FIFTY-ONE

ERLYN

ERLYN WOULD HAVE LIKED to say that everyone had come willingly, but that would be a lie. Pascia had been all in on the idea and brow-beat the others even more than Erlyn had, until eventually Roald had come to realize that he would lose any vote eight to one, at which point he had finally shut up and acquiesced to something approximating *force majeure.*

Or, in this case, the largest war fleet the Rio Alliance had ever assembled for anything larger than war games.

Admiral Pedro Santos had taken personal charge, to top it all off, and was leading the cavalry, as it were, from the flag bridge of the flagship *Guarulhos,* though she hadn't been allowed aft into that holy space to bother the man on the flight here from Brasilia.

But they were here. Finally.

She and Pascia were having tea in her quarters and watching the *Blueshift* fade, just waiting for an orderly or Council Guard to arrive and let them know.

"What do you supposed Carlos Nguema will say when

he sees us arrive?" Pascia asked as she sipped, grinning like a Cheshire Cat.

"He'll either assume the best or the worst," Erlyn replied.

"And which are we?" Pascia's grin broadened.

"Probably—*Probably*—the former," Erlyn laughed. "But the day is young."

"Yes, it is," Pascia agreed. "But I'm not, and it was past time we did something like this."

"The fleet would have never consented before this, Pascia," Erlyn teased. "Only Eduardo's signature on that letter convinced everyone that the man was serious."

"One should not blackmail the High Council," Pascia turned a bit sour now. "I might have to have words with your ex-spy Persaud when I see her."

"Anya didn't do this," Erlyn interjected before the woman could work into her anger. "She knows far better ways to make any of us look bad if she wanted to use them."

"Then who?" Pascia demanded.

"I have been paying attention to Martìnez and Flores from the beginning," Erlyn said carefully. "As Chair of the right committees, I am privy to certain things that are not even general knowledge on the Council."

"Oh?" Pascia perked up. "Who should I be bothering?"

"Pedro Santos, for one," Erlyn informed her. "But this is something else. Eduardo moved immediately, that night when he first met Eha and Aileen, just like Oluchi Pryce did. Put his best resources at Lazarus's command with a blank check when Eha was kidnapped. A blank check. Do you have any idea what kind of person Grace Savidge is?"

"Deadly," Pascia said. "You can see that in the way she walks."

"It's more than that, Pascia," Erlyn said. "She is quite literally a trained assassin. A killer. A ninja operating as a geisha, if you want to use the proper terminology, which I am assured by the correct folks in quiet corners is preferred in these circumstances."

"Oh?"

"And Martìnez told her to do whatever Lazarus needed to make sure Eha Dunham was safe," Erlyn stated. "*Whatever.*"

"Oh…"

"Yes," Erlyn agreed. "Eduardo has been maneuvering to take financial and social control of all trade into Phraettis Space since then. Successfully, I might add, as he doesn't dither, like we do. He sees a problem, or more likely Collin Lau identifies one, and Eduardo moves."

"We're here," Pascia said a bit defensively.

"Only because he threatened to form a single alliance across the nebula instead of with Rio," Erlyn reminded her. "To cut us entirely out of trade with another two hundred billion people over there, if we didn't do something entirely out of character right now."

"Attack Westphalia."

"Put a warfleet big enough to be called such a thing on the table, Pascia," Erlyn said. "I know you haven't dealt much with the man, but he's ruthless in business. Personally, rather interesting and enjoyable company, but he'd also walk three days across the desert to cut your throat, and then walk home, without ever saying a word, or even losing the smile on his face. Don't forget that part."

"You sound almost smitten," Pascia teased now.

"I doubt he'd be much fun in bed, but I'm not sure I know more than a handful of people that would be as pleasant to sit with in front of a nice fire, having brandy and a long chat on a quiet, rainy night," Erlyn countered, however close to the truth Pascia might have struck accidentally.

Politicians, as a rule, were hustlers, but very few of them were interesting or intellectual, once you got them out of the political arena. Charm but no brains. Roald Cavalcanti, for instance. Erlyn worked hard not to be just another one, and if she had started taking Fernanda Flores more serious as a role model that way, more than one person had remarked on their similarity: physically, emotionally, and socially.

Not the worst place to start.

"So what are you up to now, Erlyn Teixeira?" Pascia pressed.

"We're going to have to negotiate a new treaty," Erlyn nodded. "Two of them, as a matter of fact. In good faith. And in a very short window. Eduardo has called our bluff in ways that Eha and Lazarus simply could not do."

"And?"

"And we have to be not bluffing, Pascia," Erlyn assured her.

FIFTY-TWO

EDUARDO

EDUARDO SMILED as he studied the room. Blackmail, as he had told Lazarus, was such an ugly term. However, it was also another tool in the box when he needed it.

Normally, the bureaucratic reticence of the Rio Alliance worked in his favor, allowing him margins and openings they didn't see until he'd claimed them. Markets open for a quick killing before laws got updated or tweaked.

They tended to embody patience. That was another useful tool. One he'd taken advantage of over the last seventy years.

The time for patience was over.

The room was still a little noisy as everyone found their spaces. Interestingly, he'd ended up inviting everyone to join him aboard *Celestial Sovereign*, formerly the piratical warship *Limited Liability* under the useful flag command of one Oluchi Pryce. Only this ship had the ballroom forward that was large enough to house one hundred and fifty primary players, plus an addition three hundred or so *aides de'camp*.

On a Protector or a Destroyer, this space would likely be

guns and generators for them. Here, it was as close to Ambassadorial Neutral Ground as anyone could get.

And it let him drive the pace for this Argentine Tango.

The tables had been arranged in a peculiar manner, but that couldn't be helped. Too many people for any single conference table to hold, so he ordered all the trestle tables lined up in a loose triangle.

He sat across the base, with Fernanda and Leena on his left, and Colin, Oluchi, and Anya on his right. The power side and the money side, as it were. He smiled at that.

On his right, the High Council of the Rio Alliance. Chairman Roald Cavalcanti in the center, amidst eight others. The room was so big because each table was the same size, but only one of them was crowded.

The left arm of the triangle was centered on Eha. She had her mother and utterly cute daughter with her, as well as a few assistants he didn't know all that well, a few of them from Liberty and a few from Zhoonarrim and Oton Mari. But it was all centered on Eha.

As it should be.

Both Addison and Lazarus sat on the side with Eha, a political statement not lost on anyone present. But the addition of Carlos next to Lazarus on the other side was interesting.

Admiral Santos had ordered the man to protect Liberty and the colony on it with his life. Eduardo had spent enough time with the Gnashiiley Captain and now Admiral to understand how seriously Carlos took that charge.

Had Lazarus not ridden to the rescue at Yisan, Carlos would have tried. Eduardo caught his eye now and nodded. Carlos understood and nodded as well.

Eduardo took a breath, smiled at everyone, and rapped his knuckles on the wooden surface of the table in front of him. Cavalcanti had been aghast that he brought no gavel, but that man was something of a well-bred fool, more in love with forms than outcomes.

"We are assembled," Eduardo announced simply, once the room had fallen to a silence so sharp he could hear the life support blowers on all sides cranked up to handle this mob.

Dead silence, and yet he wondered if the echoes of his words could be heard on Earth.

Yet.

"Mr. Chairman and High Councilors of the Rio Alliance, you have had three days to read and discuss the proposed treaty assembling the worlds of Yisan, the embryonic Phraettis Alliance, and Rio into a larger political and social entity," he continued. "My Ambassador Oluchi Pryce had previously gone fairly deep into the weeds on the details that will be attached as Addenda and Codicils, but those negotiations will likely continue for as long as everyone wants to remain friends. Forever, if I am lucky, but I will not see it. I would have your words *now*."

He sat back and watched Roald Cavalcanti suck bitter lemons.

Eduardo was intimately familiar with the tides binding and driving the High Council. Intelligence reports on that group was one of the first things he read every morning, transmitted as quickly as a regular courier service could haul news from Brasilia to Yisan.

The High Council was broken. Humpty Dumpty-style.

Eduardo looked around and wondered if he had all the King's Horses and all the King's Men handy that someone might put everything back together. But best he know these things now, and not find them out later.

Best the entire galaxy understand, before the final war was unleashed.

The pause lasted past *pregnant* and almost down into *rude.*

Eduardo would teach Roald Cavalcanti the meaning of *rude* if it became *necessary* today. Fernanda had prepared an almost-identical treaty, the only difference being the space on the last page for only two signatories: himself and Eha Dunham, rather than three.

"The Rio Alliance has reservations not yet explored," the Chairman began in a voice probably intended to sound proud and stentorian, when it come out almost needy and weak.

Eduardo nodded for the man to continue, wondering just how stupid Cavalcanti really was. Interestingly, Erlyn Teixeira appeared to be chewing nails angrily, seated clear down at one end of the grouping, well away from the others emotionally. But then Pascia Nkali, the Gnashiiley Councilor, was opposite Teixeira and just as angry.

What had that idiot in the center pulled on them, two minutes before everyone walked into this chamber when nobody could do anything about it?

Eduardo felt Fernanda bristle, but only because he'd been playing poker with the woman for nearly fifteen years at this point. It wasn't a physical motion so much as the way her perfume seemed to surge, driven no doubt by adrenaline and rage underneath.

But she'd also spent the most time with these folks, excepting only Oluchi, who, interestingly, hadn't twitched.

What did that man know?

"This is a starting point to a marathon, Chairman Cavalcanti," Oluchi spoke up now, not quite sneering but not much short of it, either. "Not the end of a race. To what might we attribute this latest bout of *doubts* on your part?"

Cold. Brutal, but no doubt warranted, as Oluchi had shared some stories of his fencing with these folks.

Cavalcanti steamed. Visibly, even, so Oluchi must have known about a soft spot in the man's mental and emotional armor. But then, never sit across from a poker player when the stakes are that high.

"I note that the Rio Alliance Navy has arrived at Liberty with a significant tonnage of warships, Pryce," Cavalcanti snapped back at them. "Even the Phraettis Alliance has delivered a mass of vessels, although I am given to understand from my own experts that most of them have no business in the sort of fleet action you propose."

He paused, like a fool thinking he was going to drop a bombshell on the group and wanting the best angle for the camera to catch his profile for posterity. Eduardo decided to let him. All the better this way.

"And?" Oluchi asked, obviously willing to play the straight man here, if only for a bit longer.

"Where is Yisan's navy?" Cavalcanti thundered at the room to gasps, moans, and chatter.

At least around the back. Interestingly, nobody on these two sides of the triangle made a noise.

"Yisan was captured by Westphalia and held against their will," Cavalcanti continued, building himself up to a pretty good lather.

Pity there was no scenery for him to actually gnaw on right now, but Eduardo had no doubts the man was emulating some of those really cheesy vids that you find on the obscure channels in the dead of night when you couldn't sleep.

"It required the Rio Alliance Navy to rescue your planet," Cavalcanti roared. "What are you contributing to this war that earns you an even spot at this table?"

Masterfully done, if a bit overwrought. Eduardo could even see a sheen of sweat on the man's brow from the excitement.

Roald Cavalcanti leaned back like he had just delivered a fatal blow to a mortally-wounded foe and smiled augustly as the room roared and tittered in response.

Eduardo just waited. His smile was polite and bit paternal.

Silence was an even deadlier weapon than words, but much harder to master.

The noise and uproar took nearly two minutes to settle, like waves in a small pool caused by some fool dropping rocks into it for fun.

But fade they did. At first, eyes watched him for an emotional response. Fear. Anger. Vengeance. Anything.

Something petty and useless at this level of play.

He smiled and waited.

The emotional temperature dropped slowly back to normal, then kept going when Eduardo didn't react. Didn't respond.

Didn't *anything*.

Coldness set in. Fearful, even. Timid little mice remembering that the cat hasn't been stopped, or even thwarted.

Merely awakened.

Finally, Eduardo decided that the charade had gone on long enough.

"My fleet, Mister Chairman?" he asked innocently.

"That's right," Cavalcanti responded, trying to sound indignant and in control.

And failing.

"Admiral Nguema, could I trouble you for the final count?" Eduardo asked in a conversational tone.

It was useful, noting which heads snapped around so hard they might hurt themselves and which didn't. Who knew, or had guessed, and who were merely pedestrian bystanders today.

Eduardo had a list. No doubt Lazarus, Eha, and Oluchi did as well.

The Gnashiiley Admiral straightened in his chair and pulled out a tablet, calling up the numbers like he didn't have them in his head already.

Yes, Lazarus had been absolutely right. Again. Bringing Carlos in on the practical joke had been the perfect coup.

But then, only fools underestimated Lazarus of Bethany.

"As of this morning, Eduardo, the count is one hundred and seventy-four armed auxiliaries," Carlos called into the dread silence like an accountant with those funny, green hats. "Six of them are Protector-class or better, not counting *Celestial Sovereign*, while the rest are more properly classified as armed transports and System-scale Search-and-Rescue Patrol craft. All, however, have sufficient shielding and firepower to accompany a Rio War Fleet into battle in my estimation."

And that, ladies and gentlemen of the jury, is how you drop a larger rock.

Bedlam. Pure, delightful chaos.

Nobody had ever apparently done a proper survey of Yisan's various vessels, mostly because the oligarchs didn't like sharing such information with each other. Plus Rio's espionage service tended to pay atrociously low rates when attempting to bribe people for information.

Eduardo was dead certain that he and Fernanda both had better spies burrowed deep into the heart of the High Council's bureaucracy than Roald Cavalcanti and his people had ever managed on Yisan. Not Anya Persaud, perhaps, but close enough. And good enough.

He smiled at the Chairman. Watched the man bleed. Metaphorically, at least for now.

Publicly, which was really the important part.

Again, Eduardo waited for blessed silence to descend on

the witnesses, rather like a spider's web spun on liquid nitrogen.

"Where?" Roald finally managed to gasp out when the room was quiet.

Eduardo leaned forward and smiled.

"Given the expected numbers, Lazarus suggested that we send out a small vessel to the expected final jump rendezvous point where everyone had been ordered to assemble," Eduardo replied. "And considering the scale involved, and the already busy moorings locally, Admiral Nguema suggested that they remain there for now, especially as more than a few of them have Rio Alliance Naval bounties on them for previous acts of *illegality* that have now ended, as they are all covered by Yisan Alliance *Letters of Marque and Reprisal* allowing them a legal grounding upon which to begin preying on Westphalian shipping. That, Mr. Chairman, is my fleet."

Boom.

"Eduardo," Erlyn Teixeira spoke up now, pitched loud enough to be heard clear back on *Celestial Sovereign*'s bridge. And perhaps on Earth, as well. "Might we ask for a recess at this point? The High Council has become aware of new information that was not available previously, and will need a private consultation as we determine the best way to deal with it."

He liked Erlyn. She reminded him of Fernanda, in all the good ways. He could see what Oluchi saw in both of them, and still agreed that Anya had that extra something they both lacked.

Eduardo nodded.

"It has been moved that we recess for an hour before reassembling," Eduardo announced. "Do I have a second?"

"Seconded," Pascia Nkali replied in a voice that sounded like Death itself knocking at your door.

Pascia and Erlyn? Most interesting.

"All opposed?" he asked, glancing around the room with his own visage conveying the suicidal stupidity of speaking up now. "Hearing none, we stand recessed until ten o'clock."

He rapped his knuckles and leaned back, wondering if Roald Cavalcanti would survive that long.

FIFTY-THREE

ERLYN

ERLYN INTENTIONALLY WALKED last into the chamber they had been given for private meetings. Things that the High Council needed to work out among themselves before taking them before the larger group they had left behind in the ballroom. Interestingly, Pascia had been first in, even though they had not moved in any sort of line getting here.

Erlyn made sure the hatch was closed behind her and all the Council Guards were outside. Nobody in here but nine High Councilors. Not even aides today. One conference table, an oval with a polished stone surface and comfortable chairs all the way around it.

Human chairs. She could see cones for a Churquen, telescoping platforms for a Yithadreph or Dreeni, and several others tucked into a corner out of the way.

Eduardo was prepared to meet with representatives of the Phraettis Alliance. Erlyn assumed he'd left them in here as a statement to people like her that might understand such things.

That man was always several steps ahead of everyone else, because he could be.

Erlyn came to rest in her chair last as well, letting the others settle, all of them grumbling just a little as they did.

Pascia spoke even before Roald had his precious gavel in hand to do anything silly like formalize this.

"Roald, that was the stupidest stunt I have ever seen you attempt," she said in a withering voice directed entirely at him, as though the two of them were alone.

Erlyn noted that the round shape had Pascia sitting exactly opposite the man, instead of beside him like she normally did. Erlyn would have taken that spot, had it been empty.

"Now you see here…" Roald started to retort, loudly, but Pascia cut him off.

"No, you listen, Roald!" she roared back, an enormous voice coming out of such a tiny frame. "You already cut us off from accepting the treaty as written because you wanted to use this last minute push to extract something special when you thought that you had everyone else over a barrel. You miscalculated. Badly. Fucked up hugely and now we're going to have to clean up the mess you've just left all over the floor."

If Pascia was raging, so was Roald at this point.

"We could not have known!" he snarled at her. "Nobody knew that they had that much firepower at their command."

"Actually, I did," Erlyn snuck the words in like a dagger in a dark alley. "As chair of the Committee on Security, we have access to those numbers. If any of you had actually read the reports, you would know as well. I couldn't have told you the number arriving would be one hundred and seventy-four, but that represents just under forty percent of the armed vessels registered to any corporation on Yisan, not counting private yachts like this one."

She gestured to the luxurious vessel they rode in, because doing so might remind a few of them that this very ship had sailed up to Bajerlie Station and forced it to surrender after annihilating two Security Barcs and then decapitating the command structure by blowing up the governor in his private suite.

"You thought he was bluffing, Roald," Pascia sneered up at the tall man. "And made us all look like fools as a result. Again, I might add. Erlyn, what do your spies tell you about Fernanda Flores and the treaty document she transmitted to everyone?"

Erlyn wondered just how the woman had known to ask that specific question, even in as public as the privacy of Council Chambers. Anya had whispered it to her at a private moment, the woman still having some residual measure of loyalty to Rio, maybe wanting to keep things from reaching this crescendo of idiocy.

Erlyn made a note to ask Pascia later if she'd been bluffing when she asked that question, or had known something. She thought they had grown close enough over the last year that she might even get an honest answer.

For now, though, she focused her attention on Roald.

"That there are two versions, Pascia," Erlyn answered in a conversational voice, letting those two remain emotionally overwrought right now. "The only difference is the last page, however."

"Oh?" Pascia asked, now schoolgirl innocent, which was a fun transition on a Gnashiiley snout. Her ears even perked up.

"One copy has three signature blocks on it," Erlyn smiled. "The other only has two."

Throats might have been cut by the sudden silence that descended on everyone. Erlyn waited patiently, still not sure what Pascia's game was, but knowing that the woman would not be pushing so hard without a damned good reason. And enough votes in her pocket.

"Two, Roald," Pascia pounced now. "That means that Eha Dunham and Eduardo Martìnez might cut the Rio Alliance out entirely."

"They wouldn't dare," he hissed.

"Why not?" Pascia demanded hotly. "Eduardo might not need the military might of the Rio Alliance, if they leave us to fight Westphalia alone. I imagine that he might turn his attention to arming the Phraettis Alliance with modern technology now, making common cause with them to hold the nebula and not trading at all with Human worlds, except on his terms. Where does that leave the Rio Alliance?"

"They would never survive without us!" Roald snarled.

"Really?" Pascia asked. Then she turned to look at Erlyn, and Erlyn felt the first part of the trap close. The only question was whose legs were about to be caught in it. "Erlyn, dear, where do you suppose would Lazarus end up, if it came to that?"

Ouch.

The single most important Human in the galaxy, depending on how you framed the question, exceeding even Eduardo Martìnez on many scales.

"Well, Grace Savidge is a citizen of Yisan," Erlyn found herself saying in a clinical voice. "But I presume that Eha might reconsider Liberty as a long-term destination if all this came about, so she and Addison would likely stay on Yisan or perhaps return to Zhoonarrim. Maybe even Gowook, depending on things we can't know right now."

"Yes," Pascia nodded. "I would have to presume that Liberty might end up being abandoned if we were that foolish. I wonder what would happen to the Rio Alliance itself at that point."

Okay, more ouch.

Erlyn could smell *trap* right now in the same way that cattle smelled wolves, but she still didn't see where the woman was headed. And since she had a better idea than anybody else, Erlyn wanted to make sure she was at least last cow into the chute, if Pascia decided to be holding the stun hammer today.

"I will remind you that I am the Chair of the High Council," Roald snapped. "I make decisions for this group."

"Yes," Pascia agreed, her voice turning into the sort of purr that had the hairs on the back of Erlyn's neck standing up. "About that…"

Oh, shit.

Erlyn wondered if anyone else was really paying close enough attention as those steel jaws began to crimp enough to bite. She wondered if she should just start running now, at least metaphorically.

Or maybe literally.

"Roald Cavalcanti, it is my considered opinion that you no longer have the esteem of the High Council, and should stand down gracefully," Pascia said, invoking one of those formal terms that usually preceded a duel. Metaphorical or Literal. "Failing that, I will submit to the High Council that new elections for the position of Chair should be held immediately, as we have gotten ourselves into a terrible bind under the current administration, and risk compounding our mistake with errors that will be generations playing out."

Roald had turned scarlet as her words first sank in. Looking around the table, he turned white now. Erlyn could see enough of her fellow councilors to note that none of them were smiling at Roald right now. Scowling, perhaps. Snarling, in Juan's case.

On the one hand, the Alliance Block, Erlyn's usual allies, had just been threatened with an outcome that undid the entire purpose of the Rio Alliance, if new species chose to withdraw from Human Space rather than stay. On the other hand, the Humanist Block, the *warmongers* to use Erlyn's usual term for them, could see Lazarus and Eduardo withdrawing from things and leaving Rio to fight for itself alone.

Up until two years ago, Westphalia had been slowly winning. Erlyn presumed that if Yisan drew a hard wall in space and defended it as ferociously as she expected they would, then Westphalia would turn all their attention on Rio.

How long until they won? Especially without Lazarus?

She and Pascia had been gossiping earlier about how Roald might stagger himself into losing some important votes eight to one against, but it had only been gossip. The man was usually better at gauging the currents in the room and finding a way to end up on the winning side.

But this looked like his luck had just run out.

Or maybe he had finally screwed up enough times that nobody was willing to support him. There was always that.

The silence stretched. And stretched.

Roald opened his mouth. Closed it. Opened it again, but nothing came out.

"Roald, go out with some dignity," Ch'ani Zen spoke up quietly now, her Atomarsk feather fan flaring out into distinct points.

Again, ouch.

Like it was a foregone conclusion. A political execution playing out in the privacy of Council Chambers.

Erlyn had seen some hard maneuvering in her time, but usually the collegiality enforced by ten-year Parliamentary appointments meant that things were polite and friendly.

Until days like this.

Roald Cavalcanti looked around the room and counted votes, just as all the rest of them were doing.

Eight to one, against.

"All right," he finally whispered.

"You should stand down as well, Roald," Pascia said, not triumphant but implacable. "Make it an entirely clean break and retire to your estate."

Erlyn caught her breath, but nothing more. From the sound around her, so did several of her peers.

"Is that necessary?" he whispered, all the fire gone from him now.

"It is," Pascia said. "Let us focus on the good things you have achieved up until now."

That was defeat. Erlyn had seen it a few times, but never so stark.

So brutal.

Roald Cavalcanti, ex-Chair, set his gavel down quietly on its side, slowly thrust his chair backwards and rose. The others did as well and he shook each hand in silence before departing the chamber.

Erlyn sat back down a little shell-shocked, but that was not a unique thing in this room right now.

"Now," Pascia announced. "We have new business before us in the election of a new Chair. I nominate Erlyn Teixeira to fill the position and lead us into a new age."

Bombshell. Boom. What?

"What?" Erlyn managed, but her words were overrun as Juan Almeida, Humanist Block firebreather and one of Pascia's oldest and closest allies spoke up.

"I second the motion," Juan called in a firm voice, looking right and left as if daring the others to challenge him. Juan was many things, but among them was being somewhere past old and rapidly approaching elderly, from the white hair and wrinkled skin to the impression of immense ago.

Silence.

"Are there any other nominations?" Pascia asked, looking right and left as well.

Nobody challenged the woman.

Not even Erlyn.

"Lacking other nominations, I move to accord unanimous consent," Pascia said. "Agreed?"

"Aye," they said.

Erlyn included somehow.

More silence, made worse as Pascia picked up Roald's damned gavel and handed it to her.

"Congratulations," Pascia beamed at her with an honest smile.

"Why me?" Erlyn managed to squeak out, still utterly in shock at what had just happened.

"You are everything that Roald Cavalcanti was not, my dear." Pascia smiled. "Forward thinking, at a time when the era of stagnation needed to be over. Friendly with Eha and the Species Underground, at a time when we really need every ally we can get, lest they throw us to the wolves. And something of a godmother to Adriana Dunham. We will need Eha, almost as much as we need Lazarus. You will be able to carry us there."

"Quando no curso de eventos humanos…"
"When in the course of human events…"

Erlyn understood that a revolution had just occurred.

Another one.

How many was Lazarus of Bethany going to be responsible for, ere that man was done?

Erlyn had no idea.

But time was very short, so she took the gavel from Pascia's hands and considered what had to come next.

FIFTY-FOUR
EHA

EHA COUNTED the Human High Councilors as they entered, wondering what had been the outcome of the private meeting Eduardo had forced on them an hour ago. Then she realized that there were only eight of them entering.

A quick count and Roald Cavalcanti was missing. And nobody was saying anything, as if nothing was amiss.

Erlyn Teixeira looked like someone had just run her over with a speeder. Or perhaps just missed as she threw herself madly out of the way at the last minute.

Others began to notice now as she looked around the room. Lazarus, but nothing escaped that man. Eduardo, ditto. Oluchi. Carlos Nguema.

People used to ignoring shells and looking at the souls underneath.

The whispers started up now, an uncomfortable buzz with something of a rusty saw blade edge to it as more and more elbows transmitted messages and heads nodded in that direction.

Eduardo's face might have been carved in stone, but Eha could see the wicked gleam in his eyes. He waited until the

High Councilors settled and then slammed his knuckles down on the table top, hard enough to hurt.

"This meeting will come to order." His voice cut through the hissing like a Star Lance.

And he wasn't waiting for Cavalcanti, so Eduardo had drawn the same conclusions that she had.

The High Council had expressed their displeasure with Roald Cavalcanti, but done it in private.

Interesting.

"Madame Teixeira, you appear ready to speak," Eduardo said now in what sounded like a friendlier tone. "You have the floor."

Eha would have called on Pascia, but only because of the grin on her face right now. Her and Juan both had that same smile Addison got when someone delivered a plate of fresh *galumph* strips and *baka* sauce.

Erlyn took a visible breath and recovered some of her equilibrium. At least as much as a biped could. Eha had never understood how they didn't fall over when they walked.

"There have been…developments," Erlyn began in a voice still finding its footing.

Eduardo seemed content to wait. Eha found her tail kinking a little with anticipation.

"After consultation with my peers, the High Council of the Rio Alliance has accepted the resignation of Roald Cavalcanti, both as Chair and as a member of the Council itself," Erlyn said.

She might have wanted to say more, but the sudden roar of voices drowned everything.

Then it was gone, like a soap bubble popping, leaving an awkward and almost-as-painful silence in its wake.

"Is there a new Chair?" Eduardo asked simply.

"There is," Erlyn nodded. "Myself."

More noise, but less of it, like the second wave after the

first has done the most damage. Which was why Churquen didn't swim. There were always more waves.

"Congratulations, Chair Teixeira," Eduardo replied, with honest emotion in his voice.

Like Eha, Eduardo liked Erlyn. She couldn't say that about many of them. Even Pascia was more of an ally and less of a friend.

But Erlyn had been there for her when she'd needed someone in the Rio Alliance.

"Is there other new business we need to address?" Eduardo asked now, as if the previous however long had been something of a fever dream that had broken.

But Eduardo was playing a game measured in centuries, when the man himself likely only had a decade or three before he died, if Eha understood Human genetics properly. One hundred, maybe one hundred and twenty years. Much like the Churquen in that.

"The reconstituted High Council has voted to accept the proposed treaty with no further amendments or discussion," Erlyn continued now. "On the understanding that all sides will appoint permanent ambassadors to the other players to continue petty negotiations related to day to day tasks."

"Very good," Eduardo said, and then turned to Eha.

"Ambassador Dunham, does this meet with your approval?" he asked.

Eha understood that hint of concern in the man's voice. Rio had been shits to her at times, but looking back she could see where much of it might have been driven by Roald Cavalcanti as a person, rather than as an official position. Certainly, he had been dealing with two fractious sides and eight other strong personalities.

He had overstepped finally, and the others had apparently had enough.

That left her with Pascia and Erlyn as direct allies, but

also Ruby, Juan, Aatther, Mara, Ch'ani, and Whrlaxu, all of whom had been relatively friendly, as Eha had negotiated the twists and turns of Human and Rio Alliance politics, first as a representative, then later as a hat-in-hand beggar.

"It does," Eha replied now. "But only to a certain extent."

It was telling that neither Erlyn nor Eduardo reacted. Nor Oluchi or Fernanda. Eha wondered how far down the logic tree the folks from Yisan had gamed out various alternatives as this terrible endgame began to play out.

Eduardo nodded and rapped his knuckles like Roald had always gaveled things.

"Then we can, at least, assume approval of the treaty, pending the signing ceremony itself," Eduardo announced, but Eha understood that he was playing to the galleries. There were no reporters in here, but many people would be recording this and leaking it later.

How many of them were actual spies as opposed to bureaucrats making a little spare change on the side remained to be seen. After Esmer, apparently the Council Guards and Rio Navy had performed a brutal house-cleaning that had uncovered at least two nests of long-term, deep-cover spies.

Lazarus had been right from the very start, even when nobody but Addison and Aileen had believed him. Several players had personally apologized to the man subsequently.

"Madame Dunham, I would hear your next set of reservations, now that we can all consider ourselves treaty-bound allies," Eduardo continued.

It was an interesting way to phrase it. Treaty-bound.

The Rio Alliance. The Yisan Alliance, or whatever they ended up calling themselves when Eduardo got serious. The Phraettis Alliance, which was a term already gaining mileage in her old home.

The Grand Alliance.

"We are gathered *en masse*, Eduardo," Eha said, letting

her gaze sweep the room and the hundreds of folks here as witnesses. Humans, but also almost all of the Species themselves, missing only a handful, as various directors had answered Aileen's call for war. "The Rio Alliance Navy has arrived with a tremendous war fleet, of a scale I am told is possibly unique in the history of the Alliance itself. Yisan has delivered a second war fleet, made up of smaller vessels, perhaps, but no less willing to fight. Phraettis has delivered ships and sailors, those same folks that have previously rescued Zhoonarrim and Yisan from conquest."

Eha let the words dangle now. She might have been a spymaster for more than a decade, but that also involved a lot of psychology and public speaking, even when you only needed to motivate one other person.

Today, she had hundreds hanging on her words. They best be good ones.

Eduardo nodded, allowing her to remain the focus of all that energy, like lightning coiling to strike on the surface of a planet.

"Put simply, ladies and gentlemen, what do we do with it?" Eha asked.

She was not surprised when all eyes turned to Pedro Santos, Admiral in charge of the Rio Alliance Navy itself. He was sitting at her table, only because Lazarus, Addison, Aileen, and Carlos were already here, all in tan uniforms, and she otherwise would have had the table to herself, with Alla and Adriana among the few to come up from the surface.

Apparently, stubborn and hard-headed ran on both sides of Eha's family, and her mother had had to be dislodged from her place as Governor of Liberty, even to attend a meeting as important as this.

Eha will handle it, she would say.

And so she was.

Santos looked like he was chewing on something for a long moment before he spoke.

"As you know, I am in command of Rio's Navy," he began, quieting the few whispers that had arisen. "It was my authority that caused nine Heavy Starcruisers to be in orbit right now. Ten counting *Mannheim,* but that ship is not repaired sufficient to engage in long-distance sailing so it will remain in place, regardless. Phraettis has delivered a group that Commander Enjehn affectionately calls her *Mob of Galumphs.* Yisan has produced a significant tonnage of escorts and raiders. We even have eight Gun and ScoutWall vessels captured by Phraettis forces over the last few months."

He paused there, but Eha was not surprised. His job was probably at least as political as Erlyn's. Maybe more. And he was good at it, or someone else would have his command.

"However, I will remind everyone present that military power must remain in service to civilian authority," Santos continued now. "Anything else results in the eventual fall of any government. So I will take your orders and faithfully execute them, but those orders must originate in the halls of government, and not the Admiralty building. With the government itself, and not for it. Here, ladies and gentlemen."

And with that, he sat back and crossed his arms across his chest. Apparently, Humans had the same body language as Churquen that way. And Yithadreph, as she'd seen Aileen do the same thing.

Aileen leaned forward now: torso, ears and whiskers. Eyes turned to her instead of the Human next to her.

"I have a better question for you folks," she called to the room. "One my mother and sister habitually inflict upon me whenever I'm home visiting family and spoiling my nieces and nephews. You talk about a Grand Alliance. That's wonderful. I'm sure it looks good on paper, but what do you folks want to be when you grow up?"

Laughter greeted that question. Every parent had asked every child that, including her own. And many of the people at these tables had been the ones that liked putting round pegs in square holes, given the chance. Coloring outside the lines.

And then Lazarus leaned forward and scowled at everyone.

FIFTY-FIVE

LAZARUS

LAZARUS HAD WAITED PATIENTLY. The coup that had apparently defenestrated Chairman Cavalcanti had caught him a little off guard, but only because he hadn't believed that those folks had the brass to actually do it, in spite of the time he had spent with Teixeira and Nkali over the last however long.

The deal was done. Wonderful. Grand Alliance. Lovely.

He could already see the bureaucrats preparing to stick things into spokes and gears to slow everything down, but that also didn't surprise him. That was what they did.

It was also why the Navy had instituted a *top secret* weapons program with him and Juan-Pedro to build a better mousetrap. Without folks hovering over his shoulder and second-guessing everything they did, *Ajax* had been the result, when these bureaucrats would have come up with something else. Something less elegant.

Something stupid.

All eyes centered on him now.

There was a part of Francisco Luiz Oliveira, Capitão De Mar E Guerra and ex-Special Services killer that quailed. His old job had involved never emerging into the light, lest his cover be blown permanently. Later, he'd turned into a scientist designing better things in his relentless quest to do this one thing: Win the war.

"You have three choices," Lazarus announced now in a loud, clinical voice. "Four actually, but you're already doing the fourth and hoping that something good will somehow come of it. Namely, dithering. Eventually news of this room gets out. Nothing will stop that, regardless of how hard you try to prevent that."

He paused, scowling still, left to right, excluding his allies. Mostly.

"You can go attack someplace like Esmer again," he continued now. "We did a number on them last time, so they have likely rebuilt and reinforced the place, but there is nothing they have that could stop us from taking that system away from them and holding it against any counter attack. Not with the tonnage that we have present."

Another pause. All those classes in Command and Leadership had ground certain things into his bones, so Lazarus just let them autopilot him now. Breathing. Posture. Pitch. Projection.

How to be a Captain in the Rio Alliance Navy.

"That won't solve a damned thing," Lazarus sneered at the civilians in the room who were smiling hopefully at the thought of attacking Esmer. Bureaucrats, mostly. The ones who didn't like to think of the cost in blood, sweat, and tears that had to be paid when fighting a war.

"So you really have two choices," he said now, eyes boring in hard on the new Chair of the High Council of the Rio Alliance. Technically, his boss, since he was supposed to answer to Rod, who answered to Pedro Santos, who answered to Erlyn Teixeira. When Lazarus wasn't skirting all the rules. "First off, we can go annihilate the Innruld, and do so easily with only a fraction of this force. Hell, just Eduardo's people alone would let me scour Phraettis Space clear of every single Security Barc and Pyramid in existence in a matter of weeks. That still doesn't solve my problem."

Lazarus found his hands both palm down on the table in front of him, starting to sweat, but that was the mad energy in his veins right now rather than fear. That dream that created *Ajax*, and saw the potential for light at the end of the tunnel.

"What is number two, Lazarus?" Erlyn spoke now, in a calm voice like they were out for lunch somewhere and just *chatting*, rather than surrounded by most of the key players in the galaxy, deciding its fate. "The thing that does solve your problem?"

"We take this sledgehammer and make a few critical adjustments, Erlyn," he replied firmly. "Then we sail to Earth and destroy every single warship they have before overthrowing their government and ending Westphalia as a political and military threat to the galaxy ever again."

He had to stop there because the noise had risen to painful levels again, as people cheered, screamed, hooted, belittled, objected, or merely fainted.

Erlyn didn't even blink. Nor did Eduardo. Nor did Eha. Oluchi even smiled, like he'd won a bet with someone actually dumb enough to try Pryce's luck and experience.

None of those folks surprised him. All of them knew what he was about. And that they were on the cusp of being able to do it.

Eventually, the room settled. He'd leaned back to watch and let them howl insults and encouragement at each other, because he could go slaughter Innruld with just what Eduardo had already committed to that task, since nobody had been sure that Rio would pull its head out of its ass this morning.

Smashing Westphalia would be even better.

Erlyn had a gavel that she pulled out of a pocket and hammered to get people to shut up.

After a while, it even worked.

"I agree with you that going to Earth and smashing Westphalia is probably the only use of a force like this," she finally said, some eight minutes after he had dropped his bombshell on them. "What adjustments would you make before we went and did this thing, Lazarus?"

He did grin when he thought about it. Nobody even called him *Pancho* anymore. Only a few ever called him Captain Oliveira. And then usually only once and by old habit.

He would go down in history as a second *Lazarus of Bethany*. And that would be okay, because like the first, he really was a sideshow to it all.

"Aileen's people have heart, Erlyn," he replied. "But those ships would be destroyed in any sort of fleet battle. That didn't stop them from going with her to Zhoonarrim or with me to Yisan, so I'll take those people with me anywhere in the galaxy, and that includes Earth. But we need to rearrange crews and hulls. We did that some with Aileen's two Protectors: *P-4282* and *P-4317*. I left *PL-371* and her consorts, *P-4491* and *P-4502*, back in Phraettis Space with Rod da Silva to cover him and keep the Innruld at bay while I was here. We have captured five GunWall ships and three ScoutWall as well, and have mixed and thinned crews around to train folks. What we need to do is park all of the Phraettis eggshells in orbit here and take those hungry crews and feed them into Rio and Yisan vessels, to the point that things are a little crowded, because those sailors are the nucleus of the Phraettis Alliance Navy I intend to build. We need to keep them alive long enough to return home and forge something we can all be proud of."

He watched the woman pause and consider.

The *Galumphs* had heart, oh so much heart, but those ships were eggshells, and a battle in Earth orbit would be a slaughter among those hulls. But if Wybert of Capantzina could turn into a hero and a legend, then by God he'd make sure the rest of them did as well.

"Admiral Santos?" Erlyn asked the man now.

Pedro leaned forward and turned to look at Lazarus down the table, like he was seeing a complete stranger.

But then, the man had never really known *Pancho* Oliveira. Just the rebel son returned with a fantastic story of luck and strangers he'd met, just over that mountain.

"So I have a question for you, Lazarus," he began in a slow drawl that suddenly sounded like a trap.

Lazarus nodded to the man. He had demanded this. He could accept the costs.

What was one more Court Martial at this point? He'd already lost count of the number he owed them. And he wouldn't have changed one damned thing getting here.

"So Aileen's *Galumphs*, as you folks call them, could be fitted into Rio hulls as extra crew," Santos said. "And presumably Yisan as well. That's all well and good. How will we organize command of such a monstrosity as a fleet with over two hundred ships, once you add in all the Light Starcruisers and escorts Rio will commit in addition to eight Heavy Starcruisers?"

"Sir?" Lazarus asked, a bit confused now.

"I can command eight heavies," Santos said. "Carlos can take charge of the escorts. From what I've heard, Oluchi Pryce would make an excellent overall commander of the Yisan forces, especially after what he did at Bajerlie and other places. Aileen could help, as many of her folks will be on those ships and she's already proven herself an exceptional combat commander who has gotten high marks from the folks I've asked who served under her. Addison can take command of those eight captured hulls, since they need to really be flying as a single group anyway, to make best use of their design. But I have my own problem."

"Sir?" he repeated, feeling a little bit like a broken record.

With a corner of his mind, Lazarus saw Pryce turn completely white as the Admiral's words sank in. Anya Persaud leaned over and whispered something in Oluchi's ear, presumably to calm him.

"Pryce is the Ambassador to Yisan, as I understand it, Lazarus," Santos gestured to Oluchi, grinding on like a grain mill. "Dunham and Wolcott represent Phraettis. I suppose I would front for Rio in a pinch, along with Carlos, but this force needs a commander that all sides respect. Who has proven himself to the revolutionaries of Phraettis, the Oligarchs of Yisan, and the Rio Alliance Navy. I understand from messages Rod da Silva sent home that you have refused on more than one occasion to be promoted to a Rear Admiralcy, because that would take you off the bridge of *Ajax*. But at same time, by your own words, Rod da Silva made you a Commodore for the liberation of Yisan."

"That's right," Lazarus answered weakly, still a little at sea.

"So I propose adding both my fleet and Yisan's to your squadron, *Commodore*," Santos said, beaming now. "And following you to Earth."

Shit. Talk about blindsided.

The cheers erupting on all sides of him didn't help. Nor did the way Aileen leaned over and just hugged him, getting there even before Addison could.

But he'd demanded it, hadn't he? Held on when everyone had told him he was imagining things and that there were no spies feeding his sailing orders to Westphalia, where they could ambush him and almost destroy *Ajax*.

Setting him on the path to *Lazarus of Bethany*. To sitting here today. To doing this thing.

This was who he was, wasn't it?

He nodded to the man, to the others. The noise was so great that he wouldn't be able to get a word out anyway.

Because they were going to go smash Westphalia.

Finally.

PART FOUR
EARTH

FIFTY-SIX

LAZARUS

LAZARUS LOOKED over the bridge of *Ajax*, a little crowded now in spite of the enormous space he had intentionally designed to give it that cathedral feel he'd had as a kid.

Lieutenant Ulisses Lòpez was still handling communications along with Cormac, but they had a new boss, as Carlos had insisted that Marie Oslor be transferred over. Santos had even promoted her to Lt. Commander, and put the woman in charge of all flag communications for the entire force. And Eduardo had subsequently insisted that Collin Lau be present as a Yisan representative, since Oluchi would be aboard *Celestial Sovereign*.

Lazarus had started to put his foot down, until Anya had pulled him aside and explained things nobody had bothered to share with him prior to that. And who was he to deny folks the chance to have a little romance? Grace was still aboard, but not fully dedicated to being a bodyguard, as Xiuying had transferred over as well and brought with him a team of folks he had fully vetted to handle that task.

And Alla Dunham had finally bent enough to send a

group of Churquen and Yithadreph—traded them for Adriana really—to accompany the Ambassador.

This finally felt like the thing that he had first envisioned, that third morning, standing in the shower on *Shiva Zephyr Glaive* and finally understanding where he was. Not that second day, when he'd first learned how Aileen liked her back scratched, but later, when *Pancho* reborn had come to understand that the Good Lord had kept him alive for a reason.

And introduced him to aliens. And friends.

He paused and looked down at his own scan of nearby space on one of his side screens. Two lines of Heavy and Light Starcruisers arrayed like an arrowhead with *Mendoza* at the tip, flying Carlos Nguema's new flag as a full Admiral, with his fourth star and commanding all the Rio escorts as well.

Outside that, two wings of Rio and Yisan escorts in layers protecting the Starcruisers, with a third cluster around *Ajax* and *Celestial Sovereign* at the very center of the formation. None of the *Galumphs* were flying with this force, but he had twenty-one species represented aboard just *Ajax*, and the entire rest of the Phraettis Alliance somewhere close, including that refugee and rebel Turkan Volan, an Innruld bureaucrat that had fled Gowook with Alla when Lazarus and Wybert had blown up the Hall of Records.

Every known species.

Every *presently-known* species, he amended himself, thinking back to an Atomarsk mining freighter that had accidentally located one of the first Earth explorers to head inward on the galactic arm and forever changing the homeworld.

How many more species were out there? And how many colonies of folks that had perhaps snuck quietly away from

Innruld Space in some distant past and settled in that darkness that he was planning to explore one of these days?

Lazarus paused and counted hulls. Over two hundred. Mind boggling.

"Marie, open a general channel to *Task Force Liberty*, but mute all the captains for now," Lazarus called, looking over the group around him. Three Humans, with Marie, Ulisses, and Collin, but not counting Grace seated quietly off to one side, because she was not in any kind of uniform and had no intention of ever doing so. Ilount. Churquen. Vaadwig. Crawler. His favorite Yithadreph was aft, but her face was on a secondary screen from the flag bridge, where she was constantly offering suggestions via her own staff as to how to better stack boxes.

She grinned at him now like she was reading his ears and whiskers, like he did hers.

"You're live, sir," Marie replied a moment later, looking up at him with a nod.

He also saw the shy smile she had for Collin. It was good. Hopefully, someone had finally explained to her that Collin was likely to become Erlyn Teixeira's equal, once Yisan finally organized all the paperwork and turned into a nation. Eduardo had warned Lazarus what was coming, at the same time he had offered citizenship.

Lazarus would have three passports when this was all done. Rio, Yisan, Phraettis. It would be good.

"Admiral Santos. Admiral Nguema. Captain Wolcott. Ambassador Pryce," Lazarus began now.

Oluchi refused even a courtesy promotion, and was wearing his black outfit with the blue-lined cape, but that was Oluchi. He'd been wearing a cape the first time Lazarus met him, and pretty much hadn't changed his mind or his game since.

"Ladies and gentlemen," he continued. "Civilian leaders of all nations, please give me your attention."

As if anybody wasn't watching right now. The biggest fleet ever assembled, and God willing, the last time something like this ever needed to be done.

"We are about to embark on an epic quest," Lazarus said, finding his eyes turning to Grace and then Aileen as he found the words. His two closest friends in the galaxy, with Oluchi a close fourth behind Addison. "We sail out to break the hold of small minds and reactionary politics on the spirit of all people. I would normally avoid saying that we are here to free the Human Spirit, as so many of my friends today are from other species, but I will say it now in the sense that you are all people. All my comrades in arms. My friends. And you should all be free."

He paused and counted blue dots on his map again, just imagining what it would look like, in the night sky of Liberty, when it happened and they got to watch the biggest redshift light show in history.

"All squadrons are prepared for navigation and that long voyage of discovery and retribution that we have been able to assemble in the name of *Alliance*. We have gone into darkness and returned. We have fought tyrants and fools and cast them down. We have died and been reborn in the name of Justice. Now we will complete our mission. All vessels, on my mark. Jump."

Blueshift.

FIFTY-SEVEN

ERLYN

ERLYN HAD STAYED up late with Alla, Pascia, and the rest of the civilians remaining behind. Eduardo Martìnez had originally talked about accompanying the task force named for this world, but in the end had sent Collin instead, and remained here in the man's stead.

More negotiations. At least she'd been able to bribe Eduardo with some of the excellent coffee she'd known to pack for this trip. Alla preferred tea, and they had even started farms growing a variety of flavors, though it would still be years before they were mature enough to harvest regularly.

But it was night, and everyone was either drinking decaf right now, or in Erlyn's case, a fabulous brandy that Eduardo had brought along from one of his own estates, aged for five years in oak casks and left underground.

Sublime, and she already had access to exceptional liquor as a High Councilor.

They were all gathered on the back porch of Government House, overlooking that huge back yard where a variety of plants from Gowook had been transplanted from pots and left to grow, bringing something of home with the refugees. Not everything had taken. In life as in botany, that was the nature of things. Eventually, it would be a park for the population. For now, however, it was private and everyone respected that, even before Xiuying had added his idea of an armed defense force for the colony, tonight patrolling around and making sure nobody snuck in. The Council Guards were on the inside of the fence, but not that close.

Making themselves scarce, as it were.

Lazarus's words came over the speaker now, drawing all eyes inward and settling quiet on the throng.

"…*We have gone into darkness and returned. We have fought tyrants and fools and cast them down. We have died and been reborn in the name of Justice. Now we will complete our mission. All vessels, on my mark. Jump.*"

All eyes turned to the heavens now. The station was a permanent presence overhead, an unmoving star marking the fact that all worlds had to deal with some threat. Erlyn looked forward to the day when that was no longer necessary.

Maybe tomorrow.

A new red star appeared in the heavens now, almost a blob of light like a rose unfolding, kissing the day, and then receding just as quickly. Erlyn was certain that others had been pointing cameras at the night sky to capture the thing, but she didn't care that much.

It was just a milestone. Not an ending. Not really a beginning.

A line drawn in the sand marking how far they had come.

Eduardo happened to be close. He toasted her with his own glass and she touched them.

"I would say *To Victory*," he muttered quietly. "But this isn't about victory, is it?"

"It is not," Erlyn agreed, looking around at all the facets of galactic civilization she could see, just here in this proto-garden. "This colony is named Liberty because to the folks of Gowook who escaped with Eha and Lazarus, that's what it represents. And the flag that Lazarus carries forward now in our combined names."

"I would agree," Alla broke in now, slithering close and settling on her coil. "All of the names we might suggest, or things we might toast to are backwards looking, at a time when the future is in front of us. All of us."

Eduardo bowed his head and smiled.

"*To bridges yet to be built*," he suggested instead. "Already, there are spans from Rio to Yisan, and Yisan to Phraettis. When Lazarus is successful, there will be more bridges, including to Earth itself."

"You automatically assume he will be successful, Eduardo?" Alla asked before Erlyn could. But she would have said the same words.

"I remember that first night," Eduardo replied, his eyes finding a distant horizon now as he spoke. "Oluchi was on the guest list for a night of poker and conversation, and that usually implied a Plus One of some sort, but Pryce normally came alone, or perhaps as someone else's Plus One, depending on the season. That night he brought Eha and Aileen, which served to utterly disrupt everyone's evening and throw all their corporate plans into disarray."

Erlyn nodded. She'd gotten this same story from Eha's point of view, early on when the woman was still trying to convince the High Council to live up to itself.

Just how badly had Roald infected all of them that nobody had noticed the pushback a new alien species had created, when they should have been embraced? But again, yesterday. Roald was on the planet only because nobody had any vessels leaving for Brasilia until tomorrow at the earliest, with which to drop him along the way and let the man quietly retire with his dignity intact. He had not joined the party.

Or whatever story Erlyn would tell tomorrow to make sure that he was marked with honor. Roald had been doing what he thought was right, however wrong he had been. Misinformed wasn't the same as evil, after all.

"However," Eduardo was continuing, "everyone overlooked the *Human* who had traveled with them. Or perhaps they had seen that red outfit he was wearing and assumed he was a nobody sailor that had been rescued along the way by these strange, alien women, and would be of no import later."

Eduardo laughed now, a low, knowing chuckle.

"They didn't bother looking at the man, seeing only the shell, you see?" he said. "Fernanda and Leena and the others saw the potential for trade. Strav Ardna, may he burn in hell for a while yet, saw only scales. But there was a third traveler. *Lazarus of Bethany.*"

"What did you see, Eduardo?" Alla asked.

"Determination," the man said. "He wasn't just a sailor who had gotten marooned. He was in charge, to the point that all three of the others deferred to him. I didn't know at the time who he really was. Nobody could know, but I understood that when Strav attacked the women that I needed to move to help him. Immediately. That meant Grace, but I was lucky that I had Oluchi Pryce on the scene."

"He has told me more than once that he was bluffing your authority, waiting for you to jerk his chain short or disavow him," Erlyn interjected now.

"And I would have in a heartbeat, if I thought he'd gone wrong, ladies," Eduardo replied. "But I had also been facing that man across a green, felt table with a lot of money between us for several years at that point, and I had a very good feel for Oluchi. I told Lazarus that help would be coming, but then hung up the comm and called Oluchi to tell him where they needed to go, because I understood that Pryce had found himself on something of a personal precipice and already jumped into becoming the man you folks know. I remember the old one, and trusted that he would do the right thing. Pedro Santos, of all people, recognized that and more or less appointed Oluchi as my warlord for this mission. *And he was not wrong to do so.*"

"But you understood Lazarus, just in that one evening?" Erlyn pressed.

"No," Eduardo replied, shaking his head. "I doubt even Grace understands that man, and she's far closer than I am. I saw his purpose. His drive. His willingness to take on Strav Ardna's entire organization by himself if he had to. And he would have. Knowing what I know now, he might have succeeded, and I still wake in a cold sweat occasionally when I realize that he was not bluffing about ending Yisan as an inhabited planet had something happened to Eha and Aileen. I know Addison Wolcott now; while he might have hesitated after destroying Strav, Lazarus would have gladly scoured the surface of the planet clean of Human life. And probably been in the right, on the overall scale of things, because Strav broke faith."

Erlyn heard Alla's gasp echoing her own, but Erlyn also understood just how hard a man Eduardo Martìnez really was. He might appear tall and heavy and jovial at times, but that was the end result of the throats he had cut along the way, metaphorically or literally.

She didn't ask. Didn't ever want to know.

"So what happens to Earth?" Erlyn asked, interested in this man's take.

"They will give way, just as Strav Ardna had to give way in the end," Eduardo said. "Grace might have fired the shot that ended Strav, but only after Lazarus kicked in the door and charged unarmed into the room to let that dangerous fellow Bălan kill everything that moved. And now Lazarus has the largest, deadliest fleet of warships ever assembled, ladies. And gentlemen."

Erlyn noted the way he had paused to look around before finishing that speech. Every single head was facing this way and most of the attendees had drifted into a much closer orbit than they had been before, wanting also to hear.

"Lazarus will walk into the fire, if he has to, because he has all of us backing him, just like he had Pryce, Bălan, and Grace that night rescuing Eha." Eduardo spoke louder now. "The only question left to ask is how many more people Lazarus will have to kill before Earth and Westphalia see the error of their ways."

Erlyn let that sit uncomfortably in her stomach and added a little of Eduardo's excellent brandy atop it. She had no doubts as to the truth of Eduardo's words.

Now, they just had to calculate the costs.

FIFTY-EIGHT

ADDISON

CAPTAIN ADDISON WOLCOTT. Squadron Commander, Combined Arms Wall Team, Task Force Liberty.

He shook his head and looked at the readout showing his eight vessels. He had transferred much of his crew and his flag to the newly-captured GunWall Archer renamed *Gowook*, and flew second in line behind *Intruder*, with six Phalanxes three and three on his wings, the Scouts *Swift* and *Drifter* leading two lines.

In the old days, all of a year ago, captured vessels were eventually traded home or sold for scrap, rather than being impressed into service, so GunWall mushrooms flying with Rio Protectors was weird, and all of his Human crew agreed with that sentiment.

But it made a statement here. And that was what it was all about.

They were on the plane above the Heavy Starcruiser *Guarulhos*, just a little behind Admiral Santos, as a matter of fact, but that was Lazarus making sure that Addison's force of trained Phraettis sailors wasn't going to be immediately in the thick of any skirmish. He wasn't coddling them, but making sure they all got home to Zhoonarrim and other places, so they could spread the revolution the rest of the way across those stars.

Finish the Innruld for good.

Just his squadron could probably do that, at least until those slime turds panicked and withdrew every Security Pyramid they had left to defend Innruld itself, at which point orbital space around the old imperial capital would look like a floor with children's toys scattered across it for an unsuspecting biped to step on.

Churquen would just slither everything out of the way as they moved, but that was the advantage of a keel.

The whole invasion was poised now. According to scouts sent secretly forward by Carlos, they were as yet generally undetected. A spy in the vicinity of Liberty could have made it directly to Earth by now, according to the sailing directions, but what would they do? Alternatively, had they raced to the nearest naval base and somehow convinced the admiral in charge to do something, what could he do? Heavily defended worlds like Esmer now might have two Heavy Starcruisers and two or three Light.

Addison supposed that adding those vessels to the forces reputedly surrounding Earth might make the battle a little closer to balanced, but not even. *Ajax* was sailing right behind *Guarulhos*. And if Oluchi's mob weren't as bloodthirsty as Aileen's *galumphs* had been, they were better armed.

And there were a lot more of them.

"Sir?" now-Spacer First Class Aanthos Park asked as everyone sat in this second-to-last moorage before Earth and did all the things that needed to be done.

Ereshkiki Nisab and Thadrakho would have just worked inside a trans-space tunnel, but that wasn't an option here.

Addison turned to Park and smiled.

"So what happens when we get there?" Park asked.

Pera was listening as were others here on the bridge, heads and ruffs turned slightly his way while still monitoring their stations.

"Maybe we fight, Park," Addison replied. "If they think they have enough ships to stop us. Maybe they see the error of their ways and surrender. You're better equipped to tell me what Humans would do when presented with a situation like this."

"There will be dead-enders, Captain," Park nodded. "Always are. The question I suppose would be if they are captains and admirals, or just punk sailors like me. Do they stand a chance?"

"Park, what do you suppose would happen if three hundred Star Spears all hit the same ship at the same time?" Addison asked, gesturing with both skinny arms to indicate the number of friends they had brought to this picnic.

"Fucker'd evaporate," Park replied. Then blushed furiously, his mouth falling open and skin reddening when he realized what he'd said. And to whom. "Sir."

"I agree, Park," Addison chuckled, smiling at the man to relieve him.

Some directors didn't allow profanity on their ships. Addison had never figured out how you'd have a crew of any quality at all doing that. Ereshkiki Nisab had certainly taught him a number of older profanities that had largely fallen out of favor in the last few centuries.

"They smart enough to realize that, sir?" Pera asked now from her Piloting station.

"Lazarus, by his own words, is prepared to make a demonstration," Addison said succinctly.

Everyone Addison could see shivered at those words, but they had all seen what *Ajax* could do. At Earth, Lazarus wouldn't have to be madly backing away and maneuvering to make sure he wasn't enveloped in angry coils by a Human moving like Churquen to slowly squeeze him to death. Here, he could just sit safely in the middle of the formation and carve pieces off of any Starcruiser that got close enough.

Addison considered that *Ajax* had never actually fought the kind of battle it had been designed for, instead smashing pirates, GunWalls, and dueling Heavy Starcruisers with short blades.

"Message from the flagship, Captain," Park suddenly held a hand up to his ear. "You're to report aboard *Ajax* for a final planning session in two hours."

Addison nodded.

There wasn't much left to say, unless Carlos's scouts had found something new. But he would get a dinner cooked by Khyaa'sha instead of a Rio Mess Specialist, and maybe spend the night with Eha.

Then, the final confrontation.

FIFTY-NINE

CARLOS

ADMIRAL CARLOS NGUEMA. Four-star Admiral, after impressing all the right people along the way, and getting damned lucky.

Still weird.

There had only ever been a handful of Gnashiiley Admirals. He supposed that he had stood on their shoulders, but he'd also made it easier for others to climb up his tail later.

After so long aboard his first love *Dutra*, *Ajax* was always a weird transition as he emerged from his shuttle and saluted the security marine here to escort him to the meeting. But he understood the purpose. Lazarus and Kirov had reduced that monster beam emitter as much as they could, but it was still huge and long. Throw in all the generators a beast like that needed, and you pretty much had to have the tripod grappling hook design.

With a lot of personal space inside, because the exterior was a smoothly-rounded surface, when Carlos supposed that it could have been crunched down a little by squaring off corners, but then it would have been a pain in the ass to repair, and damned ugly, inside and out. Like a lot of other ships he knew.

He preferred elegant. Helped that *Ajax* was new, and still had the original paint job in most places. And that Lazarus had insisted on a cream color verging down towards mustard to soothe the mind of the sailors and diplomats aboard instead of that gray so common elsewhere.

And carpet in many places, which was just *weird* on a warship.

His escort opened a hatch and stepped back rigidly as Carlos entered. Even the lounge had been made pretty. Relaxing, with faux-wood paneling and trim designed to almost make it look like a bar back on Brasilia. Most everyone was already here, judging by the looks. Lazarus, Aileen, and Kuei, representing the hosts. Pedro Santos. Oluchi Pryce. Addison. About two dozen other captains who were the various squadron commanders. Ambassador Dunham, here representing everything that Pryce had been doing before he put on his dread warlord hat for Pedro.

Khyaa'sha had done something in troughs tonight, heavy on garlic and tomato from the smell that engulfed him as Carlos stepped in. The room was informal, so nobody did more than turn and nod or smile in his direction. Carlos took that as a good sign and wandered to the bar, tapping elbows and bumping fists with folks as he went by, but not being drawn into any of the small talk yet.

The bartender was Human, that was good. Of course, there was also a tea bar installed now, at the other end of the space.

"Red wine blend," Carlos said.

Felt like an Italian dinner night, so a red would complement it.

He got his wine and wandered off into whatever

conversation might grab him, but Admiral Santos turned and buttonholed him almost immediately.

"Pedro," he nodded. "That feels weird to say."

Pedro nodded and chuckled.

"I remember the first time I addressed Miguel by his first name as a peer," he said. "Just as weird. You'll get used to it."

"I suppose," Carlos shrugged. "So I understand the need for one more big meal for the condemned thing going on. What else should I worry about?"

Pedro turned serious now. They were somehow alone, with nobody within ten feet of them in what had been a somewhat crowded room. He wondered if Pedro was giving off the right kind of negative vibes to everyone else.

"We're going to go down in history, you and I," Pedro said. "Good or bad. Lazarus will have his chapter, but as senior officers here, you and I will be the ones covered in shit or glory. Even Pryce is just along for the ride, because he doesn't have the depth of training to command that many ships."

"He's more than just another pretty face, Pedro," Carlos reminded the man.

"Oh, I know that," Pedro laughed, waving one hand. "Lost enough money playing poker with him, back when he was all that was left, after Eha departed to Vilga's Stand. The man's sharp. But he's a civilian."

"Okay," Carlos said as a placeholder, unsure where his boss was going now.

"Lazarus will have *Ajax*, and everything that it implies," Pedro continued now. "That includes the ability to kill enemy Heavies from a distance. But you and I have to be ready to mix it up. To get down in the mud. To go into the corners after a puck. That's where it might get ugly."

"You think Westphalia will go down fighting us?" Carlos asked.

That had been his primary assumption while training all of these various ships to fight together. Pedro would command eight Heavies, but Carlos had six Lights and four wings of support escorts of various classes. The rest of the onion, as it were, that you would have to peel back crying, in order to get to *Ajax*.

"I don't think they have any other option, Carlos," he replied now. "At least not at first. Professional pride, if nothing else, that they have to stand like Horatio at the bridge. We won't convince them otherwise until a lot of men and women get killed. If then."

"So we should be prepared emotionally for a slaughter?" Carlos asked.

"If every ship here fires just one beam at the same Westphalian Heavy Starcruiser, at the same time, what happens, Carlos?" Pedro asked. "Star Spear or Star Lance."

"Yeah," Carlos grunted.

"So we'll have to kill our way into a position of power and authority from which Lazarus can dictate surrender terms," Pedro said.

"You won't step in?" Carlos asked, a little surprised.

"This is bigger than you and I, Carlos," Pedro nodded. "Oluchi is in rough command of three quarters of our hulls and maybe half of our overall firepower. Plus the Phraettis sailors manning every ship here. This is everybody, for all the marbles. Lazarus is the only person who can speak for us all."

Us. Carlos caught that distinction. At one time, Pedro Santos had been the total hardass commander of whom everyone else lived in terror. Not a martinet. At the same time not your friend.

Maybe he had softened some, but maybe nobody had ever seen the real man since Captain Pedro Santos put on his first star and raised his first flag.

"So I'm supposed to drive right in like a snowplow and damn the torpedoes?" Carlos asked.

Pedro compressed his lips for a moment in thought.

"Yeah," he finally said. "Pretty much that. You'll suffer the worst casualties because your Light Starcruisers will be at the front, regardless of how you lay out the escorts. We're expecting some fifty GunWalls, if everyone is present, combat ready, and reacts. That's a hell of a lot of incoming firepower, at least until they break their teeth on you and *Mendoza*. But I'll be right behind you killing them, Carlos. Never doubt that."

"Thank you, sir," Carlos said automatically. "Hope it doesn't come to that."

"You and me both, Carlos," Pedro said. "But I wanted you prepared. And your captains need to understand how vital their sacrifice might end up being. All of them because even then, most of the Phraettis sailors are with Oluchi on those ships. Like Lazarus, we need them alive, in order to build us a navy over there. We might break Westphalia tomorrow, but that just means a lot of pirates, most likely, in ships too powerful for the Nebula to handle, in spite of Aileen Enjehn and her *galumphs*."

"Don't discount those people, sir," Carlos said.

"Oh, I don't," Pedro said. "Addison has told me what kind of sailor, what kind of man Wybert of Capantzina used to be like, before Lazarus came into their lives. Any similarity to today is merely coincidental."

Carlos nodded. He'd heard similar things from folks that had gone to Vilga's Stand and then talked to their friends back on *Recife*. And again caught that reference to Wybert as a sailor and a man, rather than as an alien.

No higher esteem in the Rio Alliance Navy.

"Now, let's go circulate," Pedro pretty much ordered.

"I've said my piece. You understand the needs of the service right now, but I'm glad to have you, Carlos."

Carlos nodded and found himself alone again, just as suddenly. He turned the opposite orbit from Pedro and made his way deeper into the crowd.

SIXTY

EHA

EHA LOOKED AROUND AS ALL these directors—Captains and Admirals and Warlords combined—sat and ate. She had come to appreciate what Khyaa'sha could do with Human ingredients, in making a home-cooked meal that still wouldn't poison anyone, with meatballs in red sauce or chicken in white, over noodles of various types, with a multi-national mix of vegetables and Human bread. All that was missing was *galumph* strips that Addison would have loaded up on.

Could one see the future of the galaxy in just how a meal was prepared and served? Eha hoped so. And was willing to bet that Khyaa'sha had done this deliberately. Nobody ever appreciated what a good cook she was, nor how canny.

Seventeen species sat down to a communal dinner and broke bread together.

At her table, she had Lazarus and Grace on her right and Addison on her left. The others had been left open for randomization, but everyone was somewhat clustered by nation and squadron. That was acceptable tonight, as long as it didn't harden down into lines later.

In one of those odd lulls in conversation that came up, a Human officer asked a question.

"What happens after we break them?" he asked the table, but the man was mostly looking at Addison and Lazarus.

With a start, she recognized him as Deni Wallace, hero of Zhoonarrim and commander of *P-4282*. Aileen's flagship, as it were, and leader among the *galumphs* in more ways than one.

"I'd like to go home, Deni," Lazarus replied quietly. "Wherever that ends up being."

"Brasilia, Yisan, Zhoonarrim, or Gowook, sir?" Deni asked.

Eha noted how few of the men and women in this room could have asked a question that incisive, but Deni had been with Aileen. He understood probably better than any other outsider in the room.

Lazarus shrugged.

"Right now, I'm still technically a wanted pirate and murderer on Gowook," he said. "As is Grace. And Aileen. We'd have to have a chat with the authorities before I was comfortable there. Past that, I don't know. I haven't looked past Earth, because until we know the shape of that outcome, everything else is superfluous."

Deni subsided and chewed. The others glanced at each other, but didn't have any better ideas.

"Is there a world close to the mouth of Akeley's Passage on this side that might be colonized?" Eha found herself asking. "Trans-space equipped ships can sail that passage almost faster than Jumpdrive ships, and safer. Would that be a good place?"

"To date, I have not found a candidate I liked," Grace spoke up now.

Eha watched Lazarus stop chewing and turn to the woman, eyes huge.

"Such a world would quickly grow as important as Yisan," Grace smiled at him. "And surpass it in less than a century, if only because folks like Eduardo would eventually move their warehousing operations there from Yisan, which was a good central point when trade was only two-sided."

Eha nodded.

"And if it was a new colony, everyone could start on even footing," Eha noted.

Grace nodded back. One of those non-verbal conversations she could have with the woman after being so close and isolated, before Esmer.

"Would you like that?" Lazarus asked Grace now. "What would please you?"

"I have looked, but not yet found the answer to that," Grace smiled at him. "So you'll just have to keep working at it."

Lazarus finally smiled, but Eha wondered.

Liberty was what it was because it had been a tool to get the Species represented on Brasilia, as a prospective member of the Rio Alliance itself. And before anyone knew if Westphalia could be beaten.

Innruld was already dead in everyone's mind, so they wouldn't get a vote in the matter, unless and until they were removed from power forever.

And maybe not even then.

"There is tomorrow, and then the day after," Lazarus opined. "Tomorrow we look at fighting for our lives. Only after that do we worry about happily ever after, Deni. Does that help?"

"It does, sir," Deni said. "One of those conversations I had with Aileen, when she was still trying to figure out what she wanted to do next. Nobody got past Westphalia."

"And we cannot, until we are there," Addison spoke up.

"Plans are just dreams written down. They must yet meet up with reality to be implemented."

Eha leaned over and kissed him. She had seen more sides of this man in the last year than the previous ten had even hinted at. She looked forward, like Lazarus, to exploring them all.

SIXTY-ONE

ADDISON

ADDISON WAS COILED and twined with Eha on the nest she had built in the Ambassador's quarters reserved for her. Kissing had been wonderful, but they had not progressed beyond cuddling tonight.

"I must ask this, so please do not be offended," he said, staring into those bottomless eyes.

She smiled, as if she could read his intent in his tail muscles. Not that he doubted she might.

"Go ahead," she murmured.

"Would you consider not leaping madly into battle with us tomorrow?" he asked. "Transferring over to one of the cargo ships along to resupply the fleet? They will remain here when the rest of us charge over that hill, and you will not be at risk."

"I must be there, Addison," she replied.

He opened his mouth to argue with her, and closed it. She hadn't even raised her voice.

But she was also right, he supposed. He was speaking, asking as her mate. She was replying as the Ambassador to the Phraettis Alliance.

"It will be a terrible mess," he continued vainly. "And *Ajax* will be the target of every ship that can try to hit it."

"This is the alliance," she said. "Your idea, along with Lazarus. I must be here, just as Collin and Oluchi must be. Just as Pedro and Carlos must be. You as well, but you are not enough of a representative by yourself."

"None of the other politicians came," he tried. "Erlyn remained with Alla and Adriana, as did Eduardo."

"All of them are secure in their place, Addison," Eha said, leaning in to kiss him to soften the blow. "The Phraettis Alliance consists of Oton Mari, Bajerlie, and Zhoonarrim right now, plus other worlds beginning to resist their Innruld overlords quietly. There must still be a government built, when all this is done."

"You think they will forget you?" he asked.

"I think that each of those governors is content, at least for now, worrying about their own system," Eha replied. "Rod has enough ships remaining behind to stop the Innruld from retaking things, and every day that passes increases his strength even as it diminishes the Innruld."

"But you?"

"I am the Ambassador to the Humans," Eha said. "The Species Underground representative to our friends and allies who will make it possible to free us from the Innruld."

"Do you wish to be a leader in Phraettis?" Addison asked.

To now, she had been a spy and spymaster. A master negotiator. Possibly a candidate for the Rio Alliance High Council at some future date. What happened on that mythical day-after-tomorrow?

"I already am," she sighed. "This will simply solidify it to the point that local politicians cannot challenge me when I suggest that we do not merely replace the existing lords and keep the system in place. A tyranny of leaders is not better as a multi-species thing than it was for the Innruld. We must be free, but we must also be equal. That will require laws enshrined in a constitution that cannot be easily overcome. Nor changed. The passions of the mob must be tempered and allowed to cool, so that deliberation allows progress. That was the lessons of the Rio Alliance and their constitution, inherited from earlier structures on their own homeworld. Deliberate progress that cannot be immediately undone tomorrow. We have nothing like that now, so we must build it."

"Which is exactly why you should not be risked during this coming battle," he tried again. "You alone have the tools and experience to make sure that this dream comes to fruition later. You cannot do that dead."

"You are at much greater risk than I am, Addison," she breathed on his skin and kissed him. "They will be offended to fight one of their own, while every vessel in this fleet will be protecting me because they are protecting Lazarus."

He shrugged.

"I am a sailor, dedicated right now to war," he offered. "That will change as soon as we return home. Either they give me a new ship to replace *Shiva Zephyr Glaive*, or I will find a way to steal something that will let me go back to just hauling cargo around. Plus, they will be protecting me almost as well as *Ajax*, for those same reasons. The Combined ArmsWall Team, all those captured Westphalian vessels, are heavily populated with the Species, learning how to be sailors and warriors themselves, with Human officers leading them. We will be safe."

"And I will be safe, Addison Wolcott," Eha said. "Now, come make love to me so we can sleep."

He surrendered at that point. She was at least as stubborn as he was. Probably doubly so.

But he could not get that niggling fear out of the back of his mind.

SIXTY-TWO

LAZARUS

LAZARUS LOOKED out over his bridge and offered the same prayers to Saints Elmo, Nicholas, and Andrew that he had before departing on that first mission to test out *Ajax*. Anyone to watch over sailors and men lost at sea.

And they had, when you measured it by the longest of terms. He had become as Job, in some ways, and been cast out like Odysseus, returning safely thus far, though he doubted that the Good Lord had seen fit to make him a new messiah in any way.

He was merely the one who showed the way. *Lazarus of Bethany*, whose revival marked the greater divinity of the true Messiah, as yet unreturned. But had he not said that there were many mansions in his Father's House? Were there not places for Churquen, for Yithadreph, for Qooph, and all the others?

So he said a quick prayer and hoped that God would take pity on all the lives about to be lost, believers and fools alike, and gather them all up where they could be at peace together. That was all he was seeking with his foolish quest: a place where everyone could be free and equal, endowed by that same Creator with immutable rights.

Lazarus could no longer say **unalienable** rights. The word no longer felt right, even as Life, Liberty, and the Pursuit of Happiness were just the barest minimum he demanded. Innruld and Westphalia both would have to give way.

So he looked at a Vaadwig Second Officer, an Ilount Fusilier, a Crawler and a Human splitting duties, plus the faces of Churquen, Qooph, Atomarsk, Yithadreph and others on his various screens, and drew strength from them.

Many rooms. One mansion.

Lazarus of Bethany could find no better way to describe this day.

"Comm," he said, a term containing both Cormac and Lòpez as well as Marie Oslor and letting them sort it out. "Open a channel to all vessels."

"*You are live, Lazarus,*" Cormac replied now, so perhaps Marie and Lòpez felt the same weight of history on their shoulders and how important it was for a lifeform like a Crawler to be represented today.

Lazarus had not yet figured out how electronic lifeforms achieved souls, but he had no doubts when he looked at Cormac and Lenox that they had done so.

He drew a deep breath.

"My friends, this is the moment when history will be written," Lazarus said simply. "I am certain that by now someone has detected us, even hiding out in the darkness like this, and run to Earth crying *Wolf!* like the child in the ancient fable."

He drew a second breath now as the weight of history did return, landing squarely on his shoulders and pressing him down, but he had a lot of friends to help hold it up.

"We are not wolves," he continued. "We are not pirates.

Not marauders, nor any of the other terms that the Humans of Earth and Westphalia would use to describe us. We are Justice. We are the avenging army returned from forty years in the desert to demand our freedom from want and from fear. To live in peace and prosperity for the untold trillions of beings who will come after us. Always keep that in mind. We have come to free the galaxy, not merely to change the masters holding the chains."

He looked down and typed a few quick strokes on his keyboard, trying to keep the tears from blurring everything and mostly succeeding, even as he caught Aileen's smile right beside his hand.

"Pilot, I have transmitted a new set of coordinates to your station," he looked up and caught Kuei's shocked look back at him, ears straight up and eyes huge. He smiled at her. "Calculate standard offsets and transmit that to all vessels."

He drew a third breath as Kuei worked quickly, taking the moment to memorize everything around him before this most momentous moment of his life.

"Updates transmitted," Kuei said in a quiet voice.

"My friends, normally we would leap to a spot high in Earth's system, perhaps near the ancient wanderer known as Jupiter, before stepping down to Earth itself and challenging those people for the future," Lazarus explained. "Instead, in sixty seconds we will step directly into battle, foregoing that moment when they might think to ambush us in the darkness as we gather one last time, and instead perhaps catching them with half their forces out of place. I am done with partial measures. I am going to lead you to battle right now, and trust that all of you will watch your comrades, regardless of his or her shape. Pilot, transmit an updated countdown sequence."

The room had stirred, but everyone here knew him well enough to understand that a surprise like this was in character for him, and out of character for most other admirals and warlords.

Risk, but it heightened the rewards precipitously, and he found that acceptable.

It had been a risk leaping into the Nebula. It had been a risk kicking in the door on Strav Ardna's yacht. Or traveling to Brasilia and then Vilga's Stand.

The future was come.

Blueshift.

SIXTY-THREE

ADDISON

ADDISON WATCHED the massive blue light fade. It never ceased to amaze him, after a lifetime of trans-space tunnels, that he could just *be* somewhere in a single beat.

"Fusilier, stand by to engage," he said aloud.

Gowook and *Intruder* had Star Lances, so there was a chance that they could actually shoot someone effectively from their spot at nearly the center of the formation, a helmet guarding *Ajax*'s skull as it were. Everyone else would be defensive for now, at least until the Humans of Earth decided to charge madly into battle.

Scouts had identified more than twenty GunWalls and ScoutWalls in this system. Four hundred vessels, but most of those were assigned defensively to high-value targets. There were stations and naval bases around five of these planets, plus an enormous asteroid belt that was apparently a failed proto-planet of some sort, so the whole mass of the Westphalian Navy could not hit them immediately.

Light-speed itself meant that some of his enemies were hours from knowing what was about to happen, because Lazarus had gone straight for the throat.

Aileen had mentioned to Addison more than once that for a species without fur to protect their skin, no claws, and blunt teeth, Humans were still amazingly dangerous and willing to use those teeth if nothing else presented itself as a weapon.

But Lazarus had a fleet today.

"Movement orders from *Mendoza*," Park called, typing furiously as he listened to all the traffic.

Addison doubted that Marie Oslor would talk to them directly. Cormac might in a pinch, but *Gowook* was part of the Rio force rather than Yisan today. Carlos was his superior officer for now.

And that man had been there in the first battle ever fought in the nebula, when a desperate *Dutra* and *Star of Kilri* had stopped a ScoutWall from invading Innruld Space. Esmer had merely been a skirmish.

And Earth was going to be apocalyptic. *Hell on Earth*, as it had once been called, with that very Earth itself in front of him now.

Addison dialed back the scale of his sensor screen now, letting him take a moment to see everything within ten light-seconds of *Gowook*. Not as bad as he had feared. Still an enormous mass of death and destruction, as Lazarus had brought them out rather close to a major naval platform.

Beams were already going back and forth from the Light Starcruisers at the tip of this terrible powerspear known as *Alliance*.

"Pera?" Addison called over the chatter.

"Already on it," she replied, typing with almost as much speed as Kuei would have, but lacking that woman's perfect grace in doing so.

Still, good enough.

"Fusilier?" Addison asked now.

"Engaging," Hayesell replied. "Engineering, skip

recharging the Powerbolts until someone needs them and feed me everything on a rapid cycle. We've got a Light Starcruiser target down range we can just touch."

Addison listened to them talk and held his peace. Two hundred warships were badly outgunned by the number of forces that Earth could bring to bear, but those were scattered and Lazarus had everything like a hard, oval stone sliding across the fresh ice of a winter pond.

The only time a Churquen would willingly get near it.

Two GunWalls and a handful of Starcruisers had been in close proximity to the base when Lazarus brought them here. Addison wondered if there was another fleet like it sitting out at that spot where everyone agreed they would have gone normally, to square up for that last jump.

But they hadn't, and this enemy squadron was hardly better than what would have been at Esmer, had they been up to strength.

Completely out of their depth. Churquen and oceans.

"Firing," Hayesell said again.

Addison watched beams flickering out, light lines projected on his screen, even though they were just an eyeblink. Eight Heavy Starcruisers. Seven Light. All of the Task Force that could, firing anything that would reach.

He said a quick prayer for all the souls that would be lost and dialed his sensor array down in close.

Someone would be coming for them soon.

SIXTY-FOUR

CARLOS

CARLOS HAD THE VAN. That meant *Mendoza* was the big ship closest to the enemy, with only Protectors and semi-reformed pirates in front of him.

"All guns lock on target *Blue Three* and engage," Carlos ordered, knowing that his flag comm team would transmit that to everyone. "Everyone else engage nearest enemy as secondary."

In a standard battle, in the era *Before Ajax*, he would have picked out another Light Starcruiser and started exchanging punches at close range until someone was too bloody to continue. But even an old Gnashiiley like him could learn new tricks, from Lazarus, Addison, and even Aileen.

So *Mendoza* had identified what Carlos thought was the local Westphalian Flag Starcruiser from where it was parked and how it was moving. And told every Fusilier that could range on it to hit just that one vessel.

Helped that the ship's transponder identified it as *Europa*. Apparently Westphalia had been a tiny province in a place called Prussia, once upon a long time ago, itself located on a continent known as Europe in those days.

He had no idea what they called it now, and didn't care. *Europa* the Heavy Starcruiser had its shields on full and was trying to slither backwards away while ten thousand rats were gnawing on its leg.

"Sensors, let me know when that other Heavy Starcruiser, *Australia*, starts to get frisky," Carlos called now. "*Mendoza*, when *Europa* has had enough, we're going to sail the line straight through the hole we're blasting. That means we'll need to thread a needle for everyone behind us, because that's going to be a high-speed merge."

He looked over and caught the Captain's nod. Calling the man by the name of his command was an ancient thing, but it got the man's attention now.

"What about up three and left six, sir?" *Mendoza*'s Captain asked.

Carlos studied his screen. Yeah, that might work. Crazy, but nobody would see it coming.

"Affirmative, *Mendoza*," Carlos agreed. "But accelerate two points when you do, and make sure you and my flag team synchronize that with everyone else, otherwise we're likely to be out on our own for about five minutes, when they don't have anybody else to shoot at. Lazarus will appreciate us locating him a barrel full of fish to shoot."

The combined crews laughed at his joke, but it had a hard edge, as he expected. Everyone here had signed up for the war, hoping to free the Rio Alliance from Westphalia. Now they had their chance, but *Mendoza* was going to take one hell of a beating before it was done.

SIXTY-FIVE

LAZARUS

LAZARUS FELT like he was wading deep into the ugly parts of *Revelations*, when those final battles were unfolding and the Four Horsemen were riding. John of Patmos calling down the end of times as the various seals were broken.

Today was certainly that momentous. Hopefully, he had not deluded himself to the point that he was really the Antichrist today, although many of the people on the planet below were likely to so view him.

"Fusilier, I want you to hurt *Europa*," Lazarus said quietly.

Today was not the day for yelling loudly over the noise. There was precious little volume at this point, because Lazarus could only issue broad orders. In that, he was talking to Carlos, Pedro, or Oluchi and nobody else, and letting them break things down into movement and firing orders for everyone around them. Marie was good, but nobody but perhaps Cormac could issue useful orders to an individual captain effectively at this point.

Better not to try.

So *Ajax* was quiet. Just the blowers up a notch to contain

the heat he felt he was giving off, antiperspirant or not. Grace and Collin both watched from the side but offered nothing beyond moral support.

"*Europa*, aye, sir," Wybert replied, just as quietly, like he felt that weight and was just holding it.

Kuei didn't even have to do any of her insane maneuvering stunts today. At least not yet.

Mendoza was close enough to the main Earth squadron to be nearly engulfed now, at least on his screens, but had also brought the entire force in behind him like an arrow. *Europa* had the choice between engaging *Mendoza*, all Carlos's escorts around them, or the two wings of Heavy Starcruisers sailing in Carlos's wake.

Australia had gone straight after *Campinas*, second in line behind *Guarulhos*, for reasons Lazarus couldn't guess. But that meant that a staggering number of Starcruisers were hammering *Europa* right now, at a time when that ship had made the mistake of firing every which way.

And then Kirov spoke, like Joshua at Jericho.

The battle was happening lower than usual in orbit today, so the atmosphere lit up like northern lights, a brilliant blue and gold show that persisted for several seconds after the beam had delivered its deadly message.

Like the straw that finally broke the camel's back, *Europa* staggered, no longer in control as it tumbled into a turn they had been trying to make. On his visual screen, lights had gone out over most of the hull, save for fires and plasma leaking out of a hull no longer stable.

"Next shot, sir?" Wybert asked, which was almost out of character.

Normally, Wybert would be keyed up to score the kill at this moment. To actually break a Heavy Starcruiser into two pieces.

"*Message from* Mendoza," Cormac broke in. "*Targeting*

shifting to Australia *next, followed by maneuvering orders to go after* Terra One Station."

"Override?" Kuei and Marie both asked at the same moment.

"Wybert, conform your shooting," he ordered while he brought up the path Carlos was laying out. Lazarus and Pedro could both override the man, but Lazarus saw no reason. They were in the middle of hell right now, up on the front line, but would sail through to a point where *Ajax* could attack the biggest drydock and naval yard in the galaxy, and do so from the safety of range.

Just about the time that reinforcements could arrive.

"Follow *Mendoza* and communicate that to everyone, Marie," he decided. "Pull the escorts in a little tighter once we emerge, because the GunWalls will be swarming at that point and I want to give them a chance to get close."

"*Close?*" Cormac asked from his station. "*Why?*"

Not an insubordinate question. Merely confused and curious, as a young Lieutenant still learning the ropes in a fleet action. Lazarus had been there.

"If we engage them at the usual distance, our escorts will get pounded badly," he said. "Always expect local superiority of fire from a GunWall. If we pull them closer, then the Heavies and Lights can engage as well. Might also tempt them to try, when we can turn the tables on them."

"*Ah.*"

And that was that.

Kuei slewed the bow around and Kirov tagged *Australia* just as a hundred other beams were doing the same. The ship looked like it had been dipped in alcohol and set afire for a long moment, and then vanished.

Europa continued to tumble, lights out.

"Do we kill *Europa?*" Wybert asked, again calm and cool.

"Negative," Lazarus decided. "Pick out the next vessel

that will be closest to *Mendoza* on this new path and blast him open a corridor through, Fusilier."

The Westphalian Lights were alone now, outnumbered on Starcruiser hulls three to one, and outmassed by a factor of five. Two got mauled before the squadron chose discretion and fled ahead of his vengeance.

"Sensors, what is the countdown to an engagement sphere?" Lazarus asked now.

They had won the ambush. Normally, Rio ships would flee madly now, having *counted coup*, but this was not a hit and run raid. This was war for the future of the galaxy. They sailed methodically forward instead, aiming now at the platform that would represent the most stunning blow Lazarus could inflict on the enemy psyche.

"Seventeen minutes to seventy-five percent envelopment, Captain," Lòpez replied calmly.

"Marie, remind Oluchi that he's about to be on the front line in every direction," Lazarus called. "Time for him to earn his keep."

SIXTY-SIX
OLUCHI

OLUCHI TURNED TO MAFÊ.

"What does that even mean?" he asked the woman, ignoring the rest of *Celestial Sovereign*'s bridge for a moment as he walked towards the woman's station.

"The enemy forces that remain are about to assail us on all sides," Mafê explained calmly. "We have damaged or chased off that first group of bigger ships, so now all the escorts need to be prepared for the fact that GunWalls and others will be coming at us from all sides. Thus, an engagement sphere."

"Oh," Oluchi said. "Can we handle it?"

"Yisan's ships are better at that than Rio or Westphalia," Antonia spoke up now with a warm chuckle. "We're used to dealing with pirates coming out of ambush as much as being pirates lying in wait. Lazarus's earlier orders actually make it a little safer, as we'll have heavy ships supporting in several places, rather than someone expecting us to charge out and mud wrestle."

"I see," Oluchi said. "I am so glad I have experts who can explain it all for me."

Five queens, like always. Anya, Antonia, Mafê, Esperança, and Adamanteia. He had heard that group occasionally referred to as his *harem*. Skipping over the part where he only slept with one of them, it was not a smart designation. He still preferred *Board of Directors*, although you had to get pretty deep into some obscure incorporation documents to understand what structures Anya had set up when nobody was looking.

His five queens would never be poor again.

"So what does this ship do?" he asked the room, uncertain who should be responding.

"Nothing, until someone gets handsy," Adamanteia replied with a growl. "Then we slap them. Hard. Until then, like *Ajax*, we sit here in the middle and prepare to go into rapid turnover in any direction to bring the Star Lance to bear as needed, but we have several layers of ships around our own sphere first."

Oluchi was glad he'd taken up poker, instead of three dimensional geometry. And that he could just sit here and be another pretty face as these fantastic women *handled things*. He returned to his chair and caught Anya's hand in his own.

"Should I say something inspirational here?" he asked loud enough to be ignored once he sat. "Buff up the fleet, as it were?"

"Oh, you have been," Mafê grinned at him over her shoulder. "We've been transmitting messages and pep talks to squadrons and commanders with your signature since yesterday. You probably need to study it all later so that when folks ask afterwards you can look like you knew what you were doing."

Oluchi laughed. These women **got** him. Which was why they'd gone from suspicious strangers that first time at Liberty to his Board of Directors.

He reached for the travel mug of coffee he'd almost forgotten about and took a sip instead. Lazarus made it look so easy, but then, he had Addison and Aileen helping, and Kuei and Wybert executing.

Not as good as five queens, but a pretty good team.

SIXTY-SEVEN

ADDISON

ADDISON FIGURED he had something of an advantage, at least emotionally. His squadron sat just above *Ajax* in the formation and a shade aft. GunWalls would be staring straight at the planet beneath them as they charged in to attack, and that would cause more than one of them to shy off a bit. Come in at a flatter angle.

Something, so their brains didn't register this as *diving into the ground*. Or *shooting at their homeworld*.

At the same time, the design of his own GunWalls left him with a distinct combat advantage. They were generally coasting forward now, and could rotate the entire forward half of the ship up and around like an inchworm. Or a Churquen with an itch.

Fold to bring the gun around and pound away. *Gowook* and *Intruder* could engage from here, but the others, led now by *Drifter* and *Swift* as Scouts, couldn't really do anything, given the chaos of maneuvering around them and the number of ships all trying to engage.

But Lazarus had warned him that Westphalia would be particularly upset that their own ships had been turned against them today. The usual rule was that they got traded home, just like crews, or scrapped if they were too badly damaged.

Not *captured*.

Tough. The Phraettis Alliance needed them. Needed the hulls, the crews, and the experience this battle would give.

Addison held off on taunting them with a picture of his face, though. There was crazy, and then there was stupid.

"Engagement orders from Pryce," Park called. "Targets coming in from high and right for us to watch. Nobody close enough to shoot currently."

"That will change soon," Addison replied. "Pera, work with Hayesell to get us flying on a path where he and *Intruder* can engage now. Range be damned, since we both have Star Lances."

"Aye, sir."

Addison watched his screens. GunWall coming. They'd popped high and wide over the pole of the planet and were sliding down now, shooting at the outermost ring of Yisan escorts. Everyone was firing back as best they could, but Addison gave up trying to count the number of ships around them. Instead, he color coded them by distance and all of a sudden the whole mass looked more like an onion he was watching being peeled. Yes, that served nicely.

The two Archers began to fire. The Humans had a creature Addison had found endlessly fascinating, called an eel. It sat down in the rocks until something swam overhead, and then lunged out to bite it, a black, armless Churquen that swam.

Utterly bizarre, but highly efficient. *Gowook* was a moray now. Except that they were only nipping, instead of dragging someone down into the depths to be munched.

"We're drawing counter-fire," Park called to the room.

"Not surprising," Addison replied. "Let Oluchi and

Carlos both know that we're starting to draw more attention than we deserve. I would expect at least one GunWall will come directly after us, even if that gets them pounded on all sides in the process. Worse, someone might tell them what *Gowook* means."

Chuckles from his bridge crew, but that was the point. All those correspondence courses he had taken from *Ajax*'s computer. All those training videos on how to be an officer, and then a commander.

Even a hard-headed old snake like him could learn a thing or two.

He just had to survive to get home.

SIXTY-EIGHT
LAZARUS

LAZARUS WAS surprised when Khyaa'sha appeared, bringing coffee in mugs, but then he got a sniff and realized that it was hot chocolate, spiked with a little rum in his case.

Ye Gods, that sounded really good right now.

He shared a smile and caught her knowing grin. How much better did *Ajax* run because that woman was in charge of feeding all her little ducklings?

"Yes," Lazarus said, grabbing his cup. "Thank you."

She just laughed and went to take Kuei and Wybert their own hot prize.

Around them, the battle had moved to a fevered pitch, GunWalls growing reckless with abandon as the invaders inexorably approached the main Westphalian base. Weirdly, almost no ships were directly in front of the arrowhead that represented Carlos and Pedro. It was like the arrow had already entered flesh and passed through, with the sides and rear under constant assault.

"Maneuvering orders from *Mendoza*," Marie called now. "He's bringing the entire formation to a halt shortly and spreading the Starcruisers back and out into a sphere around *Ajax*."

"Will we be in range of the station?" Wybert asked in a conversational tone.

"Affirmative," Marie replied. "*Optimum* was his term."

"Excellent." Wybert drummed all ten of his feet, even through the pad, hard enough to make a sound. "Gunners, you are released to local control. Engage as you bear but call for help as you need it."

Lazarus nodded. Three Star Lances weren't much, in the scale of this battle, but *Ajax* would also be at the center of all attention for any enemy ship that could get a clear shot.

"Lazarus, it would be a long shot from here and unlikely to do much damage," Wybert continued in a more personal tone. "Should I take it anyway, or wait until I have a hammer in hand?"

Lazarus studied the boards. Without turning on his gyros, there was nothing to shoot at anywhere in the forward twenty-degree cone worth the effort. At the same time, the Kirov was just barely close enough to still cohere on impact, but it would be attenuated at this range.

Pretty, though. Northern lights that might be visible from the ground.

He wondered if anyone had told the billions of Humans below them what was going on, or if this was still a top secret naval battle that the brass would later deny.

Earth had never been attacked by a hostile fleet before. Even Rio had never come this deep.

But they didn't have the resources or the technological advantage until today, either.

"Go ahead, Wybert," he replied. "Light the skies up bright enough that it can be seen from the ground."

That silly face, with four mandibles and five eyes came around in utter confusion.

"Aurora borealis, you dork," Kuei muttered loud enough to be heard.

"Oh!" Wybert brightened. "Right. Coming up."

Lazarus shook his head and grinned when Kuei glanced back. Some days, you forgot you were dealing with Wybert of Capantzina. The old goofball and not the modern killer.

Kirov spoke again. The range was too great, and from the image Lazarus wondered if Wybert had overridden the beam controls and defocused it even more than he would have for a close-in shot.

All the heavens turned blue and then faded to gold as he watched. Certainly, nobody would ever forget that image.

"Damage minimal," Wybert announced. "Art has been committed. Stand by for warfare."

Yup, goofball. With the galaxy's deadliest powerspear in his capable hands.

"Maneuvering orders from Pryce," Marie said now. "Shifting resources unto the upper forward quadrant and asking ships with arc to retarget."

Lazarus spun his image around to see what was happening.

Ah. Two GunWalls were moving after *Gowook* and Addison's squadron, in spite of two layers of escorts in the way and the Heavy Starcruiser *Fortaleza* drifting slowly back to cover the rear of the formation.

He hated fanatics. Death or Glory berserkers that charged mindlessly into battle. That was exactly what he had on his hands. Or rather, Addison did. *Fortaleza* had already stopped cold and now began backing rapidly, using the Wolcott Retrograde to try to interpose itself, but the space was too great. Even *Ajax*'s two dorsal Star Lances were shifting to get some shots into that mess.

Lazarus wondered if he had a suicidal Westphalian Wall Commander on his hands, ordering his ships to their death.

On the one hand, that many fewer maniacs to death with tomorrow. On the other, it just meant that many more maniacs to deal with today.

A flash of light fogged his scanner screen, blotting everything out.

"Oh, shit," Lòpez cried. "One of the Archers just exploded."

Lazarus felt his stomach fall. There were only two Archers in his formation. *Intruder* and *Gowook*.

One of them had just *exploded?*

"Who?!?" he demanded, even as every head had turned to the man in shock.

Gowook meant Addison.

"Stand by," Lòpez said. "The plasma cloud is still clearing."

Plasma cloud meant that a beam had hit metal and penetrated, like a bullet into soft flesh rather than merely an arrow. Had hit something fragile and flammable.

Lazarus had only ever seen a handful of ships actually explode in battle. GunWalls were delicate around that central hinge that gave them such tremendous maneuverability, so he'd known a number that had been broken there by a lucky hit.

But not explode.

"Wybert, tune your next shot down as tight as you can get it," Lazarus said cruelly.

If he had to avenge Addison Wolcott right now, he was going to give the man a Pharaoh's funeral, by sending a frightening number of Humans dressed in gray to escort his friend.

"Tight?" Wybert ask, confused.

"I want you to send a message to that station," Lazarus said. "I want you to sign your name on the commander's kitchen nook."

A light bulb came on in all five eyes.

"Aye, sir," he said, snapping into *automatic* and *killer* now. "Engineering, I want you to overload the Kirov for this coming shot. Dump everything you have into the stream, regardless of the risk of burning out cables and generators. Am I clear?"

Lazarus wondered what they thought of that order back aft. Ereshkiki Nisab was not a warrior, so he normally put H'Brige Slani in charge during these times, preferring to just keep things rolling cleanly day to day.

"Acknowledged, Fusilier," H'Brige replied now. "Stand by for overload in ten seconds."

"Cormac?" Lazarus asked.

Human eyes might not pierce that cloud of plasma and debris, but he was willing to bet that a Crawler could.

"Intruder *has been destroyed,*" Cormac replied in a sad voice.

Lazarus could not help the sigh of relief that escaped his lips, but he also wasn't the only one.

"Order *Fortaleza* to shield that squadron with their own bodies now," Lazarus called, uncaring who actually transmitted. As long as nothing happened to Addison.

It might be just like Yisan, all over again, when he had feared that a raging Addison Wolcott might annihilate that planet with the Kirov, had anything happened to Eha. Only this time, the Ambassador to the Phraettis Alliance might demand excessive retaliation on the planet below.

And Lazarus might just do it.

"Firing," Wybert said in a casual voice that still managed to completely disrupt Lazarus's thought processes.

Probably on purpose. Nobody really ever gave the man the credit for brains that he deserved.

Lazarus watched on the big video display at the front of

the bridge, zoomed in fairly tight on the station now as *Ajax* approached.

Sledgehammer.

On his boards, Lazarus watched a number of green lights representing engineering statistics go yellow. Two dropped to red, but those were both heat warnings that could probably be ignored for now.

He hoped.

H'Brige had just routed *everything* she had: main generators, battery arrays, shield reinforcements, and even the engines that weren't needed right now as the fleet coasted sedately along.

All of it into Juan-Pedro's dream of building a better weapon, and striking an orbital platform with a powerspear instead of an enemy Heavy Starcruiser like *Europa*.

The effect was catastrophic, as Lazarus had always suspected it might be.

At Esmer, they had been at pains to strike from specific, calculated angles and distances, tuning the beam to destroy offices and control spaces, while not annihilating the warehouses themselves, nor breaking the station apart.

Wybert had no such compunctions today. Nor did Lazarus, when push came to shove.

Shields failed. Whatever the locals over there had done to reinforce them had been inadequate. But then, whoever expected an enemy warfleet to sail right into Earth orbit, drive off the defending fleet, and then take potshots at things?

Obviously, these people had never truly understood what *angry* really meant.

"Second shot?" Wybert asked serenely.

If there was something scarier than a furious Ilount, a calm one with a bloody powerspear in three hands might be it.

Lazarus watched the cloud of plasma billowing off the near side of the station. As with *Europa*, lights seemed to be failing. Gravity might be out in places, as would inertial dampers and other things.

Living on this platform might shortly be like experiencing the inside of a can someone was furiously shaking.

Addison had survived when *Intruder* exploded instead. Glancing at his boards, Lazarus saw where *Fortaleza* had made good by literally charging to put itself in the path of that GunWall. Oluchi's people had shifted inwards as well, everyone rotated down and in. *Celestial Sovereign* had even opened fire with their own Star Lance.

That GunWall that had claimed *Intruder* might be molten scrap in another five minutes.

"Fire a second shot, Fusilier," Lazarus said. "I want their undivided attention."

"That's likely to draw all guns down on us," Kuei said, possibly with anticipation.

She might need to get *crazy* if that happened. Might even have been looking forward to such a thing.

"Yes, it is," Lazarus agreed, knowing that particular gleam in the woman's eyes right now. But he had seen it at Esmer. And Zhoonarrim.

She could handle whatever it was that needed doing.

"Firing."

SIXTY-NINE

ADDISON

ADDISON BLINKED FURIOUSLY to clear his eyes. He'd left an optical display tuned to an image of nearby space earlier, just because he liked seeing stars out a windshield when he flew, after so many years on *Shiva Zephyr Glaive.*

He was still seeing stars.

"Park, what just happened?" he called.

A strangled gurgle caused him to look over at his sensors tech. Spacer First Class Aanthos Park had turned a color of Human that looked unnatural. Practically white. Bizarre.

"*Intruder's* gone, sir," he whispered.

"Gone?" Addison asked, aghast.

"Aye, sir," Park nodded. "…gone."

Addison blinked both sets of eyelids now and flinched to the tip of his tail as he looked where the other Archer had been flying, ten seconds ago.

Just like that. Any of us could vanish with the snap of your fingers.

"Fusilier, all gunners in the squadron, go to rapid fire with everything you have left," Addison ordered. "Take them out before they finish us off."

That GunWall had charged. And gotten lucky. And wasn't stopping now to try to back out of the tail trap they'd wandered into.

Addison wondered if they might yet decide to just ram these traitor GunWall ships flying Rio transponder codes, to get even with the shame. At Oton Mari, he'd wondered if some crazed Innruld commander, seeing the end of their rule, might sacrifice his own Pyramid to take out the rebels.

The same option was on the table today.

"Send out an urgent call for help, Park," Addison replied. "Anyone who can fire this direction needs to hit those ships now."

"Heavy Starcruiser *Fortaleza* is moving to intercept, sir," Park called over the sudden din.

Addison held his breath for nearly ten seconds as *Hell on Earth* erupted around him. Other squadrons, other ships were doing things, but his entire world had just been reduced to twenty GunWall ships attacking eigh of hist. Seven. Six, with *Swift* suddenly going dark from damage.

He didn't have long until it was *none*, even as the forward gunshield held.

Then it looked like an eclipse, suddenly blotting out the sky overhead.

"Park, what's happening?" Addison cried in a voice not all that far removed from a primitive snake on the surface, suddenly confronted by the gods themselves.

"*Oh, wow…*" Park whispered.

Addison blinked away tears and wiped his face as he understood.

Celestial Sovereign was leading the Heavy Starcruisers *Guarulhos*, *Campinas*, *Recife*, and *Teresina* as they charged into the fray, firing everything they had at anything that moved. With *Fortaleza*, five of the eight Heavies in the fleet, coming to rescue him.

"We're being hailed by Admiral Santos, sir," Park managed to say.

"Main screen, Park," Addison said, unable to contain the wonder in his voice as five angry wargods unleashed their unimaginable fury, pounding that GunWall to molten scrap before his eyes.

Pedro Santos appeared. Even for a Human, the worry was evident on his face, lines that hadn't been there yesterday.

"Captain, tomorrow you'll be someplace safer than an Archer," Santos said simply, but those words contained a love and respect from the man that Addison had never seen, had never even imagined might reside under that gruff exterior. He looked a lot more like Lazarus now. As if a mask had been stripped away to show the man underneath. "That I promise you."

"Thank you, Admiral," Addison said automatically, not really capable of higher thought.

His screens showed what happened when a wall of angry leviathans were unleashed.

As Addison watched, he noted that the GunWalls weren't even being given an opportunity to strike their flags. But then, none of them even survived as fighting vessels for more than sixty seconds.

Awe inspiring on the one hand. Utterly frightening on the other.

But thus would the Humans of Westphalia be beaten.

As would the Innruld.

For now, he felt a little coddled.

And that was just fine.

SEVENTY

LAZARUS

LAZARUS WATCHED the second cloud of plasma and spare parts puff outwards from the platform. The whole station had a distinct wobble now, a precession that would rotate across the stars over the next few days.

Assuming he didn't just blow the damned thing to hell right now and be done with it.

"What's happening with the fleet?" Lazarus called, uncaring who answered.

"*Addison is safe,*" Cormac replied in such an emotional tone that Lazarus snapped around to see a camera pointed back at him.

Rather than ask, Lazarus rotated his scanner screen to show the overhead, and then dialed the magnification back when it was obscured.

Holy Mother of God…

Five Heavy Starcruisers, flying in a wing formation like geese headed south for the winter. Shattering *everything* in their path.

Lazarus watched an entire GunWall get churned under like an avalanche, unable to even process the impossible image right now. Maybe ever. Around the rest of the fleet, the remaining GunWalls suddenly panicked, facing three other Heavies and all the remaining Light Starcruisers and escorts that had gotten just angry. Gotten *mean*.

Two hundred deadly warships, minus casualties like *Intruder*, but not that many of them.

*Come for **all** your souls.*

Earth Command had been surprised, that much was obvious. Or had sent half the fleet out to engage where they expected the Rio invaders to come out of that first jump.

While that meant that they might be receiving frantic calls to return right now, Lazarus didn't think it would help. Around him, individual Westphalian ships began to blink out, dropping into jump to escape being crushed like a tin can by the side of the road. That just left larger gaps in the GunWalls.

As Lazarus watched, it turned into a cascade, as local superiority in firepower turned into *run-or-die* decisions for so many enemy captains. They might reassemble later, but it wouldn't be for hours at a minimum. Maybe days, if everyone went a different direction right now and then had to gather themselves up later.

Lazarus doubted that they had a carefully-orchestrated plan for what to do when something like this happened. Might as well plan for being struck by lightning.

In under four minutes, all Westphalian vessels had withdrawn, leaving no enemies within four light-minutes, which was about as safe as they could get. Some had probably gone to where the other fleet might yet be waiting. Lazarus would deal with them when it became necessary.

"Marie, hail the station," Lazarus said. "Get me the senior admiral still around. Let's see if he thinks today is a good day to die."

Cormac and Lòpez were both busy from the sounds,

routing things around, but at this point, Carlos, Pedro, and Oluchi were in command. Lazarus had done the things that needed doing. First, he had killed *Europa*, still lying there dead in the middle of the Rio force, slowly tumbling on its long axis and wobbling lengthwise, but nobody had chosen to finish them off, and he was fine with that. Second, he had blasted that station hard enough that it might join *Europa* if they weren't lucky.

"Admiral Johnson-Walker on line, sir," Marie turned now to look at him with a hard smile on her face.

"Main screen," Lazarus replied with an equal look.

Let the man see what he had faced today. Human, Vaadwig, Ilount, Crawler. Let him see the future of the galaxy, just in the command crew of *Ajax*, adding a Churquen and a Yithadreph.

Let him know fear.

Admiral Johnson-Walker was a base admiral. Lazarus knew the type. Living ashore in luxury and adding fifty or seventy-five pounds from all the good eating without any of the exercise. Broken blood vessels in the nose and cheeks from all the wine consumed with so many fine dinners. Eyes showing his whites right now.

Pedro Santos was still in as good of shape as his sailors coming out of basic training, because that man worked at it every single day. He had even taken command of the Rio Fleet for his mission.

This Earthman just gave orders and expected people to execute them.

Lazarus sneered at the face, even as he saw the fear take root.

"Admiral," Lazarus let himself grow calm now. "Your fleet is chased off or destroyed. Your station is damaged and at risk of being blown up shortly. All I have to do is tell my Fusilier to finish you, and it will be all over except for the life pods dropping down onto the surface ahead of large pieces of metal deorbiting. Do you understand me?"

"Who are you?" the man cried, sounding more like a poor shepherd when a Messenger from God has arrived.

Weren't their first words always "*Human, fear not!*"?

"I am Francisco Luiz Oliveira, Rio Alliance Capitáo De Mar E Guerra, and Commodore of *Task Force Liberty*," Lazarus said in a grinding tone. "Perhaps you know me better as *Lazarus of Bethany*."

That name elicited a gasp. That was good. Lazarus was not feeling particularly benevolent right now. *Intruder* could have been *Gowook*. *Ajax* might have turned inward and begun firing on the ground at that point. There were several important cities below him right now.

"What are your demands?" Johnson-Walker wheezed.

"Your surrender," Lazarus said. "This station. This fleet. This system. **All of it.**"

The gasps on the screen were echoed by the gasps around him, but everyone here should have known by now what kind of man Lazarus of Bethany really was.

Grace wasn't surprised, for which he was eternally grateful.

"I can't do that," Johnson-Walker cried.

"Then I will blow up your station and go annihilate your fleet, Admiral," Lazarus continued methodically. "After which I will have to find a way to convince the politicians on the ground that I am *serious*. I'm sure I can kill enough people today to convey that message to *whoever manages to survive my* **wrath**."

More gasps. More fools, he supposed.

This was the endgame, when the black king has nowhere to go to escape as knights and rooks closed in inexorably from all sides.

"Earth will surrender to me right now," Lazarus snarled.

"Then you will negotiate a peace with the rest of the galaxy good enough to convince me that I don't ever need to return to this system again. Because next time I will bring a fleet one hundred times as powerful as this one, and end Westphalia as a thing. ***AM I CLEAR?***"

He leaned back and cut the line himself.

Let that jackass stew in his own juices for a while, assuming he hadn't already pissed himself.

Grace had risen while he'd been focused elsewhere. No words, just a hand on his shoulder, but all the weight of the galaxy evaporated from his back as he looked up at her smile.

Add Human technology to a Phraettis fleet made up of sailors who had grown up under an Innruld boot, and let's see just how tough the Humans of Westphalia *thought* they were.

"Station attempting to contact us again," Marie said ambivalently. "Do we answer?"

Lazarus smiled evilly enough that Marie cringed, and then opened the line he had just closed.

The admiral started to speak, to say something. Maybe to have an opinion. Lazarus overrode him with a roar that got everyone's attention before he spoke in a quieter, almost-civilized tone.

"Call the ground and tell your President that he is my welcome guest aboard *Ajax*, along with his Cabinet or Privy Council, or whatever you call it," Lazarus said. "I will personally guarantee their safety and transport them to Brasilia in luxury. *Ajax* has Ambassadorial facilities aboard, as well as an Ambassador to the Phraettis Alliance. The Ambassador to Yisan is one of my warlords here with the fleet, but I can convince him to put aside the sword long enough to chat with you as well. Do you understand me?"

Johnson-Walker's eyes were huge. It helped that Lazarus was broadcasting this in the clear, so every receiver in the solar system would be able to pick it up, considering the transmitter strength behind it. That included people hiding in bunkers on the ground right now, wondering if the sky was about to start falling.

"Once everyone is on Brasilia, they can chat with the Rio High Council, Yisan's leaders, and the Phraettis Ambassador to work out whatever ransom everyone thinks is acceptable. These terms are not negotiable. If you choose to fight me after this, I will destroy everything. *Everything.* Once the politicians are all gathered, I will, however, wash my hands of the situation and leave you all to God's Infinite Mercy while I go back to my own life. Reply on this line when you are ready to accept my conditions. Otherwise, I suggest you start heading for a lifepod **right now**."

He crossed his arms and smiled at the man. Grace stood beside him, and would be in the camera image. A moment later, another hand on his right and Lazarus realized that Aileen had come forward to lend him her strength.

He could do this. All of this. He had those two supporting him.

SEVENTY-ONE

EHA

EHA JUST HELD ADDISON, almost as tightly as he was wrapped around her.

"That close," he whispered in her ear. "But Lazarus's luck rubbed off on me and they hit *Intruder* instead, so I'm safe."

"Is the war done?" she asked, almost unwilling to hope.

"I am," he replied and she grabbed him tighter. "Whatever Pedro Santos thinks, I just want to go home and go back to being a merchant captain."

"You cannot," Eha reminded him, leaning back now enough to see him, the wall of his cabin, and the spartan quarters he kept aboard *Gowook*.

But it was barely smaller than *Shiva Zephyr Glaive*, and he'd done that for a long time.

"Cannot?" Addison asked, also leaning back just enough to study her face.

She wondered what he saw.

"What is left?"

"Lazarus convinced them to surrender," Eha reminded the man, feeling all that adrenaline still coursing through his body, even though the battle had ended almost nine hours ago. "We still have to manage to bring representatives to Brasilia, and hammer out the shape of the future. If Westphalia is willing to bend far enough, we must include them, or this war will just start up again in a generation. I must be there. I need your help. Your support. Your love. Best you be wearing a uniform that reminds everyone who you are."

He sighed, and she hugged him close. Tomorrow, perhaps, she would tell him that Adriana wasn't going to be an only child for long but for now, she just held him close and let the day slough off his scales like water.

SEVENTY-TWO
OLUCHI

OLUCHI HAD REVERTED to the colors that he'd worn on that fateful day when he first met Lazarus of Bethany, though this was a new outfit Thadrakho had worked up for him much more recently. Black slacks. Silk shirt in canary yellow with a standing collar. Black opera cape lined with white silk.

And the thigh holster, filled. Plus that sword he'd taken to carrying at Heechua. He didn't figure he'd need either today. Or possibly ever again if he was going to model himself on Eduardo going forward, but Oluchi felt like he needed to make a statement this time.

After all, everyone had taken to calling him the *Warlord from Yisan*. Best to reinforce that while he could, so that he had that much more of a legend to work with later. Never let a sucker get an even break, and he still had a lot of money to make when this was all done.

Oluchi smiled over at Anya as they waited for the flight bay to finish pressurizing after the Westphalian shuttle landed. She was dressed in a suit modeled on what a proper businessman might wear on Brasilia, but cut to remind you that she was an amazing woman. She didn't have a gun on her hip, but they also had a hundred or more marines around them right now, and dress armor was still armor. Dress rifles were all charged and ready to commit mayhem at the drop of a hat.

Not that Oluchi expected anything. The Humans were still in shock, last he'd heard, and would be days regaining their equilibrium.

Humans? He supposed so. Rio was a *mostly* Human place, as was Yisan. However, Oluchi and Anya also represented a number of interests and banks in Phraettis now, none of whom were *Human*.

If nobody had remembered to revoke all those various ambassadorships and things they had bestowed on him up until now, whose fault was that?

Anya smiled at him, as if she could read his mind. Honestly, he was about as deep as a mud puddle most of the time. Still, she leaned close to kiss him, so he must be doing something right.

"Could you two save it for later?" Lazarus groused from his other side.

"No," Oluchi grinned at the man. "I don't think so. If they can't deal with it, that's not my problem."

Grace chuckled, then leaned in and kissed Lazarus on the far ear, which just elicited more good-natured grumbling from the man.

Oluchi looked around now. Lines of officers and crew members drawn up and looking severe. Not just from *Ajax*, but several captains, both admirals, and a lot of marines. A LOT of marines. Most of them were Human, as expected, but there were Moah, Gnashiiley, and Atomarsk as well. Around the outer edge of the room, all the other species, in the forms of Aileen's Galumphs, were watching

The inner airlock door beeped and opened now. Oluchi heard the sudden intake of air, multiplied across several hundred people to the point it was audible over the sound of the air systems. Shoulders came back. Heads came up.

Everyone else got all military and formal.

Oluchi slouched to his left side, which just happened to rest his hand on his pistol. Statement of purpose, if you will, from the *Warlord of Yisan*.

Traditionally, you rolled out a red carpet for important dignitaries and then waited for them to walk all the way across the bay to you, like poor gigolos with hat in hand. Instead, Lazarus had forgone the carpet and started walking now. Oluchi fell in on his wing, as always, with Anya and Grace as well.

Pedro, Carlos, and Collin Lau joined them. Eha and Addison. Even Aileen.

Thank God Wybert was on the bridge with Kuei, or he would have insisted on standing here with that powerspear in two hands.

We're here to impress them, not make them wet their pants.

Oluchi smiled as everyone came to rest. Behind him, Lucas Lam and a squad in simple uniforms rather than combat gear took up a line.

The shuttle door opened and steps descended.

Oluchi watched the first man come out. Old and stuffy. Gave off the air of a British Butler from Central Casting in an uncomfortable suit of a cut long-since out of style. Rail thin with a beak of a nose and gray hair slicked back with something shiny.

Well-polished shoes, when Oluchi's were perfect for those times when you had to run suddenly or climb out a window and down a brick wall as someone's spouse came home early. But he was armed and the other fellow had nothing but his wit and his sniffing disdain for the whole scene.

You lost, princess, so get over yourself or keep your mouth shut.

Oluchi let those pheromones waft over the fellow. And anybody else in the shuttle. He'd honestly thought that the Humans of Earth were going to test Lazarus yesterday by deciding to die fighting rather than surrendering.

That would have lasted for about five seconds.

Even that chunk of the Human fleet that had been hiding out near Jupiter like ambush predators had gotten the order to stand down, having jumped close and been all set to go down in a blaze of glory. Everyone had heard the President and followed orders. Without Lazarus having to blow up the station or start destroying cities from orbit. He could have.

Now, everybody on this side more or less came to something approximating attention. Helped that they weren't all sailors to begin with so they didn't try to look like it.

The Butler approached Lazarus and bowed his head enough to be polite. Lazarus bowed even deeper, but he'd won and everybody else had to live with that knowledge for the rest of their lives.

"The President of Westphalia," the stuffed suit announced, turning to one side and coming to a sort of attention facing a sidewall so he didn't have to look at anybody.

Oluchi had seen images of the man who was emerging. None of them had been recent, or he had aged a decade in a day. More likely they'd all been touched up by professionals before release.

Got to keep that pretty face going, you know…

Better suit. Dark gray with pinstripes. Not as good as Eduardo's were, but Oluchi didn't figure the man needed to look as sharp on a daily basis. Lord knows he had the budget, but Oluchi had rarely met a politician who understood how to wear a suit.

Seventy, plus or minus. Anglo-Germanic in the way of

that particular racism that seemed to bubble up every few centuries going back millennia. East Asians and Africans were both more numerous, but the Americas had been the center of emigration out into what eventually became the Rio Alliance when they broke away.

"Mr. President, welcome aboard *Ajax*," Lazarus said carefully. Politely. "There will be a short reception for you and your staff, and then we will show you to your Ambassadorial Suite and prepare to return to Brasilia."

Shell-shocked. Oluchi knew the look. Some fool who thought three Jacks would be enough and had gone all in on the pot, only to discover a punk in an opera cape was sitting on four deuces.

It happened.

The President nodded mechanically. Automatically. Others began to emerge, none of them in any better shape.

But yesterday, they had been kings and queens of the galaxy.

I should introduce you folks to the Innruld sometime, so you all can understand together.

Again, Oluchi didn't do anything but smile.

A sailor, an assassin, a spy, and a gambler walk into a flight bay…

"Lieutenant Lam," Lazarus spoke louder now, letting his voice carry over the whole space.

Lucas stepped around the end of the line, facing the Butler, and came to precise and rigid attention.

"Sir."

"Lam, you will hereby take charge of security for our guests, just as you did Eha Dunham when she first arrived on Brasilia," Lazarus ordered. "You and your people will keep them safe from any and all threats. Do you have any questions?"

Oluchi remembered that first, fateful day. A young officer

from *Recife*, told to go with the aliens, and then refusing to just turn them over to the Council Guards. Admiral da Silva had given him a commendation, and a hug for that.

Lucas had earned the right to stand here.

"No, sir."

He turned now and bowed deeply to the Earthers.

"I am Lieutenant Lucas Lam," he said politely. "I will protect you."

Simple as that. A promise almost as good as Lazarus or Addison destroying Yisan, had anything happened to Eha.

Lucas turned to face the Rio folks now, his face hard and professional. Oluchi grinned.

The Earthers were even more faded than their normal pancake makeup suggested, but Oluchi was facing them with two Churquen and a Yithadreph, in addition to the Humans.

It was rude to think of these people as *marks*, but Oluchi really didn't have a better category to place the Earthers.

It was, however, a good thing he wasn't here to take all their money…

SEVENTY-THREE
LAZARUS

LAZARUS STUDIED THE ROOM. The President, his First and Second Wives, plus what appeared to be a couple of spare mistresses, *plus* a lot of bureaucrats dressed up to make the journey none of them ever envisioned in their worst nightmares.

However, this was a reception. Cocktails and finger food produced by *Ajax*'s Mistress of the Wardroom, who took exceptional delight in personally supervising her *Human* staff in keeping the food troughs topped off and warm. Lazarus thought that Khyaa'sha might be rubbing it in a bit, but she'd lived her whole life under Innruld authority, and that went a long way towards explaining today.

Lazarus had a glass of fruit juice in one hand. It wasn't that he couldn't hold his whiskey right now, but it was going to be a long night and he needed the sugar.

Grace hung on his elbow like a simple mistress or wife, not fooling anybody but the Westphalian folks. Long, bronze sheath of silk that clung in all the right places and showed off others. She wasn't as curvy as Anya if you liked them that way. On the other hand, there probably wasn't anybody in this room in as good a shape, with the possible exception of Pedro Santos, for entirely different reasons.

Like him, she held a glass of juice and sipped, a merry twinkle in her eyes.

He watched Eha and her folks *chat* with the President. Oluchi and Anya were there, as were a number of other folks. Not sharks just waiting, though one might get that impression from the way the Presidential party seemed to circle the wagons rather than mingle.

"So," Lazarus turned to Grace now. "I think we've finally reached the point where your original orders from Eduardo have run out of space. What's next?"

She chuckled.

"My *orders*, as you call them, were to keep you safe and out of trouble," Grace grinned. "I don't honestly see you taking up monastic vows and retiring from the galaxy anytime soon."

He chuckled as well.

"No, but as soon as we get to Brasilia, I'm functionally done with the Rio Alliance Navy," he replied. "My current enlistment contract runs out in another year or so anyway, and I intend to file paperwork to resign my commission sooner rather than later. Go help liberate Phraettis Space. That way, I become much less of a menace to the galaxy."

Her laugh this time was full-throated, head back. Other heads looked over with a touch of surprise or concern. He felt a blush take over.

"Sorry," she finally managed after she got control of herself again. "You even said that with a straight face."

He blushed again. Or more. Something. This woman really did get him.

"As for you, I suspect that any number of people will want to hire you for something," Grace said. "You will be entire history books by yourself, and *Ajax* will be chapters in the history of the galaxy."

He shrugged. She wasn't wrong, but he didn't like to think of that. There were still nights where he woke in a cold sweat, back on the bridge of *Ajax*, just out of jump and already trapped in the middle of a Westphalian GunWall's killzone, with twenty-eight friends dead or dying and the rest madly scrambling for life pods.

Right before he jumped into the oblivion of the Phraettis Nebula to die.

Where it all began…

Pedro Santos had been talking to the other group, then circled the room for the bar as Lazarus absently tracked him. Now he was approaching.

"Should I wander off?" Grace asked as the man got close.

Lazarus wrapped a fierce hand around her waist and held the woman against his side.

"Never," he said. "Understand me?"

Rather than answer, he got a kiss and then she turned to greet the newcomer.

Admiral Pedro Santos. Senior Officer of the Rio Alliance Navy. One of the commanders, one of the victors of the greatest naval battle in history, watched them from a polite distance, before nodding to himself and taking a step to *personal.*

"I would ask *What next?*" he began without preamble, "but none of us will know that answer until we get to Liberty and pick up Martìnez and the High Council. And then, we can only deliver them to Brasilia and hope that everyone behaves long enough to come to some conclusion."

"My personal war might not be done, Admiral," Lazarus replied.

"Please, call me Pedro, Lazarus," he said. "You haven't been promoted because you refused, but in my mind you have several stars on your collar already and I intend to treat you as such. I understand that your war is not done yet, but if you'll bear with me for a few days, I believe we can set things to right there as well. I'm more concerned about you. I owe you an apology. As do a lot of other folks who might never get around to doing so, but I wanted to make sure you knew. You were right. You have been right any number of times when people like me doubted you. But you have upheld the highest possible standards of the Navy in pursuing your goals, so I also want to thank you."

The man stepped back and actually saluted. Lazarus had one arm around Grace and a glass in the other, so he simply bowed in shock and tried not to blush too hard. Or let the man see the tears welling up.

"Have we truly won, then?" Lazarus asked when the Admiral stepped close again.

He'd been so wrapped up in his personal wars on so many fronts that he'd lost track of the *Efforts of Empires*, as an old professor had once called politics at that scale.

"I think we are close enough that the others can carry it the rest of the way, Lazarus," Pedro nodded. "Now that you've gotten us this far. Chair Teixeira will have a completely different approach to damned near everything, and I wouldn't be surprised if they offered Cavalcanti's spot to Eha when this was done. Will she take it?"

"I honestly don't know, Pedro," Lazarus replied. "Liberty was colonized because she wasn't sure that Rio would help any other way. That the Innruld might last for another generation before our side of the galaxy could be put to rights and Adriana could see to freeing all her cousins and kin herself. But we have a Grand Alliance now, with three nations and possibly a fourth if those folks can decide to be part of the future instead of a can in the road that needs to be crushed by the weight of a passing vehicle. Only Eha knows the answer to what she plans to do next."

Pedro nodded again, as if that was the answer he had been seeking, or at least expecting.

"Then I will leave you to your evening," he said, bowing more formally now and withdrawing.

Lazarus found that he really didn't have it in him to talk to more people, so he steered Grace towards one of the quieter corners.

"What do you want?" she asked as they got safely ensconced.

"I don't know," Lazarus replied, feeling a wave of exhaustion crash on his shoulders all at once. "For my entire career, fighting Westphalia and defeating them has been my sole goal. Everything was keyed towards that day, and now that it's here I'm a little lost."

She leaned in and kissed his cheek to comfort him.

"You don't have to decide today," Grace reminded him. "Nor tomorrow. If nothing else, some quiet time on Yisan is in our future. I don't know when."

"Soon," he nodded. "I just don't know how to relax. It doesn't require me to finish off the Innruld, and I've given just about everything I have over the last three years. I might be done."

"Oh, I doubt you're done, Lazarus," she smiled at him. "I don't think you'll ever be done."

"That's what frightens me."

SEVENTY-FOUR

AILEEN

AILEEN STUDIED ALL the storks around her. Many of them held significant rank on a *mere commander*, but nobody was even eyeing her sideways tonight. Well, the Earthers, but they didn't count. None of those goobers had ever imagined someone like her. Rights and legends and everything.

She looked around the room and counted all the species in here. Men and women from her original *galumphs* that had gone on to Yisan with her and Lazarus. Heroes, anywhere you went in the galaxy.

Anya Persaud sidled close now, Oluchi off somewhere no doubt fleecing more rubes of their hard-earned credits. Aileen just watched the woman like *sturee* circling.

"So," Persaud began in a drawling tone best delivered in a backroom of a bar. "What does the Hero of Zhoonarrim plan to do when this is all done?"

She liked Anya, but right this moment Aileen wasn't sure she could trust the woman as far as she could throw her. Still, *Anya*. Oluchi's better half, if you asked Aileen, in spite of everything that man had done for Eha and Lazarus.

"Dunno," Aileen countered. "Got a lot of options on the table."

There. Leave it at that.

Technically, she did. Cargo Command would take her in a heartbeat. Line probably would as well. Aileen was certain that she could arrange financing for a ship, if Addison ended up being too married to Eha and her job to go adventuring in the new galaxy. There was even Yisan. Hints and suggestions that would probably crystallize into contracts and job offers as soon as she looked halfway serious.

Eduardo was like that.

"I have been approached by…several, unrelated groups of folks." Anya smiled so brightly that Aileen wondered if the woman would catch fire at some point. "All of them representing pools of money looking to invest in trade."

And she left it at *that*. Nice counter. Been spending a lot of time around Oluchi obviously.

"And?" Aileen asked, enticed just exactly the right amount.

She wondered who had prepped this woman. Lazarus? Grace? Addison? Somebody was getting tickled over this, that was for certain.

"And I believe that any such trade task probably runs much more efficiently with an expert Cargomaster making decisions," Anya said quietly. "I wanted to see how you might feel about being hired to run something like that. We'll have cash. What we won't have are connections or expertise over in Phraettis Space."

Must have been Oluchi. None of the others were that sharp. Unless Eduardo was fronting the woman money. Except he wasn't, last Aileen had checked. Fernanda Flores had been putting money into Oluchi and Anya. Aileen remembered her from that very first night on Yisan, according to the rumors.

Going into business sounded enticing.

"I'm not sure I'm ready to sit behind a desk," Aileen countered back.

Hell, she still had to go have a long, involved conversation with Briston Moora, hopefully still back at Zhoonarrim or maybe Oton Mari now. Safe instead of on the crazy front lines with her. She needed to figure out where they were as a *they*, even as she watched so many of her friends reaching for that elusive happily-ever-after.

Anya just smiled at her.

"Oh, I'm certain that any such job would involve a lot of time in the field, Aileen," Anya winked. "Travel to exotic locations and help set up networks. Figure out what everyone needs, what they want, and the most efficient way to route cargo runs around the galaxy to get things where they need to be."

Yup, Pryce must have told Anya her weakness. Efficiency.

She'd been a Master of Cargo on *Shiva Zephyr Glaive*. Those six Shippers had just been the next scale up from that. The *Mob of Galumphs* the one after that.

What was the next step? Building the trade network linking the entire galaxy together?

Aileen had to fight to suppress the maniacal giggle that wanted to emerge right now. Probably inappropriate given the company at this party. They might think she was carnivorous or something.

Hey, you storks, remember that it's not cannibalism if I eat Humans!

But she didn't say that with anything more than the set of her ears and the way she made eye contact with some peon that had come with the Earth party and had the unfortunate luck to be eyeballing her right now. The man turned white, dropped his eyes, and shuffled behind someone else quickly.

Anya chuckled.

"So that's a maybe?" the woman asked in a leading way.

Like they had already settled everything except the number in the spot for pay and shares conferred, as well as two signatures.

She smiled up at Anya. Really smiled, remembering that Oluchi Pryce thought Persaud was that good.

"A definite maybe," Aileen grinned. "Assuming Eduardo or Eha don't outbid you."

"Let them try," Anya replied hungrily. "I'll send you some contract language to review, later in the week. We have several options out there, all trying to gain first-to-market advantages, but all hamstrung because the expertise they need is all currently aboard *Ajax*. Which is why so many have reached out to me and Oluchi."

"Any of them from Earth?" Aileen asked, a bit flippantly, but Anya turned dead cold in the blink of an eye, before relaxing a moment later.

"That would be telling," she grinned. Then winked and walked off, leaving Aileen a little off center.

Two days and the merchants of Earth had already reached out to Anya and Oluchi to make deals?

Shit, maybe Lazarus really had won, and nobody had realized it. If the traders came over, the government really had no choice.

But then, the President of Westphalia was all of about fifteen yards away right now, smiling like he was holding in a painful fart.

Aileen pasted a smile on her face and headed that way.

She wanted to introduce herself to these new Humans.

SEVENTY-FIVE

ERLYN

CHAIR ERLYN TEIXEIRA of the Rio Alliance High Council.

It still hadn't sunk entirely in, in spite of the two weeks wearing the cloak of authority that came with it and talking to Eduardo and Alla Dunham on a daily basis.

She was suddenly in a much more interesting place than she had imagined. Hell, Erlyn had always assumed Pascia or maybe Ruby Martins would be the next chair when Roald finally stepped down. She'd never imagined that she would be maneuvered into the job.

She took a breath and stared at the door in front of her. Everyone was already present, save for her and seven compatriots arranged to join last. Two marines stood guard, within reach on either side and looking a little pale as they side-eyed her.

Erlyn forced a smile at the two of them and opened the hatch to the ballroom. Eduardo was acting as host today, because his yacht, now returned and leading the parade as it were, was really the only space in the Liberty System big enough and luxurious enough for this coming meeting.

Not that she hadn't considered asking for tents to be raised on the surface below to make a point. If it hadn't been the cold season down at the colony right now…

Erlyn had settled every butterfly in her stomach by her third step into the room. Eduardo, Collin, and Oluchi rose immediately as she did. Eha and Alla came to a more erect posture on their coils as Aileen stood next to them.

The President of Westphalia caught the hint and shot up a moment later, a bit tardy, but that was lack of time spent being less important than anybody else in the room.

He'd get used to it.

She walked to the grand arrangement of tables and stood behind her seat. A quick meeting yesterday had settled on as much of a curve as you could get out of straight tables eight feet long and put into a circle. King Arthur, from ancient Earth legend, and all that. He was a cultural hero to Westphalia, so that might help.

Not like she was going to ask the man's opinion either way.

Erlyn waited for the other Councilors and they sat more or less together, bringing everyone else to rest. She glanced around and noted a gallery had been set up to one side, with both Westphalian observers as well as Erlyn's Yisan and Phraettis allies seated there. Lot of tan uniforms involved, and only about half of them on Human shapes.

She smiled at Lazarus and Grace and then extended it to the group surrounding her, all four sides of this equation.

Erlyn pulled a gavel from one of her pockets and rapped it once as a placeholder.

"This meeting will come to order," she said in a conversational tone.

Then she let the silence hang for a long moment as she smiled at the President of Earth.

"We want peace, Mr. President," she announced simply,

reiterating the common request that had been rebuffed time and again by this man and his predecessors. "Failing that, Lazarus has already made it clear that wiping out your entire fleet and then perhaps bombarding your bases and governmental buildings from orbit might be necessary to get your attention. And a chore he's willing to pursue if it came to that. I'd rather not."

The man across from her didn't flinch, but she already knew from her spies that he was a cold, calculating character. It was his people on either side of him, as well as the gallery, that gasped now.

And she was only slightly bluffing. Lazarus might not do it, but she had any number of folks who would be willing to take a sister ship of *Ajax* and sail out with it. Rio was building a pair right now, but that was generally secret.

That genie was out of the bottle, and the next naval revolution would involve building shields tough enough to survive that level of firepower. She had hope, but the galaxy was teetering on mutually assured destruction right now, as not even *Ajax* could resist its own Kirov's Lance.

"I have spoken with Yisan and the…with Phraettis," the man replied now, almost calling Eha, Alla, and Aileen *the aliens* but stopping himself in time. "What does Rio demand?"

"Trade," Erlyn said simply. "Mutually recognized boundaries that are not violated by warships. What you do on your worlds is entirely up to your government, but we always welcome immigrants here in Rio. The planet below us is named Liberty, and represents our Phraettis friends, even as their governor sits on my left right now. There are two worlds in this system, and we plan to open both of them soon for approved settlers looking to make themselves a better life."

She knew the story of Lazarus's grandfather, who had

actually fled Earth originally, coming to Brasilia. Liberty might entice others, but she would have rules about who was allowed. Only those folks symbolically important.

Like a group from Earth directly, for instance.

The President leaned towards one of his aides and the two muttered something back and forth for a moment before he looked up.

"That's it?" he asked. "No reparations? No apologies? Nothing else?"

"We don't need your money," Erlyn sneered at him now. "Nor your permission. We have two hundred *billion* new friends to trade with. To bring up to our level of technology over the next generation. There are enough worlds out there that we can expand in three directions and never bother you again. As long as you behave, we won't. If you wish to join us as treaty partners, like Yisan and Phraettis, we can start negotiating that now."

"What about the Innruld?" he asked carefully.

Erlyn gestured broadly with one hand palm down, sweeping to her right.

"The Innruld will be removed from power," she said simply. "What Phraettis does with them after that remains their decision, but I wouldn't expect that a **xenocide** is all that likely."

She even smiled as the man cringed just a little. A reminder that Rio's other enemy might be hunted down and eradicated like vermin, when she was offering him something so much better.

It helped that Pryce and Persaud had already whispered in Erlyn's ear about trade opportunities that had come up from folks in the Earther party. The President of Westphalia was seated on an unstable throne, and it even looked like he had come to recognize that.

She turned to Eha now and nodded, ceding the floor.

"The Innruld must be broken entirely," Eha said in a simple tone, bereft of any emotional loading. Like discussing the price of a pound of coffee. "We have the assistance of our current treaty allies for that, so it will not be long now."

Erlyn liked the way Eha added that tiniest of stress on *current* as she spoke, perhaps suggesting that Westphalia might yet redeem themselves. The man also seemed to catch that, as he leaned forward a little. Like maybe he saw an opening where Westphalia might be able to *redeem themselves* a little now by piling in on the Innruld.

Kicking the worse punk when he's down, as it were.

Erlyn had never done that. Pinky-swear.

But she also leaned in, knowing why Eha had opened that door.

All it would take is a little push now to deflect Westphalia onto a better road toward tomorrow.

She could win Lazarus's war for him that way, too.

SEVENTY-SIX

ADDISON

ADDISON DIDN'T LIKE the way this meeting room had been set up, but it didn't feel like an ambush. Just Admiral Santos, Carlos, and Lazarus right now, in a chamber small enough to be cozy but not claustrophobic.

Humans had a thing about personal space that Churquen didn't really understand, but Addison also knew he was much more flexible than they were.

They were seated when he entered, so Addison took a spot on the only cone chair and joined them.

"So now what?" Lazarus asked the obvious question once Addison settled. "Where do we go from here?"

"This does not leave this room," Pedro said, turning to each of them in turn and getting nods. "The negotiations are likely to take weeks to even begin to reach some sort of useful consensus, according to Erlyn. We've already noted that Westphalia might be interested in helping us go stomp on the Innruld, as a way to buy themselves into our good graces."

"Caught that this morning," Carlos agreed. "Think they're serious?"

"I think they want a slice of the pie and are expecting us to do something silly like conquer Phraettis Space and maybe set up some sort of protectorate or something," Pedro offered. "Just goes to show how stupid and short-sighted they are. Bull-headed, as it were."

"So what are we doing?" Addison asked now. "What doesn't leave this room that it is so important?"

"You, Addison Wolcott," Santos said.

"Me?"

"This is not going to be even leaked, because I do not intend to file the correct papers until sometime after I get back to Brasilia from here," Pedro replied. "Having had to spend a lot of time supervising things and it must have slipped my mind."

Addison felt his scales clench in. He liked Pedro Santos, but the man was up to no good right now. However, Lazarus was smiling, so he must have been approached earlier and given his blessing, whatever it was that was coming.

Addison steeled himself.

Pedro grinned at him.

"It's not that bad," he said. "And you get to blame Lazarus for it anyway. Mostly his idea."

Addison turned his best scowl on the man he'd found floating in space after Wybert had blown up his ship. Lazarus grinned as well. Carlos was practically beaming.

"Addison Wolcott, it is my distinct pleasure to promote you to the rank of Vice Admiral in the Rio Alliance Navy," Pedro said now, his voice filled with pride. "Admiral Carlos Nguema will transfer his flag to the deck of the Rio Alliance Heavy Starcruiser *Recife* and detach a squadron for a mission. Vice Admiral Wolcott, you will transfer from *Gowook* and very quietly raise your own flag aboard the Rio Alliance Light Starcruiser *Ajax* and join *Recife*. Your selected squadron will have priority on refurbishment here and we have already sent messengers ahead to our Yisan allies to prepare them to keep you going with minimal delay. Once at Zhoonarrim, you will come under the overall command of Admiral Rodrigo da Silva and assist him in eliminating the threat of Innruld or Westphalia to our Phraettis allies."

Addison felt all his scales flare out so far that it was actually painful. Lazarus and Carlos were smiling and both reached out to put hands on his shoulders.

Vice Admiral Wolcott? Of the Rio Alliance Navy? What the hell was the galaxy coming to?

"I want *Mendoza,*" Carlos said in the break. "They deserve a chance to see the future with me after all we've been through recently. I presume you'll let us have all the GunWall ships, since that's where a lot of the *galumphs* ended up?"

"Already covered, Carlos," Pedro beamed. Then he turned to Addison. "I want you to finish the job before Westphalia has a chance to get involved, Addison. That's why a Gnashiiley and a Churquen will be the ones holding the hammer, in spite of the number of Humans involved. At some future point, my plan is to see if I can convince the High Council to transfer *Recife* and *Mendoza* to the Phraettis Navy permanently, to become the kernel of your new fleet. Allies, not subjects. What say you?"

Addison stammered before he settled himself and draw a deep breath.

"Thank you, Pedro," he managed. "I'll do you proud."

"You've already done me proud, Addison," Pedro said. "I promised you that you would be safer than the bridge of *Gowook.* This is the best way I know to do it."

"What do we do with the Innruld?" Addison asked.

"Rod sent me messages suggesting that there might be folks interested in xenocide," Pedro sobered now. "As Chair Teixeira noted with the President. I would appreciate you not doing that while wearing a Rio Navy uniform, Addison."

He flashed back to that conversation with Cormac, so long ago. What would they do on the day when that was an option? When they would both perhaps have to think about it as Eha would want.

What would she want?

"Am I allowed to tell Eha?" he asked.

"I presumed you would," Pedro nodded. "I'm merely asking this one last mission from you and Lazarus before you both put aside the tan."

Addison nodded. Rio would not want that stain on their conscience or reputation, but that wasn't the same as not doing it, if the Species Underground decided that would be the fate of the Innruld. And with *Recife* and *Ajax*, plus *Mendoza* and some of the other Light Starcruisers and escorts, the Innruld would have no say in the matter.

Not that they deserved one.

"Okay," he said. "I can do this. It will be up to Eha how it all plays out, but we can eliminate any threats to Phraettis Space right now. And then we'll build the future."

Addison wondered just what that future would look like.

SEVENTY-SEVEN

EHA

EHA HELD him close and let the tears flow. It was all wonderful, and she could not think of anyone better suited to the job than Carlos and her Addison.

He held himself a little rigid, but that didn't surprise her one bit. Addison had never been comfortable in any sort of spotlight, preferring the quiet of sailing and smuggling to being promoted to any sort of senior position with the Species Underground.

"You'll do fine, Admiral," she leaned back enough to watch his eyes as she teased him. "And I have another exciting surprise for you, before you leave."

"You're pregnant," he said calmly.

"How did you know?" she gasped. "I'm not showing at all."

"I could not think of anything else that might even approach the news of ending the Innruld as a threat," he said before his brain caught up to his mouth. Addison's scales flared. "You're serious?"

"I am," she beamed. "By the time you get back, Adriana will be an older sister."

"Oh my God," he managed as he hugged her tighter before finally relaxing.

It was good.

"What are you going to do about them?" Eha asked him after a few moments.

He leaned back and uncurled from her enough to blink.

"I have given this much thought, since that first moment when I reeled a Human into my airlock," Addison replied, turning quite serious now. "Cormac and I have even had more than one conversation when the others were not around."

He paused there and Eha found herself balanced up on her central keelstrake rather than flat on the floor.

"You were able to recruit me, once upon a time, because ending the Innruld as a species was not a thing outside my desires, Eha Dunham," he finally continued. "But Rod and Pedro have both mentioned that such an act is not acceptable from a Rio Alliance Flag Naval officer."

She just let him work it out, rather than prodding the man. Addison Wolcott could not be chivied or hurried along. He would get there in his own time. Just one of the reasons she had fallen in love with the man before she could ever tell him.

"But Pedro specifically talked about Lazarus and I doing one last mission in tan," he said. "Breaking the power of the Innruld with *Ajax* and *Recife*. He also talked about things that might come after that. After I had retired from the tan that I never wanted. That would be a time when the Underground formed itself into this thing we have been calling the Phraettis Alliance. They might decide to end the Innruld."

Eha nodded. Addison would hold that power in the palm of his hand. There was nobody else in the galaxy she would trust as much. Not even Lazarus, though she would never tell that man.

He would always be a close second, but only second, just as Oluchi would stand just barely third. Fourth place might be Erlyn, but Eha wasn't sure she could see the woman in that great of a distance.

"We must decide tonight then," Eha said after a moment of consideration.

"Tonight?" Addison gasped now. "Why tonight?"

"Because it must be done in the heat of anger," she said. "Or not at all."

"Not at all?"

"If the rage of the Species Underground is so great that they chase all the Innruld down and annihilate them, history will look on it entirely differently than if we first break their power and only then calmly call a congress and decide to commit xenocide afterwards," she said. "Not that they do not deserve it, mind you, but we will be judged on very different scales by history."

She lapsed into silence and just listened to his heart race, pounding in time with hers against her keel.

"We can destroy them," he said quietly. "*Ajax* makes that possible."

Eha nodded. *Ajax* could sit above the planet Innruld itself and obliterate everything on the surface of the planet, should Lazarus choose to do so. Yisan might have suffered a similar fate, driven by an even greater rage in the heat of the moment.

But not now.

"Do you trust me?" she asked.

"Explicitly," he replied without hesitation.

She hugged him all the closer for that.

"Break them," she said. "Nothing more."

"Okay," he replied, not necessarily seeing her logic, but accepting it unquestioningly.

"Turkan Volan," Eha continued.

"Who?"

"He is a rebel, living on the planet below us," Eha said. "And an Innruld, the one who fled with us from Gowook because all the work he had done for the Species Underground would be found out eventually when we fled and they would have executed him just as readily as any of the rest of us."

"Oh."

"He is the exception that proves the rule of how bad the Innruld are," Eha noted. "But he is also an example of what they can become, should they choose."

"So kill the Security Pyramids, destroy or capture their Barcs, and chase them unrelentingly back to Innruld?" Addison confirmed. "Then what?"

"Cut off all trade and communications," she said. "Until such time as they overthrow their own government and decide to petition the Phraettis Alliance for membership."

"Would we take them?" he asked, aghast.

"Turkan Volan."

"Turkan Volan," he nodded. "If one of them can change, so can the rest."

"Exactly," Eha agreed. "*Pancho* Oliveira became *Lazarus of Bethany*. I have read their ancient religious books enough to understand that he sees himself as dead and then reborn via a miracle. I will talk to our own Innruld rebel and ask him to start writing letters home. Once the rest of his kind are broken, they might be more willing to listen to reason. The President of Westphalia is not coming willingly to our side, but is being driven by merchants and oligarchs seeing the potential riches of Phraettis Space being denied them as long as this war persists. And no war is ever profitable for more than a few, well-connected folks, either smugglers or those making armaments, at least according to the Human histories I have read."

"The Humans of Westphalia will break as well?" Addison asked. "This was not a fool's errand, going to Earth?"

"It was a shock to the system," Eha replied. "Just like Lazarus's attack on Gowook. Or Oton Mari. Or Oluchi and Antonia going to Bajerlie. The Rio Alliance is strong enough to resist that. Yisan barely hiccupped when their own time came, according to what Oluchi has said about Heechua."

"There will be folks baying for blood," Addison said.

"Let them lead the charge at the beginning," Eha ordered now, suddenly feeling like Erlyn's peer. Or perhaps Eduardo's. "Let them sate themselves on the warriors and bureaucrats who uphold Innruld Space. Let them be used up in the fighting, so that cooler heads who remain afterwards will listen to your orders as well as mine, when it becomes *necessary* later."

Necessary.

Lazarus used that term with a specific intent more than once. Things he might not rather do, but was driven to by circumstances. Like killing Strav Ardna and everyone aboard that yacht. Like blasting enemy Starcruisers again and again with Kirov's Lance, not because he was excited, but because he needed methodical shocks to their system to convince them to give way before his rage.

Like overthrowing the power of the Innruld but not ending them as a species, simply because she asked.

"*Necessary,*" Addison echoed her.

But then, he had known Lazarus longer. Had seen that man do those things that were essential to survive and make it home safe. To save the galaxy.

To kill people for no other reason than it was *necessary.*

"Will we eventually live on Brasilia or Gowook?" he asked her now.

Eha blinked in surprise.

Like Addison or Lazarus, she had been living in the now for so long that she hadn't really given it that much thought.

Liberty was also an option, as was Yisan. Zhoonarrim. Whatever newly enshrined colony Grace eventually decided upon, near the mouth of Akeley's Passage.

Home.

She had been a spy and a spymaster for more than twenty-five years now.

Others would have opinions, but she could ignore them.

Eha Dunham could make her own future.

How she wanted.

Finally.

"We will figure that out when you come back to me, Addison Wolcott," she decided.

And she kissed him.

Because she could.

SEVENTY-EIGHT

LAZARUS

LAZARUS STOOD next to his command station on the bridge of *Ajax* and just let the fresh, clean smell of his ship embrace him.

One last mission, with everyone who had been there at the beginning. In a way, they were all going home.

He was at the other end of that original mad escape. That first test flight to make sure that everything on *Ajax* was working, before they went and gathered up the first full crew and set out to maybe change the future.

He had a letter from Ernesto da Silva, his first Quartermaster on that flight, captured, interned, and eventually traded home when it became clear that he hadn't known anything useful about Rio's new secret weapon. And another from the daughter of Commander Joao Lopez, Wybert's predecessor as Fusilier, who had also written, thanking him for making sure that her father's body had gotten safely home.

Lazarus didn't want to think of this as an ending, even though it was. It was also a beginning, just as his escape had been.

The door to a grand new adventure he could have never imagined.

He looked around now, as the room had fallen to silence, all eyes on him.

All his friends. All of them.

Addison and Aileen, seated next to Grace. Kuei and Wybert and Cormac at their stations. Lucas and Xiuying had both come forward from their usual duty stations, as had Lenox the MedCrawler. Khyaa'sha and Remahle. Ereshkiki Nisab and Thadrakho had joined him, leaving the engines and power systems in the capable hands of H'Brige Slani and her people for a few moments.

All of those friends who had been there from the beginning, or joined him at Yisan when it became necessary for Lazarus of Bethany to start a war for the future of all species and the entire galaxy.

Only Oluchi was missing, but he and Anya were aboard *Celestial Sovereign* for this trip, the man being unwilling to separate from his Board of Directors of the piratical raider *Limited Liability*, whatever other lies and evasions he might try to offer.

Lazarus had not been fooled. As Lazarus had the smugglers of *Shiva Zephyr Glaive*, so Oluchi had his five queens. His Board.

Lazarus sighed with something almost approaching joy and took his station.

His friends smiled. All of them.

"Fusilier, what is your status?" he called now, walking through the book.

"All guns are locked down," Wybert of Capantzina replied firmly. "All my gunners are on standby."

"Engineering, check in, please," he turned to H'Brige's image on his board.

"All systems in the green, Captain," she smiled at him. "Jump drives are charged and ready."

"Marie, contact *Recife* and let them know our status," Lazarus ordered.

She had stayed, even though technically she was supposed to return to Carlos and *Recife*. But she had also had a quiet conversation with him in the privacy of his office about superstitions, and Lazarus was in no position to argue with her logic. Collin Lau had come forward from his new spot aft as Eduardo's Ambassador to Phraettis, since Oluchi was a Warlord now and possibly going to be a competitor to Eduardo Martìnez one of these days.

But that was the future. Today, they were simply all here because they were needed in Phraettis Space.

Alliance.

"Fleet signals, Captain," Marie replied a moment later. "Squadron is standing by for the order from Vice Admiral Wolcott."

Lazarus was fast enough to see Addison's scales around his eyes flare before they quickly flattened again. He would enjoy teasing the man, as Lazarus had once been a mere deck swabbie on *Shiva Zephyr Glaive*. Before working his way up to stevedore.

Addison Wolcott had been his last Director in any service. And his friend.

Addison took a deep breath now and straightened on his cone chair.

His mouth opened but his voice broke so he closed it and swallowed.

Everyone waited quietly, knowing that history would be made today.

Lazarus smiled at him, lending him some strength.

"Marie, you will raise the standard of the Phraettis Alliance and transmit it to all vessels," he finally managed.

"Pilot, on acknowledgment, you will transmit a jump sequence to the squadron and then take us out."

He collapsed somewhat then, but Lazarus just grinned at the entire galaxy.

It was an ending, but it was also a beginning, and this time *Lazarus of Bethany* had no doubts about his success.

Blueshift.

EPILOGUE

LAZARUS LOOKED around the big living space laid out before him. Sunken living room with a stone fireplace. Several comfortable couches and chairs. Marble tile floors.

He had Grace on one arm. She was smiling, but not as wide as Eduardo was.

"It's only been ten months," Lazarus said with profound awe. "This colony had nothing when we flew by on the way to Phraettis Space to finish the Innruld off."

"And you and I both knew that they would fold like the house of cards they were, Lazarus." Eduardo beamed. "Originally, I had intended each of these as estates sitting on huge tracts of land, but Grace corrected me. Now you, Addison, and everyone else have their own houses, all cozy with a few hundred others in this little village, while the surrounding two hundred square miles will be held as a permanent wilderness. Think of it as a wedding present. And a thank you for coming to my rescue after Yisan."

"You came to mine when I first arrived," Lazarus reminded him.

"That worked out pretty well," Grace chuckled in his ear. "Thank you, Eduardo."

Lazarus pulled her close and kissed her. It was finally real. Westphalia would be a generation or a century getting over themselves, but they had an entirely new galaxy to trade with. The Phraettis Alliance was slowly building itself into a thing, after the Innruld had been chased back to their homeworld and broken as a power.

And Lazarus of Bethany didn't have anybody else that he needed save.

Including himself.

"What's next for the mighty, conquering hero?" Eduardo asked when they came up for air.

"I would like to be retired for a while," Lazarus said sincerely. "Being me, I'm sure I'll grow restless in a year or two, and need to go do something, but it can wait."

"Oh?" Eduardo asked, suddenly engaged in that business sense he did. "Like?"

"Grace has suggested we form a security company the exact opposite of a band of pirates," Lazarus replied. "Get paid to hunt them down, because everyone is aware that piracy will only get worse for a while."

"You don't sound terribly enthusiastic," Eduardo noted. "What's the thing that really lights a fire in your soul?"

Lazarus held on to it for a moment, but decided that Eduardo was one of those friends who would understand. And probably demand to be involved and help. That would be good.

"Build something like a Light Starcruiser," he replied. "Like *Ajax*, but without the Kirov."

"And?"

"And go sailing into the darkness, Eduardo," Lazarus said. "The Human sides of known space are being explored, but there are whole quadrants of the galaxy beyond the

Phraettis Nebula that the Innruld never explored. I'd like to grab some of my old friends and go see what's out there."

Eduardo laughed with joy.

"You would be the right man for the job, Lazarus of Bethany," he replied. "Send a note to me or Collin when that itch finally gets to be too much. Trade exploration instead of military conquest sounds like a grand adventure. But for now, I will leave you two alone to enjoy your new home and settle in. I'm staying just down the block for now, in the house that will belong to Anya and Oluchi, once I can convince those two to come home to dinner."

He bowed to them and left. Lazarus turned in place and just reveled in it. His own home. He'd grown up in poverty on Brasilia, then lived for twenty plus years in military housing, never owning much more than he could stuff in a footlocker.

He finally had a home. A place of his own.

"Twelve months until you're climbing the walls?" Grace asked with a smile.

"Sixteen, maybe," he smiled back. "Maybe eight until I'm designing a bigger, better version of *Dutra* and asking someone to build it for me."

She kissed him again.

"I'll send a note to Carlos and see what he thinks," she said.

Lazarus kissed her and wondered what that future might hold.

And who might be out there.

READ MORE

Be sure to read all the books in the Lazarus Alliance series!

Escape
Return
Rebellion
Revolution
Liberation
Retribution
Alliance

Available at your favorite retailers!

ABOUT THE AUTHOR

Blaze Ward writes science fiction in the Alexandria Station universe (Jessica Keller, The Science Officer, The Story Road, etc.) as well as several other science fiction universes, such as Star Dragon, the Dominion, and more. He also writes odd bits of high fantasy with swords and orcs. In addition, he is the Editor and Publisher of *Boundary Shock Quarterly Magazine*. You can find out more at his website www.blazeward.com, as well as Facebook, Goodreads, and other places.

Blaze's works are available as ebooks, paper, and audio, and can be found at a variety of online vendors. His newsletter comes out regularly, and you can also follow his blog on his website. He really enjoys interacting with fans, and looks forward to any and all questions—even ones about his books!

Never miss a release!
If you'd like to be notified of new releases, sign up for my newsletter.

http://www.blazeward.com/newsletter/

Buy More!
Did you know that you can buy directly from my website?

https://www.blazeward.com/shop/

Connect with Blaze!

Web: www.blazeward.com
Boundary Shock Quarterly (BSQ):
https://www.boundaryshockquarterly.com/

ABOUT KNOTTED ROAD PRESS

Knotted Road Press fiction specializes in dynamic writing set in mysterious, exotic locations.

Knotted Road Press non–fiction publishes autobiographies, business books, cookbooks, and how–to books with unique voices.

Knotted Road Press creates DRM–free ebooks as well as high–quality print books for readers around the world.

With authors in a variety of genres including literary, poetry, mystery, fantasy, and science fiction, Knotted Road Press has something for everyone.

Knotted Road Press
www.KnottedRoadPress.com